EVOLUTIONS

VOLUME I

NOVELS IN THE *NEW YORK TIMES* BESTSELLING
HALO® SERIES

Halo®: The Fall of Reach by Eric Nylund
Halo®: The Flood by William C. Dietz
Halo®: First Strike by Eric Nylund
Halo®: Ghosts of Onyx by Eric Nylund
Halo®: Contact Harvest by Joseph Staten
Halo®: The Cole Protocol by Tobias S. Buckell

BEYOND

There is majesty here
   Beyond reason
   Beyond understanding
Vast in its implications
   What wonders; offered around each new corner—
   Over every skyward peak—
   Or hidden deep; within in the shadows of each
      sunken valley
The questions raised
   In astonishment;
   In fear—
If such glories can be divined, yet forgotten
   Lost to time;
   Strewn about the entirety of stars
What then are we—
   Be us man,
   Or be us monster
In light of knowledge, so vast—
   So far beyond
   Superior; even to our dreams
What matter, then, our petty confrontations
   When weighed against the sins we sow
What matter, then, our fate amongst the cosmos, eternal
   In light of the Halo; its luminous glow

BEYOND

imperfection from her painting hung there in the pink sky. Real. Baleful. Moving steadily and purposefully to the horizon. Something was coming. Something was wrong.

Soma the Painter folded her glass easel, hurriedly packed her things, and began the long climb down to Wharftown.

ONE

"How was this information discovered?" the Auditor asked, looking up from the report.

"Triangulation of devices. A trade beacon, a medical station, and a painter's jetbrush," replied the Prelate.

"Are we spying on our citizens now?" A raised eyebrow.

"Not exactly. But there are measures in place to collate unusual observations. They're blind-checked by automatons, not intelligences. We only bubble such reports to the surface when a catastrophe or Xenovent expresses itself."

"That sounds like spying to me," said the Auditor. He gestured and the report vanished. "What measures have been taken?"

The Prelate cleared his throat and adjusted the front fastening of his clerical robe. His smooth, aqualine features hardened slightly as he spoke. "None. None beyond a resupply balloon for the damaged medical station. And this meeting." Self-consciously, he smoothed his thin black fur with a palm.

"Send word to the Didact. Our test has come."

tions or scolding. Instead they simply brought gifts, food, technology, and repairs. Seaward was tolerated, encouraged even, by distant, benevolent friends who asked for nothing in return but the trades of energy and art that financed its existence.

Soma's hand hovered above the glass, the delicate steely wand of the jetbrush held confidently between stained fingers. Her creased, sun-worn brow wrinkled further, its bluish fur furrowing as as she stared dutifully at the horizon and squinted to keep the brightness out of her rheumy eyes. The jetbrush winked its ready state, absorbing light, tiny whirling motors ready for painting.

As the two suns moved lower, their proximity to each other increased, and momentarily, both seemed to shine more fiercely. And, as if acting on some unheard order, the clouds responded, their pink gossamer suddenly finding vermillion flame, then green, then blue. A flitting rainbow of hot color, then just as quickly fading back to pink.

Soma blinked tears back, resisted the photic urge to sneeze, wiped her eyes with a small silk handkerchief, and looked at the glass in front of her. Sure enough. Some of the colors were there, strewn not quite accurately on the skyscape she'd prepared.

Wonderful, she thought to herself. She examined the pattern and then frowned. The jetbrush had also laid down a flaw with its capture of that momentary light. A dark gray streak. A dirty charcoal imperfection drawn through the center of the other hues in a floundering arc, trailing a sickly yellow smoke behind it.

Disturbed, she glanced back at the sky itself. The

lifestyle, one demonstrated perfectly in her sagging skin, her telling wrinkles. She'd come here to love life, but also to age and to die.

At 417 years of age, Soma was young to be taking this path, but hardly unique. Wharftown was filled with her peers, and more besides, scattered thinly, perhaps a million souls planted here on the massive planet Seaward, unromantically called G617 g1 by outsiders adrift on endless ocean, just as the world itself was adrift in endless space, hanging on a lonely binary system at the galaxy's trailing edge. This was the last stop before intergalactic space and lifeless void. A fitting waiting room for death's cool arms.

And the citizens of Seaward were all, as their society measured it, wealthy. The world itself was a secret, publicly and officially a lifeless ball of dirt, a place truly worth ignoring. Those who could afford it had found a private, expensive sanctuary from society, and great power and influence had been poured into purchasing anonymity for this beautiful, verdant world.

Wharftown sat on a rocky shard of volcanic surge, a thousand miles from the equator. There was little there but dwellings, parks, and one of the few significant stretches of arable land, most of it terraced in pretty defiance of the towering hummocks and fangs of basalt.

Here on Seaward, contact with society proper was limited. Communications were almost nonexistent. Supplies sometimes came silently by transorbital balloon, jettisoned by unseen starships, inflating at the bottom edge of the stratosphere, then drifting gracefully to land their cargoes. They seldom came with messages or instruc-

PROLOGUE

Soma the Painter was waiting for the suns to dip a little lower in the sky. The thing she was waiting for was called *Twofire*, an optical effect caused by the light from two suns passing under the horizon and reflecting on scattered clouds above. It was beautiful, and she was trying to capture it in real time, spraying smart-pigments onto a glass surface from her color-sensing jetbrush.

From her position on the hill above Wharftown, she had a perfect view of the azure expanse of sea, with distant whitecaps beyond the reef now picking up motes of pink. She ignored the bucolic bustle of the town below and concentrated.

She had moved here for these moments; silence, unsterilized air, sounds of nature, the minuscule dangers of a real place—stinging plants and quarrelsome insects. Like the inhabitants of the town below, Soma had given up her armor in order to experience life more intimately. No more lenses, no more n-barriers, no more omniscient guides. She had come here seeking a primitive

SOMA THE PAINTER

Forerunner trilogy. But you guys have the intestinal fortitude.

Bon appétit.

Frank O'Connor
Redmond, Washington
September 2009

We can dive in, visit the bridge of Admiral Cole's latest command, or hide in an abandoned spacecraft with the life ebbing out of us. We can wander the desert of a distant world in the cloven shoes of an Elite. We can explore the ravenous appetites of the Gravemind through Cortana's tortured gaze. And we can do all this in a single book.

The first anthology I ever read was called *Great Space Battles*. It assembled short stories built around completely unrelated illustrations, and wove together a universe from the art it represented. I remember thinking what a wonderful way to read: in bite-size chunks. We have the luxury of an already established fiction and a vast range of characters and worlds at our fingertips.

Some of these stories are short and sweet and will melt in your mouth. Others are heartier fare, but they'll taste like a perfectly cooked chateaubriand. They'll all add ingredients and menu items to the Halo table and they'll all taste remarkably different.

The iron chefs catering this affair are a mixture of masters. In this volume we have stories from the Titans of Halo Fiction: Erics Nylund and Raab, and Tobias S. Buckell. We have newcomers too: B. K. Evenson and Jonathan Goff, both bring some new ingredients. Even I've been in the kitchen, cobbling together something partway edible. I hope.

This anthology is certainly a smorgasbord and may be a lot to consume before we move back to the main course of novels, starting in 2010 with Greg Bear's new

INTRODUCTION:
WHY SHORT STORIES?

BECAUSE THE Halo universe is almost as vast and boundless as the real thing. And because Halo fans enjoy a broad spectrum of flavors and moments from the games and the extended canon. In fact, no two Halo fans are quite the same. We have hard-core fans who only enjoy one game type, on one map, with one weapon. We have fans who are enthralled by the tactical exploits of UNSC commanders. We have fans who wish to explore the deepest mysteries of a forgotten civilization. We have fans who want to drop from orbit with the ODSTs. We have fans who view the entire canon through the lens of the Master Chief's faceplate.

Moreover, we have fans who can't wait years between novels to get their next fix, that next glistering nugget of data about their favorite part of the worlds Halo has created. Short stories allow us the luxury of sampling those flavors and moments. Like a box of chocolates, to borrow a Gumpian phrase.

HALO®
EVOLUTIONS
VOLUME I

HEADHUNTERS   *Jonathan Goff*
     art by Garrett Post   201

**THE IMPOSSIBLE LIFE AND THE POSSIBLE DEATH
     OF PRESTON J. COLE**   *Eric Nylund*
     art by Jonathan Goff   249

ACKNOWLEDGMENTS   345

ABOUT THE AUTHORS   347

ABOUT THE ARTISTS   351

CONTENTS

INTRODUCTION   *Frank O'Connor*   1

SOMA THE PAINTER   5

BEYOND   *art by Sparth,*
       words by Jonathan Goff   11

PARIAH   *B. K. Evenson*
       art by Levi Hoffmeier   13

STOMPING ON THE HEELS OF
   A FUSS   *Eric Raab*
       art by Alexander Kent   71

MIDNIGHT IN THE *HEART OF*
   MIDLOTHIAN   *Frank O'Connor*
       art by April Martin   103

DIRT   *Tobias S. Buckell*
       art by James Bible   133

ACHERON-VII   *art by Sparth,*
       words by Jonathan Goff   199

HALO®: EVOLUTIONS, VOLUME I

Copyright © 2009, 2010 by Microsoft Corporation

A Tor Book
Published by Tom Doherty Associates, LLC
175 Fifth Avenue
New York, NY 10010

www.tor-forge.com

ISBN 978-0-7653-5475-4

First Edition: November 2009
First Mass Market Edition: November 2010

Printed in the United States of America

0 9 8 7 6 5 4 3 2 1

EVOLUTIONS

ESSENTIAL TALES OF THE HALO UNIVERSE

VOLUME I

TOR®

A TOM DOHERTY ASSOCIATES BOOK
NEW YORK

PARIAH

B. K. EVENSON

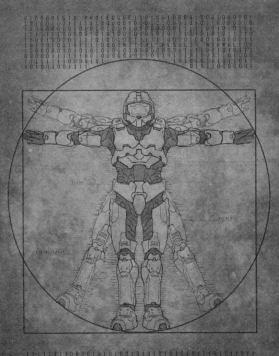

PROLOGUE

"Will you tell me your name?" asked Dr. Halsey. She made no move to squat down in front of the boy, to smile, to do anything at all to come down to his level. Instead she remained standing, her posture neither friendly nor threatening, but simply as neutral as she could make it. Her gaze was steady, interested.

The boy looked at her from across the room. He was only six but the boy's gaze was just as steady as hers, though there was perhaps a trace of wariness in his eyes. *Completely understandable*, thought Dr. Halsey. *If he knew why I was here there'd be more than just a trace.* He held his body just as noncommittally as she held her own, though she could tell by the tightness in his neck that that might change any moment, without warning.

"You first," the boy said, and then moved his mouth into something that could pass for a smile.

His voice was calm, as if he were used to being in charge of a situation. Not afraid, then. Not surprising, thought Dr. Halsey. If the report she'd read was correct, he'd managed to survive on his own, in the Outer Colonies on the planet Dwarka, on an illegal farm in the middle of a forest preserve one hundred kilometers from nowhere, for nearly three months after his parents had died. Surviving under normal circumstances on a harsh world still in the process of being terraformed was hard enough. But for someone who was barely six years old it was inconceivable.

"I already know your name," Dr. Halsey admitted. "It's Soren."

"If you knew, why did you ask?"

"I wanted to see if you'd tell me," she said. Then she paused. "I'm Doctor Halsey," she said, and smiled.

Soren didn't smile back. She now saw more than a trace of suspicion in his gaze, suspicion that sat strangely in his face alongside his straw-colored hair and his pale blue eyes. "What kind of doctor?" he asked.

"I'm a scientist," said Dr. Halsey.

"Not a sigh—, not a sigh—"

"No," she said, and smiled. "I'm not a psychiatrist. You've been seeing a lot of psychiatrists, haven't you?"

He hesitated just a moment, and then nodded.

"Because of your parents' deaths?"

He hesitated, nodded again.

Dr. Halsey glanced at the holographic files displayed discreetly on the interior of her glasses. His mother had apparently succumbed to a planet-specific disease. Treatments were readily available, but a family living off the grid wouldn't have been aware of that. Instead of reporting immediately to the planetary officials as was required by law, the boy's parents had dismissed the symptoms as those of a cold and had kept working. A few days later, the mother was dead and the stepfather sick. Soren, perhaps because his younger immune system had adapted more readily to Dwarka, had never become ill. He had, according to his stepfather's dying wish, buried the bodies of both of his parents, then continued to live on in their farmhouse until supplies were almost gone, finally setting out by foot to cross 112 kilometers of blue-gray forest and arrive at the beginning of authorized farmland.

Was she right to consider him for her team of Spartans? Certainly he was bright and resourceful. He was tough and clearly wouldn't give up easily. But at the same time, what would it do to someone to go through that experience? Nobody knew how traumatized he was. Nobody knew for certain what it had done—and might still be doing—to him. Probably not even him.

"Why are you here?" he asked.

She looked at him and considered. There was no reason to tell him anything; she could simply do as she and Keyes had done with the others and make the decision for him, flash-clone him and kidnap him for, as she'd started telling herself, the *greater good*. But with the other children she'd in part assumed they wouldn't understand. Here was a boy without parents who, despite being only six, had had to grow up fast, much faster than her other recruits. Could she tell him more?

"The truth is," she said, "I came to see you."

"Why?" he countered.

She returned his even gaze. Suddenly she made her

decision. "I'm trying to decide if you're right for something I'm working on. An experiment. I can't tell you what it is, I'm afraid. But if it works in the way we hope it will you'll be stronger and faster and smarter than you could ever imagine."

For the first time, he looked slightly confused. "Why would you want to do something like that for me? You don't even know me."

She reached out and tousled Soren's hair, was pleased when he didn't flinch or shy away. "It's not *for* you, exactly," she said. "I can't tell you much more. It won't be easy; it'll be the hardest thing you've ever done—even harder than what happened with your parents."

"And what have you decided?" he asked.

"I've decided to let you be the one to decide," she said.

"What if I say no?"

She shrugged. "You'd stay here on Dwarka. The planetary authorities would arrange a foster home for you." *Not much of a choice*, she thought. *He's between a rock and a hard place.* She wondered again if she wasn't being unfair putting the choice on the boy.

"All right," he said and stood up.

"All right what?" she said.

"I'm coming with you. When do we leave?"

Later, back on board, when she spoke with Keyes, showed him the vid of her conversation with Soren, he asked, "You're sure about this?"

"I think so," she said.

He just grunted.

"As sure as I am of taking any of them," she said. "At least he has a notion of what might happen to him."

"That's an awful lot to lay on a child," said Keyes. "Even one who's grown up fast."

She nodded. Keyes was right, she knew. The terms for the test subject known as Soren were different from those of the others—he was coming into the program in a different way from the very beginning. She'd have to remember that and keep an eye on him.

ONE

What neither Doctor Halsey nor Lieutenant Keyes knew—and what they would never find out, since Soren, though only six, was smart enough not to tell them—was what really happened to him during those three months alone. That was something that Soren, or Soren-66 as he would come to be called, didn't like to think about. It had been terrible when he realized his mother was dead and that the reason she was dead was because his stepfather had been too worried about going to jail for his illegal farm to take her to a doctor when she got sick. By the time his stepfather was convinced there was no other choice, it was too late; his mother was already gone.

But his stepfather had refused to face it. He moved Soren's mother's body into the box room and locked the door, telling Soren that it was not possible to see her, that she was too sick and needed to be alone to recover. That had lasted a few days until finally, late one night, his stepfather had had too much to drink. Soren stole the key and crept slowly through the door to see her there, lying on a pile of flattened boxes, the skin of her face tight and sallow. She smelled bad. He had seen and smelled enough rotting animals in the woods to know that she was dead.

He cried for a while and then sneaked back out of the room, shutting and locking the door behind him, returning the key to his stepfather's bedside table, and then sneaking out again. In the kitchen he sat brooding, wondering what to do. His stepfather was responsible for his mother's death, he sensed, and as far as he was concerned he should have to pay. Just thinking about it made him tremble.

Thinking this and things like it led him to get off his chair and take the sharpest knife off the counter. He knew it was the sharpest because his mother had never let him use it without her help. He had to stand on his tiptoes to reach it. It was big, heavy. He stood staring at the low flicker on the blade in the half-light and then slowly made his way to his stepfather's bedroom.

His stepfather was lying in bed, still asleep, groaning slightly. He stank of liquor. Soren pulled the chair closer to the bed and stood on it, looming now over his stepfather. He stayed like that, clutching the knife, trying to decide how to go about killing the man. He was, he knew, small, still a child, and he would only have one chance. *The neck*, he thought. He would have to jab the knife in quick and deep. Maybe that would be enough. He would fall onto his stepfather and stab into his neck at the same time and then before his stepfather could do anything he would start running, out into the forest, just in case it didn't kill him. Fleetingly the thought crossed his mind that to do something like this might be wrong, that his mother would not approve, but having grown up off the grid on the edge of the civilized universe, living under a man growing illegal crops and possessed of a mistrust for the law, it was hard to know where wrong ended and right started. He was angry. All he knew was that his mother was dead, and that it was the fault of this man.

Years later, when he thought back to the situation, he realized there were nuances to it that at the time he had no chance of understanding. There was something seriously wrong with his stepfather, an inability to face up to his wife's death, that had let him simply block the death out. Yes, he'd been wrong not to take her to town at the first sign of illness, but his behavior afterward had been less maliciousness and more a sign of how deeply troubled he was. But at the time, all Soren knew was that he wanted whoever was responsible for his mother's death to pay.

He waited there poised on his chair for what seemed like hours, watching his stepfather sleep, until light started to seep in. Then he waited a little more, until his stepfather stretched and rolled over in his sleep to perfectly expose his neck.

He leaped forward, bringing the knife down as hard as he could. It turned a little in his hand as it struck, but it went in. His stepfather gave a muffled bellow and flailed around him but Soren was already off the bed and running out the bedroom door. He was just opening the outer door when his stepfather appeared, red-eyed and swaying in the bedroom doorway, the knife jutting out between his neck and shoulder a little above his clavicle, his shirt already soaked with blood. He cried out again, a monstrous sound, like an angry ox, and then Soren had the door open and had plunged out into the crisp morning air, vanishing into the forest.

He was well-hidden within a clump of bushes by the time his stepfather came out, the knife out of his flesh now and in his hand, the wound sprayed with biofoam. The man was grimacing, clearly in pain.

"Soren!" he cried out. "What's wrong with you!"

Soren didn't say anything, pulling himself deeper into the bushes. His stepfather came in search of him. Whatever was wrong, the man claimed, could be sorted out if Soren would just come out and explain it to him. He passed very close, so close that Soren could hear the ragged sound of his breathing. His stepfather nearly stepped on his hand, and then he continued on deeper into the forest, occasionally stopping to call out his name.

That was as far as Soren's plans went. He couldn't, he felt, go back into the house, not now that he had tried to kill his stepfather. And yet, where was he to go? They were in the middle of nowhere, miles away from anything.

The first night was difficult, the air cold enough in the dark that he kept waking up shivering, his teeth chattering. He kept hearing things, too, unsure whether it was his stepfather or the animals of the forest—and, if the latter, whether they were just small rodents or something larger that might be carnivorous. His mother had always warned him not to go far into the forest. "It's not like the parks back home," she had claimed. "It's not safe."

He awoke at dawn, hungry and bone tired. He crept to the edge of the clearing and watched the prefab house from the safety of the brush, wondering if he could sneak in and get some food. He was getting ready to do so when he caught a brief flash of his stepfather through the window, standing just inside, waiting for him.

He slunk back into the forest, stomach still growling. He wanted to cry, but the tears just didn't seem to come. Had he done the right thing, stabbing his stepfather? He wasn't sure. In any case it hadn't worked, had only made things worse. He should have had a better plan, he thought, or at least figured what to do next. This was no time for crying, he decided. He had to figure out what to do next.

The first thing was to have something to eat. He couldn't get into the house for the food in there—he should have thought of that before stabbing his stepfather, should have taken some food out of the house and cached it in the woods. But it was too late for that now. He would have to make do.

At first he tried to catch an animal, one of the toothless squirrellike creatures that slid silently as ghosts around the trunks and boles of the trees. But after only a few minutes he realized they were much too fast for him. Next, he tried to sit motionless to see if they would come to him. They were curious and got close, but never quite close enough for him to grab one. Maybe he could kill one by throwing rocks? He tried, but mostly his aim was off, and the one time he hit one it simply gave an angry chitter and scuttled off. *Even if I catch one*, he suddenly realized, *how am I going to cook it? I don't have anything to start a fire.*

What could he eat, then? Some of the plants were edible, but which ones? He wasn't sure. His family had never harvested from the forest, sticking instead to their prepackaged provisions.

In the end he stepped on a dry, rotten branch and heard it crack, an eddy of bugs pouring out of the gap and quickly vanishing into the undergrowth. He heaved the branch over and saw, along the underside, pale white larvae, worms, large-jawed centipedes, and beetles spotted orange and blue. He avoided the beetles—if they were that brightly colored there must be something wrong with them—but tried both the larvae and the worms. The larvae had a nutty taste and were okay to eat if he didn't think too much about them. The worms were a little slimier, but he could keep them down. When a few hours had passed and he didn't feel sick, he turned over a few more fallen logs and ate his fill.

Before night fell he started to experiment, moving a little farther away from the house and making several beds out of the leaves and needles of different trees. One type of leaf, he found, raised a row of angry, itchy red bumps along his wrist when he touched it; he made a mental note of what it looked like and from then on avoided it. He tried each of the other beds in turn until he found one that was soft and a little warmer. He was still cold during the night, but no longer shivering. He was far from comfortable but he could stand it, and even sleep.

In just a few days, he had started to understand his patch of forest. He knew where to go for grubs, when to leave a log alone for a few days and when to turn it. Watching the ghost squirrels, he learned to avoid certain berries and plants. Others he tasted. Some were bitter and made him sick to his stomach and he didn't return to them. But a few he went back to without any ill effect.

He watched his stepfather from the bushes. He was there to see him in the morning, when he came out of the house and went to the crops or to the processor that refined them into a white powder, and there to see him as well at night. Each time his stepfather left the house he carefully locked the door, and though Soren had tried a few times to break his way in, the windows were strong and he wasn't successful.

Maybe I'll make a trap, he began to think. Something his stepfather would step in or fall into or something that might fall on him and crush him. Could he do that?

He watched. His stepfather took the same route to the field every day, a straight and straightforward line along a dirt track his own feet had carved day after day. He was nothing if not predictable. The path was clear enough that there was little chance of hiding something on it or digging a hole without his noticing. Nor were there trees close enough to drop something from above.

Maybe it had been enough, he tried to tell himself. Maybe he could just forget about him and leave. But even though he told himself that, he found himself returning, day after day, to stare at the house. He was growing stronger, his young body lean and hard, nothing wasted. His hearing had grown keen, and his vision was such that he could now see the signs of when something had passed before him on the paths he traveled. When he was sure nothing and nobody was listening, he told himself stories, mumbled whispered fables, versions of things his mother had told him.

Several years later, thinking it over, he realized that he had become trapped, neither able to go into his house nor leave it behind completely. It was as though he were tethered to it, like a dog chained to a post. It might, he realized when he was older, have gone on indefinitely.

And indeed it did go on, Soren growing a little more wild each day, until something suddenly changed. One morning his stepfather came out and Soren could see there was something wrong with him. He was coughing badly, was hunched over—he was sick, Soren realized with a brief shudder of fear, in the same way Soren's mother had been. His stepfather went to the crops, weaving slightly, but he was listless, exhausted, and by midday he had given up and was headed back. Only he didn't make it all the way back. Halfway home, he fell to his knees and then laid there, flat on his stomach, his face pushing into the dirt, one leg jutted to the side. He was there a long time, unmoving. Soren thought he must be dead, but then as he watched his stepfather gave a shuddering breath and started to move again. But he didn't go back to the house. Instead, he crawled his way to the truck and tried to pull himself into it.

When he failed and fell back into the dust, there was Soren, above him and a little way away, his face expressionless.

"Soren," said his stepfather, his voice little above a whisper.

Soren didn't say anything. He just stayed there without moving. Watching. Waiting.

"I thought you were dead," said his stepfather. "I really did. I would have kept looking for you otherwise. Thank God you're here."

Soren folded his arms across his tiny chest.

"I need your help," said his stepfather. "Help me get into the truck. I'm very sick. I need to find medicine."

Still Soren said nothing, continuing to stand there motionless, waiting, not moving. He stayed like that, listening to his stepfather's pleading, his growing panic, followed by threats and wheedling. Eventually the latter passed into unconsciousness. Then Soren sat down and stayed there, holding vigil over the sick man, until two days later his breathing stopped and he was dead. Then he reached into his stepfather's pocket and took the keys and reclaimed the house.

It wasn't easy work to drag his mother out of the house and bury her, but in the end, his fingers blistered and bleeding from several days of slow digging, he managed. His stepfather he buried less from a sense of obligation and more because he wasn't sure what else to do with the body. He liked to tell himself in later years that he had buried him to prove that he wasn't like him, to prove he was more human, but he was never sure if that was the real reason. He buried him where he had fallen, just beside the truck, rolling him into a hole that was just deeper than the body and mounding the dirt high around him.

He stayed in the house for a few days, eating and building up his strength. When the provisions began to run low he finally managed to shake the house's grip on him, walking out into the forest, making his way slowly in the direction that he thought a town might be. He was in the woods for days, maybe weeks, living off berries and grubs. Once he even managed to kill a ghost squirrel with a carefully thrown rock and then slit the fur off with another rock to eat the spongy, bitter meat within. After that, he stuck to berries and grubs.

And then, almost accidentally, he came across a track that he knew wasn't made by an animal and followed it. A few hours later he found himself standing on the edge of a small township, startled by how the people stared at him when he emerged from the underbrush, his clothing tattered, his skin covered with dirt and grime. He was surprised by the way they rushed toward him, their faces creased with concern.

TWO

With such experience under his belt, life on Reach in the Spartan camp seemed less of a challenge to Soren than it did to many of the other recruits. After living in the woods alone, he felt he was ready for anything. He was quick to figure out the best way through an obstacle course. He could fade quickly into bushes and undergrowth when on mock patrol. Camouflage was a way of life for him: He faded into the background too when in groups, wanting neither to come to attention as one of the leaders of a group nor to be seen as an outsider. He stuck to the anonymous middle.

But despite that, there were times when he noticed Dr. Halsey standing at a deliberate distance, watching him with an expression on her face that he could not interpret. Once, when he was nearly eleven, she even approached him as he ran through an exercise with the other children, standing at a slight remove, as he hesitated, wondering which team to join. He couldn't decide if he was having trouble because she was scrutinizing him, or if he always waited until the last minute to make his choice and it just took her presence to make him realize it.

"Everything all right, Soren?" she asked him, her voice carefully modulated. Officially he was now Soren-66—a seemingly arbitrary digit for recruits, decided by the Office of Naval Intelligence for reasons they kept to themselves—but the doctor never called him by the number.

"Yes, sir," he said, then realized she wasn't a sir, or even, for that matter, a ma'am and blushed and looked guiltily at her. "Yes, Doctor?" he tried.

She smiled. "Don't get distracted by irrelevant data," she said to him, and then gestured idly past him, at the two teams already running for the skirmish ground. "And above all don't let yourself get left behind."

Don't let yourself get left behind. The words echoed for him not only through the rest of the exercise but for a long time to come, haunting him long after he was sure Dr. Halsey had forgotten them. There was, he slowly came to sense, something different about him, something that the other recruits either didn't have or didn't care to show. For that matter, he didn't show it either: as he grew, he was very careful not to let any-one see anything that would make him different, would make him stand apart.

When he was very young, six or seven, he had been less careful. He hated sharing his room, found it excep-tionally difficult to sleep hearing the sounds and the breathing of his fellow bunkmates. In their breathing he heard his stepfather. Sometimes he waited until they had fallen asleep and then slipped slowly out of his bed to hide under it, sleeping in the damp, musty space near the wall. He felt safer there. But when one morn-ing he had slept late and hadn't returned to his bed before the others had started waking up, the way they looked at him made him feel less safe. No, he would have to play along, would have to learn to go through the motions that all the others seemed to make so naturally. He wanted not so much to *fit* in as to *fade* in.

But after a while, it didn't seem like an act anymore. He liked many aspects of the life of being a recruit. He enjoyed the challenge of it both mentally and physically. Having grown up off the grid, he had never been around people who were going through the same things he was; at times, particularly when they were darting through the forest together or crawling their breathless and silent way through a ditch full of mud, it was like being surrounded by many other versions of himself. It was comforting. Indeed, he felt closer to the other recruits than he had to anyone but his mother. Dr. Halsey, too, was the next best thing to a mother to him, though often distant, often preoccupied. But there was something about her that he found some strange kinship with.

He still needed time to himself, still found himself figuring out ways of being off on his own or, if not on his own, of creating a kind of momentary and temporary wall between himself and the others as a way of trying to think, to breathe, to be more fully himself. He realized very early on that he was never going to be a leader. He was not very communicative, but his instincts were honed and good and he was willing and able to follow orders. The others knew they could count on him. He felt in this the beginnings of a sense of meaning and purpose to his life, and he felt better than he had ever felt. He was keeping up. He wasn't letting himself get left behind.

And yet he was still haunted by the past. Sometimes, particularly late at night, in the dark, he couldn't help but think about what had happened when he was younger. He knew that whatever it was that made him different from the others came from that. At first the past was something he tried to push away, tried to forget, but as he grew older and smarter his thoughts about it became more and more conflicted. In his early teens, he began to see his stepfather less as a monster and more as someone who was scared and confused, somebody disastrously flawed, but someone who was also human. He fought against that realization, kept pushing it away, but it continually surged back over him. He had watched his stepfather die—it had been so quick, almost no time at all between the first symptoms and that strange transition from life to death. Which made him wonder, with a disease that moved that quickly could his mother really have been saved?

All in all, he was neither the best nor the worst. He was a solid recruit and trainee, someone who, though haunted by his past, was doing his best to move beyond it. Perhaps, he thought, for the moment that was all he could ask for. Perhaps for now it was enough.

THREE

He was fourteen now, and standing at attention on the other side of Dr. Halsey's desk. Her face, he noticed, was drawn and tight, her responses a little jerkier than usual, as if she hadn't been getting enough sleep or was overworked. She hid it well, but Soren, himself an expert on hiding things well, saw all the cues he was learning to suppress in himself.

"At ease," Dr. Halsey said. "Please take a seat, Soren."

"Thank you, ma'am," he said, and sat, a single fluid movement, nothing wasted.

She was whispering quietly to herself, scanning a series of electronic files. The files were holograms whose contents were visible to her but which he saw only as an image of a small brick wall, an image of CPO Mendez on the other side of it with his finger pressed to his lips. *Someone has a weird sense of humor*, he thought.

"Do you mind if I ask you a question?" she asked.

"Of course not, ma'am," he said.

"Dr. Halsey," she said. "No need to make me sound any older than I am. Do you remember when we first met?"

"Yes," said Soren. Hardly a day had gone by without his thinking about that meeting and everything it had led to.

"I wonder, Soren, do you remember what I said, how I gave you a choice?"

Soren wrinkled his forehead briefly, then the lines cleared. "You mean whether to come with you or stay on Dwarka? Or was there something else?"

"No, just that," she said. "You were young enough that I didn't know how well you'd remember. How do you feel about your choice?"

"I'm glad I made it," he said. "It was the right choice, ma'am."

"I thought we already talked about your calling me that," she said, smiling. "I wondered at the time whether I was right to give you a choice. Lieutenant Keyes wondered too. Whether you weren't too young to have that burden placed on you."

"Burden?" he asked.

She waved the implied question aside. "Never mind," she said. "The reason I've brought you here is to give you another choice."

He waited for her to continue, but for a moment she simply stayed there, staring at him, the same unreadable expression on her face that he'd noticed before, when he had caught her watching him during exercises.

"You're still very young," she said.

Soren said nothing.

Dr. Halsey sighed. "You've trained well, all of you. But training is only the first step. We're on the verge of the second step. Would you like to take it?"

"What is it exactly?"

"There's only so much I can tell you," said Dr. Halsey. "There's only so much the bodies that we have can do, Soren. So we want to augment them. We want to modify your physical body and mind to push it beyond normal human capabilities. We want to toughen your bones, increase your growth, build your muscle mass, sharpen your vision, improve your reflexes. We want to make you into the perfect soldier." The smile that had been building on her face slowly faded away.

"However, there will be side effects. Some of these we know, some we probably can't anticipate. There's also considerable risk."

"What sort of risk?"

"There's a chance, a nontrivial one, that you could die during the augmentation. Even if you don't die, there's a strong risk of Parkinson's, Fletcher's syndrome, and Ehlers-Danlos syndrome, as well as potential problems with deformation or atrophy of the muscles and degenerative bone conditions."

He didn't understand everything she was saying, but had the gist of it. "And if it works?"

"If it works, you'll be stronger and faster than you can imagine." She tented her fingers in front of her, staring over them at him. "I'm giving you an option that the others won't be given. I am offering you a choice, while your classmates will simply be told they are to report for the procedure."

"Why me?" asked Soren.

"Pardon?"

"Why am I the one who gets to make a choice? Why not one of the others?"

She turned her gaze to the desk in front of her, her voice distant now, more as if she were speaking to herself than the boy. "What the Spartans are is an experiment," she said. "In every controlled experiment you need one sample whose conditions are different so as to be able to judge the progress of the larger group. You're that sample, Soren."

"We're an experiment," he said, his voice flat.

"I won't lie to you. That is precisely what you are,

and you—an experiment within the experiment. An exception to a rule," she said.

"Why me?" he asked again. "You could have chosen anyone."

She shrugged. "I don't know, Soren. It just turned out that way."

He was silent for a long time, staring straight in front of him, sorting it all out in his head. Finally he looked up.

"I want to do it," he said.

"You do?" said Dr. Halsey. "Even knowing the risks?"

"Yes," he said. And then added, "I don't want to be left behind."

Strange, Dr. Halsey thought after he had left. What had he meant by not wanting to be left behind? Where had she heard that before?

She shook her head to clear it. "Déjà," she said. "You were listening in, I take it?"

"Of course, Dr. Halsey," said the AI's smooth voice. Her hologram flickered into existence on the desk beside her. Created specifically for the Spartan project, her self-chosen construct was that of a Greek goddess, barefoot and holding a clay tablet.

"Any thoughts?"

"Is that a rhetorical question?" asked Déjà. When Dr. Halsey didn't respond, she continued. "You didn't tell him everything," the AI said.

"No," said Dr. Halsey. "I didn't."

"I would be remiss not to point out that, as the individual responsible for the intellectual development of the Spartans, you've given him faulty information about how a control generally works in a scientific experiment. The control group generally is the group that does not experience the conditions of—"

"I know that, Déjà," said Halsey, cutting her off.

Déjà nodded curtly. "I would also be remiss not to point out that Soren-66 himself is precociously intelligent and has almost certainly realized that the reasons you gave for allowing him a choice were false."

"And what were my real reasons?" asked Dr. Halsey.

"I don't know," said Déjà. "I have a feeling, however, that I'm as confused about that as *you* are."

Dr. Halsey nodded.

"But if I had to guess," said Déjà, "knowing you as well as I do, I would say that it was a way of easing your own conscience. You just wanted to tell him. You wanted to tell one of them. You wanted to see if just one of them would make the choice for himself."

Dr. Halsey sighed. "Yes," she said. "You may be right. Thank you for being honest with me, Déjà."

"No need to thank me. I can't help it," said Déjà. "It's in my programming."

Dr. Halsey brushed her hand through the hologram and it disappeared. She leaned back in her chair. *I've given him a burden to live with*, she thought. *I've let him make his own decision, but Déjà's right. I've shifted the burden of responsibility back to him if anything goes wrong. A child. Carrying my sins.*

Let's hope nothing goes wrong.

FOUR

He was dreaming but even in the dream it was as if he couldn't wake up, as if he had been asleep for days and days. In the dream he was back in the forest again, but in addition to the cold and the hunger there was also something stalking him, a strange creature, almost human but not quite: deformed somehow, its mouth cast in an odd leer, its body lumpy and irregular, dragging one of its feet behind. It was always just a little way behind him, never quite catching up with him, but he couldn't seem to shake it, either. He could hear it there crashing through the woods behind him. Every so often it would give a cry of pain that was so piercing that it was all he could do to keep going. How long had he been walking? He ate what he could grab from the ground around him and kept going, dead on his feet, half-asleep, until suddenly he took a wrong turn and found the path before him blocked. And there the creature was, just behind him and on him before he could escape. It plucked him up off the ground like a toy and hurled him. He smashed through limbs and branches and came down hard, the forest around him fading to white as he died.

Only he wasn't dead. What he saw, all around him, was a blank, uneasy whiteness, filled with a slow buzzing. And then the whiteness slowly resolved into a piercing light. To either side of him, dim shapes began to take form, resolving into heads, the heads themselves covered with white cloth caps, the faces hidden behind breathing masks. Beneath these heads, he saw, the clothing that covered the bodies was spattered and stained with blood. It took him a moment to realize the blood was his own.

One of the heads was speaking, he realized, a low rumbling coming out of it, though he couldn't understand what it was saying. It stopped and one of the other heads started to make a similar sound. *What's wrong with them*, he wondered. And then, *What's wrong with me?*

Then a set of fingers waved itself over his eyes. He tried to follow them but could do so only at a slight remove, his eyes moving always just a little late. A head dove down closer to his eyes, suddenly becoming crisply, painfully defined.

"Is he supposed to be like this?" the head asked, its voice muffled through the mask. Then other heads were there, suddenly looming toward him, crisp and almost as if too close. There was a flurry of movement, too, shouting, and then everything became too slow, everything moving oddly and slowly, as if underwater.

This is real, he suddenly realized. *This is really happening.* Then abruptly the buzzing increased and the thought slipped through his mental fingers and was lost, to be replaced by another dream, another nightmare.

In the dream he was sitting in a chair but couldn't move. There was nothing restraining him, nothing blocking his arms or his legs; he simply couldn't move. No, wait, he could move a little, could move his eyes very slowly back and forth. At first the room was indistinct, as if the chair were simply sitting in the middle of a vast pool of darkness, but, very slowly, it began to take form around. Not a chair, he suddenly realized, but a bed: He was lying in a bed—how had he ever thought he was sitting upright in a chair? There was a blanket he recognized, but he couldn't quite place it. The shape of the bed was familiar as well, the shape of the room familiar, too, but he was unable to place where he was until the door at the far end of the room opened and his stepfather, impossibly large, stooped and shouldered his way in.

I'm in my mother's room, he thought. *In my mother's bed.*

And upon thinking that, he began to realize that he wasn't the only one in the bed, that he wasn't alone. But he couldn't turn his head to see who the other person was. His stepfather stood in the doorway, more shadow than man, a strange piping noise coming from him—something with all the structures of a language but impossible for him to even begin to understand. He appeared to be pleading, exhorting, but maybe it just seemed that way.

And then suddenly the other person in the bed moved, began to speak in the same birdlike piping, and though he still didn't understand a word of it he realized, by the sound and tenor of the voice, that it was his mother. She moved and he saw just the edge of her hand, the skin gray and beginning to rot, to come apart to show a thin strip of bone below. He wanted to scream, but all he could do was let his eyes dart frantically about in his sockets as she slowly shifted in the bed, her hand carefully feeling his face. She gave a low hiss and began to pull herself up.

He was just beginning to see her face when a sudden intense pain washed over him, as if someone had worked broken glass into his veins. The dream wavered and spun and reduced itself to a small white dot on a black field and then, with a hiss, was gone, leaving nothing but darkness behind.

How long did that last? Impossible to say. He had no sense of time passing, no sense of anything but that limitless void, a vague sense of himself as part of it, but even that seemed to be blurring around the edges, any sense of himself as an individual being threatening to slip away.

And then, very, very slowly, the darkness was broken by a small white dot, a dot which grew larger and larger and in the end swallowed everything around him.

And then it swallowed him as well.

He awoke to find himself screaming. He was restrained, tied down to some sort of table or bed, and he felt like he was on fire, his skin itching and burning. The veins on his arms stood out and pulsed and felt as if they were being torn slowly out of his skin. He flexed his wrist and pulled and the strap around it started to tear. It felt like a series of plate-glass windows were shattering beneath his skin, the muscles quivering and contorting over and into one another.

There were men and women in white coats all around him, but keeping a little distance, except for one, trying to approach him from just behind his head, almost out of sight, with a raised hypodermic. They were all moving slowly, too slowly, as if something was wrong with them, as if they were underwater. He tugged at the strap again and it tore like paper, and then he tugged at the other wrist and both hands were free.

He was still screaming, couldn't stop. He reached out and grabbed the hand with the hypodermic in it and squeezed, was surprised how quickly his fingers reacted and even more surprised to hear the bones in the man's wrist cracking like dry wood as they snapped. The sound the bones made was uncomfortably loud. He caught the hypodermic before it hit the floor, jabbing it into the neck of a man on the other side of him, who went down without a sound. The other hand was already tearing the straps off his legs. Some of the others had started to turn now, turning to flee the table, but they were moving so slowly—what was wrong with them? The pain was making it hard to think. He lashed out, struck the nearest one in the back with his fist, was surprised to see the man's body slam into the far wall and then collapse, leaving a blot of blood on the wall where he had struck.

Then he was out of the bed and running for the door, but something was wrong there, too—he was having a hard time keeping his balance. The whole world seemed to be coming at him at an angle, and his legs weren't working in the way he expected. He was loping more than running, one shoulder close to the ground, steadying himself against the floor every few

meters with an outstretched hand. He seemed to have
stopped screaming, though sounds were still pouring
out of his mouth, a kind of intense glossolalia, a language without meaning. He barreled through the remaining white-coated figures and they scattered at the
slightest touch, thrown to the floor, screaming and
groaning. And then he was out into the hall.

Which way? he wondered for the slightest fraction
of a second and then darted left. Where was he? It looked
familiar, it was somewhere he knew, but the pain was
still making it difficult to think. What had they been
doing to him?

He reached the end of the hall sooner than he'd expected and slammed into the wall, crumpling the panel
with his momentum before turning left again and continuing on his way. Was the wall that weak? Yes, he
thought, he knew this place, he knew where he was, the
Spartan compound, and then a wave of pain burned
through his head and he stumbled and went down
screaming.

Almost immediately he was up again. To the end of
the hall, he remembered, then right, and then the outer
doors. Then he'd be out and free, somewhere where
he—where *they*, he corrected himself—could never find
him.

An alarm was going off somewhere, the halls strobed
with a red light, but the strobe too was moving too
slowly. Again he didn't stop in time, running into the
wall at the end of the corridor and skittering off it before turning right and making for the outer doors.

But between him and it was a line of five or six

Marines, kneeling, pointing their weapons at him. And there, standing just behind them, hands on his hips, was CPO Mendez.

"Stand down, soldier!" the man's voice boomed out. And for just a moment Soren-66, hearing the command from the man he'd been taking orders from for more than a half dozen years now, slackened his pace.

But the pain and the confusion, the sensation he had of being trapped, of being hunted, quickly took over, and he sped up again.

"Stand down!" Mendez called again. Soren was almost on them now. He saw the muscles in the forearms of the Marines tighten slightly as they prepared to pull the trigger, and he suddenly found himself galloping on all fours, like a dog. As Mendez gave the order to fire, he leaped.

He heard the shots, oddly muffled. It wasn't bullets they were firing, he realized as he saw the blur of red flash by his elbow, but tranquilizer darts. They passed harmlessly below him except for one that he felt stinging in his ankle. He came down and smashed into the line of Marines and was through them, tugging the dart loose as he made for the doors.

He rammed into the doors, found them locked. He hit them hard with his shoulder and they gave a groaning sound, starting to yield. He hit them a third time and at the same moment felt the stinging of tranquilizer darts in his back and legs.

He bellowed in pain and frustration and turned to find himself confronted again by the row of Marines,

Mendez standing in front of them now, giving every impression of being in control of the situation.

"I asked you to stand down, soldier," stated Mendez. "Will you comply?"

The tranquilizers were starting to take effect. His tongue felt heavy in his mouth. The pain, which had been so visceral, so intense, was now receding into the background. He took a step, found his legs threatening to go out from under him. He started to turn back to the door, stumbled. The hallway lurched, righted itself. He turned back and found now, just behind the line of marines, an out-of-breath Dr. Halsey.

"Don't hurt him!" she was shouting. "Please!"

"Dr. Halsey!" he cried when he saw her. "What have you done to me?" Arms outstretched, he took a single step toward her and collapsed.

FIVE

When he woke up he was in the brig, his wrists now in titanium wristlets, each of them hooked firmly by a titanium chain to a ring in the wall. He tested them. They were too strong for him to break out of easily.

When he stood, he realized there was something wrong with his legs. They were strong, the muscles differentiated and much larger than before, but the muscles had done something to the bone, twisting them, curving them in odd directions. One leg was more or less normal, just a little bit bowed and twisted. The other, though, was gnarled and a good six inches shorter, and seemed more comfortable when folded up. That leg's ankle was rubbery and left the foot flopping. He could still stand but only at an angle, leaning far to the side, and he was more comfortable, he realized, if he used a hand for balance as well.

His arms, too, were rippling with muscle and seemed almost impossibly strong. They were for the most part fine: They were hardly deformed, relatively straight. But the fingers of one hand had become twisted and bowed, functioning now less like individual articulated digits and more like a single pincer or claw. *I've become a monster*, he thought.

He was still trying to take in his new body when the door opened and Dr. Halsey entered, an armed Marine to either side of her.

"Hello, Soren," she said.

He stood motionless, watching her. She in turn looked him over, both of them waiting out the other.

Finally, she turned to one of the Marines and said, "I don't think I'll need you."

"According to CPO Mendez—" the Marine started.

"This is a science facility and here, I outrank Chief Petty Officer Mendez," she said. "I want you to leave." She turned to the other Marine. "Both of you," she said.

"Is that an order, ma'am?" asked the second Marine, his voice calm.

"Yes, it is," she said.

The second Marine quickly saluted and went out. The other, after a moment's hesitation, followed.

"There," said Dr. Halsey. "That's a little bit better. I'm sorry about the restraints. They weren't my idea, but even I was overruled on that point. I'm afraid I don't have any means to remove them." She came closer and sat down on the cell floor, deliberately within easy reach of him. If he'd wanted to, he could reach out and break her neck. "Let's just do our best to pretend they're not there," she said.

Soren stared at her a long moment, then slowly sat back down, gathering his body awkwardly under him.

"How are you feeling?" she asked.

"I don't know," he said. His tongue felt awkward in his mouth, as if he were using it for the first time. "Not very good. I'm having a hard time thinking."

"That's probably the medication," she said. "They had to give you something for the pain."

He closed his eyes, remembering how his body had felt like it was being torn apart from the inside. "Is that normal?" he asked.

She shrugged. "We're still figuring out what normal is. Some people seem to have pain. For some of them it goes away. For others, it's always there."

He nodded.

"We thought you were going to die," she said, and reached out to touch his arm. He let her touch him for a moment then slowly pulled the arm back and out of reach. "You've been comatose for nearly three months. Again and again they thought you were going to die. It reached the point where we decided to disconnect life support. You flatlined for almost four minutes and then your heart started beating on its own again."

"I wish I had died," he said flatly.

She shook her head. "You may feel that way," she said, "but your body doesn't. It could have let go at any time, but it never did."

He tried to think that over, shook his head. He gestured at his legs, his gnarled hand. "What happened to me?" he asked.

"Your body reacted badly to the muscular enhancement injections and the thyroid implant," she said. "Basically your muscles grew in ways and directions that we couldn't predict and then tried to crush or twist the bones beneath them. We were able to use the carbide ceramic ossification process to stabilize and strengthen the bones and to stop it before it became too severe, but as you can see we had better luck with some limbs than others."

She watched him and waited for him to say something. When he didn't, she went on.

"Unfortunately, what that means is that there's a constant tension between your muscles and bones. It's like your body wants to tear itself apart. That may manifest itself as pain within the bone itself, as muscle pain, or as both. The pain may be intense, almost unbearable."

"I know," said Soren.

"With medication, the pain will be bearable. Some of us believe that as your body adjusts to its new state that the pain might diminish or go away entirely."

"Is that what you believe?" asked Soren.

"Do you want me to be honest?" Dr. Halsey asked.

"Yes," said Soren.

Dr. Halsey sighed. "No," she said. "I think the pain will diminish but I don't think it's likely that the pain will ever go away."

He nodded, his lips a grim line.

"On the other hand," she said. "You're stronger than even we imagined. The straps on the operating table were strong, with a titanium microweave through the cloth. They were overengineered to hold any of the other Spartans in place, but they weren't enough to hold you."

They were silent a moment. "How many of us are left?" he finally said.

She shrugged. "More than half," she said. "Almost half of you are dead. With another dozen or so, the modifications didn't take." She reached out and touched his arm again. "I'm sorry, Soren," she said.

He refused to meet her eyes. "I made the choice," he said. "I have nobody to blame but myself."

A moment later she stood and, without a word, left. Soren stayed where he was sitting on the floor, staring.

SIX

A week later he was out of the brig, released on his own recognizance. Some of the other Spartans, he saw, were in as bad or worse shape than he. Fhajad had uncontrollable muscle spasms and was confined to a wheelchair. René and Kirk had had the same difficulty that he had, but their bones were so twisted and deformed that they were now floating in gel tanks, unable to move on their own. A few others were even worse, kept in isolation chambers, comatose and always on the verge of death. Somehow he didn't find it comforting to think that their fates had been worse than his own.

After a few weeks the pain seemed to have diminished a little, though they kept him drugged enough that it was hard to say. The drugs did help with the pain but he hated the confusion they caused within him, the sense he had of having to plow through ideas, of not being able to finish a thought. That started to get as frustrating to him as the pain had been.

He slowly began to scale back the medication, palming a few of the pills each time he was given them, then more and more. The pain was strong and intense, but definitely slightly less than when he'd first awoken. He found he could stand it. *I can live with the pain*, he tried to tell himself. *What I can't live with is not being able to think*. Sometimes, though, he would make an imprudent twist or just move wrong and find himself on the verge of passing out, his forehead beaded with sweat.

He kept at it. Everything felt rawer to him, but yes, he could stand it. His head was clearer in a way, though the pain, like the drugs, could make it difficult to think. Still after a month he was palming all the pills, pretending to take them but instead taking them back to his room and dropping them into a drawer. In another two months, the drawer was almost completely full.

It was true that he was insanely strong. Early on, in a fit of frustration, he punched the wall in his room and was surprised when his fist tore through the metal panel as if it were thin plaster. He moved the bed so its post partially hid the damage and was careful from then on out.

It's not hopeless, he started to think as time went on. He was stronger than he'd ever been—faster, too, despite his awkward gait. And even if his arms and legs had suffered somewhat he still had everything he needed to be an excellent soldier, better than any normal, unmodified human. *I'm still a Spartan*, he told himself.

But not everyone, he found, agreed. When he tried to report back for active duty, CPO Mendez took a long, hard look at him and then said, in a voice gentler than any Soren had heard him use, "Walk with me, son."

They went down the hall together, an odd pair: Mendez straight and tall, his stride brisk and confident, Soren massive, but hunched and leaning, weaving as he went.

"Sweet William?" Mendez asked him, taking out a cigar.

Soren, looking surprised, shook his head.

"Ah," said Mendez, after first biting off the ends, "sometimes it's difficult for me to remember that you're all only boys. Filthy habit, this. Don't start it young."

"Yes, sir," said Soren.

Mendez got the cigar lit and sucked on it hard. The end glowed red and then ashed over, the smoke slowly oozing out of his nostrils. "I can't do it, son," he said.

"Can't do what?" asked Soren.

"I can't have you in active service."

"But I'm strong," said Soren. "I'm even stronger than the other Spartans, and almost as fast as some of them. I can keep up and I'm smart and . . ." Seeing the stern expression on Mendez's face, he let himself trail off.

"Nobody doubts your courage, son. And I for one don't doubt your ability. But if I put you in a team with the other Spartans, you know what'll happen?"

"What, sir?"

"They'll always be thinking about the ones who didn't make it, the ones that died while they went on. They'll feel a special obligation to look out for you and keep you alive that will affect their ability to perform. It'll hurt their focus, keep them from having that edge when they really need it. Right now, without you, they all move and think in a similar way. They work like a well-oiled machine. But there's something to be said for the symmetry they display, the instinctual camaraderie. You're good, no doubt about that—hell, I could see that on the day you woke up and went apeshit—but being on a team with other Spartans just isn't going to happen."

"Respectfully, sir—"

"Plus body armor," Mendez said. "It just won't fit you. Plus the difficulty of firing a weapon with that hand. No," he said, stubbing the Sweet William out on the floor. He reached out and put his hand on Soren's shoulder, looked him straight in the eye. From his look, Soren suddenly could see how hard it was for Mendez to say all he was saying, that he wished things could be different. "I'm sorry, son. Just be patient and maybe something will come along for you. But this, this just isn't it."

"CPO Mendez is right," said Dr. Halsey, just as he'd known she would. "He doesn't mean to hurt you, but he has to do what's best for the rest of the recruits and for the program."

"But it's not what's best for me," said Soren.

"Who says it isn't?" asked Dr. Halsey. "It's not what you want, but that doesn't mean it's not what's best for you."

"I want to serve," he said. "I don't want to be left behind."

"I'm sorry, Soren," she said. "You can't serve in this way. You'll be able to serve, but not in a combat position."

"All I want is to be given the choice," he said. "You always were willing to give me a choice in the past. Can't you do it again this time?"

She shook her head. "I'm sorry, Soren. Not this time."

SEVEN

Later, when he thought back to it, he saw that as the turning point. It shut too many doors for him, damaging him, closing parts of him off. And it was stupid, he tried to tell himself. They should have used him, they should have figured out something specially suited for him and his uniquely deformed body. It wasn't that he wasn't as good as the other Spartans—even Mendez had had to admit that. In some ways he was better than them, stronger. Sure, his skin and his brain sometimes felt like they were on fire, but he was learning to control that, learning to get around it and even focus it.

They could have found something for him, something that fit him, but instead they strapped him with a desk job within the compound, an ordinary run-of-the-mill job that just about anybody could have handled. They said it was temporary, but as time went on, it felt more and more permanent. Barely sixteen and already retired from active duty, already a paper pusher. It was as if they hadn't even tried to think of the right job for him. It was hard not to feel resentful.

Which was why, almost six months later, when one of the technicians—a fellow named Partch—began talking to him about revolution, instead of reporting the man he began to listen.

Partch started slow, just bits and pieces, hints. Sure, he said, the UNSC was much needed and important—we couldn't live without them. But didn't they sometimes come down too hard? Didn't they sometimes do things that were carried out with the best of intentions but, when you looked at them closely, were just simply wrong?

"Like with you, for instance," said Partch, once Soren had confessed what had happened to him. "Why aren't they making proper use of you? Strong as a bear, quick, smart too: It's a damned waste, if you ask me.

Yet they're still putting wet-behind-the-ears Marines right in the line of fire."

At the time Soren didn't respond, but later he couldn't help but think that yes, it was a waste, Partch was right. Soon, it wasn't just that he wasn't reporting Partch: He'd started to search him out. He listened, very rarely revealing what he was feeling about what Partch was saying, but listening, listening. Finally one day he said, "So what can we do about it?"

Partch shook his head. "I don't know," he said. "It's hard to know what to do to fix the system when it breaks. People are afraid of change; they'd rather limp on with a broken system than do the hard work of making a change. If you're not careful, before you know it you're labeled a terrorist."

"But there must be something I can do," said Soren.

"A guy like you," said Partch giving him a sidelong look, "sure, there's a lot you can do. But will you?"

"I think I would," said Soren.

"Even if you knew that others might see you as a terrorist? Do you care more about what people think, or about doing what's right?"

"I've never cared what people thought," said Soren, lying.

Partch gave him an appraising look. "No," he said. "I daresay you haven't."

It went on like that for a long time, Partch talking and hinting, and Soren becoming more and more eager to take part. It was exciting, like he was part of something, like something was happening. As he heard news of the other Spartans, he needed that, needed to feel like he was involved. His allegiances changed almost imperceptibly until, almost before he knew it, he found himself on the side of the rebels. Yes, he began to think, the USNC was too powerful for its own good; it had become a big bully. Yes, the colony worlds had the right to function in whatever way they wanted, had a right to be independent from the United Earth government if they so wanted. It was crazy to think otherwise. Yes, he was eager to help, yes, and since that was the case, what was he doing here?

"Be patient," said Partch. "We . . . they need people like you. But we have to wait for just the right moment. And let's take someone along with us—something as a souvenir."

EIGHT

Partch had a card that opened the lock—whether he had stolen it or had been given it as part of his job, Soren did not know. Inside was some sort of geological research laboratory. On one metal table was a simple wooden box with a metal screen in the place of its bottom, a sealed plastic tub next to it. Here and there, loose on tables or bolted to the ceilings and the walls, were precision instruments, things mostly unfamiliar to Soren.

They went in, Partch setting the door to stay slightly ajar behind them.

"Why not close the door all the way?" asked Soren.

"I'm not sure the card will open it from the inside," said Partch.

Stolen or rigged, then, thought Soren. *Never mind*, he thought, then recited in his head one of Partch's lines: *When the government goes bad, we all have to do things that we normally wouldn't do until it's back on the right track again.*

"It's the sixth cabinet," said Partch. "I disabled the alarm this morning from my panel. And I've put in a loop for the AI to look at for the room and the hall. Not easy, if I do say so myself, and not something likely to last long. Do you think you can open it?"

"What's in there?" asked Soren.

"Something important," he said. "Something we need."

Soren nodded, staring at the cabinet. It was made of a brushed metal, perhaps steel, the doors seemingly quite thick. He reached up and put his hand over the top edge, felt the door's top lip, gave an exploratory pull. It didn't move.

"I don't think I can do it without a prybar," said Soren.

Partch nodded, took a flat titanium-alloy bar, flanged at one end, out of his backpack.

"You came prepared," said Soren.

Partch just smiled. Soren took the bar and forced the end of it in the slight channel between the two doors, grunting, barely denting the metal slightly to either side, working it in until it had gone as far as it'd go.

Then, putting all his weight into it, veins popping out on his arms, he pulled.

For a moment Soren thought that even the crowbar would not be enough. He felt his arms burning, and a black hole began to open in his vision, the pain he always felt under the surface becoming reactivated by this new stress of muscle on bone. Then there was a creaking sound from the cabinet door and it buckled just a little around the lock.

He let up and forced the bar in deeper, and then bore down again. The door creaked again and buckled further, then this time came free. He handed the crowbar back to Partch who put it away, and then he opened the cabinet door fully.

Inside was a titanium case, about thirty centimeters long and fifteen wide, maybe ten centimeters deep.

"What is it?" asked Soren. "What's inside?"

Partch just smiled. He was just reaching for it when they heard a voice from behind them.

"I don't suppose you'd care to explain yourself," it said.

Soren turned, his expression immediately going flat and neutral. It was one of the Spartans, not one that Soren had known well, someone he'd only rarely been teamed with before washing out. Randall, his name was. He wasn't dressed in uniform or battle gear, was dressed down in a simple black T-shirt and loose gray cloth pants. His face was as neutral as Soren's.

"Hello, Randall," said Soren, thinking quickly. "Problem with this cabinet, with the lock mechanism. Sometimes it won't lock, sometimes it won't open."

"I know you," said Randall. "Soren, right? Used to be a Spartan. But you're not a technician."

"No," said Partch, "but I am. The lock had frozen and I couldn't get it open. I asked for his help to unjam it."

"At this hour?" asked Randall.

"The lab is swamped during the day," claimed Partch. "They didn't want us clanging around during office hours."

Randall looked back and forth between them. "All right," he said. "You don't mind if I verify, do you?"

"Of course not," said Soren.

"If we weren't supposed to be here, the alarm would have gone off," added Partch. "But no, by all means, you should verify."

Randall nodded, his lips tight. "Let's go then."

Soren immediately started for the door. Randall moved back and out into the hall to let him come, keeping a safe distance. *He's smart*, thought Soren. *Well trained.* He started down the hall, Partch just behind him, Randall taking up the rear.

"Where are we going?" asked Partch.

"Nearest com-link," said Randall.

Soren stopped and turned, miming a puzzled expression. "But the nearest com-link is back in the roo—" he said, and then leaped.

Randall saw the blow coming and shifted just a little, but still took a glancing blow in the shoulder; they tumbled down to the floor together, rolling back and forth. Randall kicked him hard and then tried to wriggle free, but Soren wouldn't let go. Randall was faster,

Soren knew, but he was stronger. If he just didn't let go of his hold, he might keep the advantage.

Randall kicked him hard in the face, but Soren was already working his way up the man's body. Randall kept kicking, trying to work his arms into position for a choke hold, but before he managed, Soren had straddled his hips and locked both hands behind Randall's back. He gave a shout and squeezed as hard as he could.

Pain shot through his own arms and chest. Randall gave a groan and started to struggle harder, dragging Soren down the hall with him. *Hold on*, thought Soren. *Just hold on*. He squeezed harder, burying his face against Randall's chest as the latter pummeled his arms and head and then tried desperately to reach behind his own back to break Soren's fingers.

Not the way you're used to fighting, is it? thought Soren.

Randall was shouting now, then suddenly he went limp.

Too soon, thought Soren, *he's faking*, and held on.

But Randall kept still. Partch, Soren realized, was talking to him, pounding him on the back, his face just a few inches from Soren's own.

"What?" hissed Soren.

"Snap out of it, man. I tranquilized him. Let go of him before you kill him. Let's get out of here."

He turned his head to see the tranquilizer dart embedded in Randall's shoulder. The "faked" limpness. Carefully he unclasped his hands and worked his way free. Randall was fighting the drug, not quite under, but could move little more than his eyes. Soren felt his chest. Maybe a broken rib or two, but probably that was all. And he wouldn't be out for long.

"Let's get out of here!" said Partch again and started down the corridor.

Soren took a last look at Randall and then started after him. Partch moved in a rapid walk, fast enough to look to the compound's AI like he had somewhere he needed to be five minutes ago, but not fast enough to seem like he was running. Soren tried to follow his lead, quickly realizing he was heading toward the compound's airfield.

"There's an older Longsword," Partch said as Soren caught up with him. "It's pre-prepared and hacked for us, complete with a dumb AI construct that I fast-grafted to convert him to the cause. We make for that and get it in the air, get away from the base, and to the drop point as fast as we can."

NINE

But before they had even entered the field, alarms started sounding. By the time they were in the Longsword and taking off, a good half-dozen ships were being crewed, ready to take off in pursuit. *Plus*, thought Soren, *the planet is surrounded by Orbital Defense Platforms. This is a crazy idea.*

The first warning shot flashed past them before they had even cleared the atmosphere, shaking the ship slightly. It was quickly followed by two more, precision shots, even closer, that shocked the ship from end to end. Partch looked scared.

"Evasive maneuvers, Captain Teach!" he instructed the AI.

The latter flickered to holographic life on the console before them. His construct was a pirate captain, bristling with pistols, with a gold-toothed grin and an ebony beard in braids.

"Have been evading all along, lads," Teach said. "There's just too many of the bastards." He put one hand to his ear, pretended to listen. "Signal coming in—care to hear it?"

Partch, holding on to the arms of the chair with white-knuckled fingers, just nodded.

"Longsword," said a voice that Soren did not recognize. "You have not been authorized for takeoff. Return to base immediately."

"Seems like they should have sent out that *before* they started firing across our bow," said Soren.

"Well, they did," the AI admitted. "But I knew you wouldn't want to parley with such scallywags."

Partch groaned. A shot caught them, burning across the wing, inflicting light damage and giving the Longsword a worrying wobble. The atmosphere was thinner now but they still hadn't broken free of Reach's gravitation.

"How long until we reach our rendezvous?" asked Soren.

Teach gave a hearty laugh. "Astronav is unstable after that hit," he said. "I can't say that we're likely to go anywhere we want at all, even once we're free of the planet's gravity."

"Oh God, oh God," said Partch. "We're going to die!"

"We'll have to turn back," said Soren. "Teach, let them know we surrender."

A blow caught them from behind, spinning the craft almost all the way around. Black smoke, Soren realized, was billowing around them.

"Never surrender," said Teach, his hologram flickering. "Besides, too late for that. Systems are being shut down before they go critical. A pleasure knowing you, lads."

He vanished. The lights flickered and went out. The craft spun and spiraled, slowly stabilizing. Then gravity began to sink its claws into it and it started down.

"Buckle in," said Soren to Partch. Backup power kicked in, stuttered once, then went out again. He flicked the controls over to manual. The engines were gone but, unlike some of the other USNC spacecraft, the Longsword had enough of a wingspan that he might manage to bring it down even without the engines. The flaps he could manually control—at least in theory. He'd never flown one before, but he'd flown sims of the Longsword's various predecessors and variants, back when he was a Spartan, and crash-landing was one of the scenarios. It should work. With a little luck, they might even survive.

He engaged manual, grabbed hold of the stick with both hands, and pulled back, trying to level the craft out and bring it down as softly as he could. The fighters behind him were no longer firing, able, no doubt, to see that the Longsword was in trouble.

They were going faster now, a slow whine building around the aircraft. It was hard to hold the stick in place. Partch, he saw, was passed out from fear, g's, or a combination of both.

They were just above the clouds now, then moving down and through them, the Longsword buffeted back and forth by odd crosswinds. He let the craft settle a little further until they burst out of the bottom of clouds, and then he banked, trying to get a clear view of what was around them. Kilometers of farmland in most directions, more inhabited towns and districts in others, but there, in the distance, almost out of sight, a shimmer of green that he hoped was one of Reach's vast swathes of deciduous forest.

"Teach," he said, "Any life left in you?"

There was no response. He would have to try to eyeball it, figure out how to come down in a way that would get him close enough to the forest for a quick escape while still letting him land on open ground.

He circled once and saw the pursuing ships still there, just coming through the clouds now, hanging back a little distance, waiting. He pointed toward the green line and started down.

He was, he quickly realized, too high, but better too high than too low. He dipped and corrected. There, that was more or less right. Yes, he saw as they came closer, definitely forest. He'd have to come very close and then try to bring the Longsword along its edge, keep it there more or less once they hit the ground. Then, if he survived the crash, he'd simply disappear.

Lower now. Nearly able to make out individual trees. This was the tricky part, banking just right and then correcting and then descending, trying to keep it all straight. Partch awake and screaming now. *Ignore it if you can*, he told himself. No, not quite, coming in too close to the trees. Starting away again, but too late, the wing clipping the treetops and starting to come asunder. Out of control now, shaking and shuddering, the craft falling to pieces around him. An engine torn free and crashing through trees as if they were toothpicks. *Hold on, Soren*, he thought, *hold on*. One part of his mind was screaming, screaming. The other part was calm, cold. *Why worry, Soren?* that second part was asking, as the plane around him caught fire and, screeching and falling apart, gouged a half-kilometer-long channel along the ground. *You've lived through much worse*, it was telling him. *You should be able to live through this*. Partch, he saw from the corner of his eye, was dead, his neck broken, his eyes glazed over. Soren's arm seemed to be on fire. He could see the ground and the sky through cracks in the craft as what was left of the fuselage turned over and over again. Metal burning and grinding around him, he waited for whatever god that controlled the farce that was his life to flip some charred and malformed cosmic coin and decide his fate.

EPILOGUE

There was a knocking on the door. Or rather a rapping on the doorframe: The door had already slid open, revealing Chief Petty Officer Mendez, still in fatigues, an unlit Sweet William jutting from one corner of his mouth.

Dr. Halsey looked up from her desk. "Well?" she said.

"I've been to the site," said Mendez, taking the chair at the other side of the desk. She could still smell the smoke in his clothing. "I've looked at the wreckage. Not much left. Most of the fuselage is gone and what's left is mangled, hardly worth much even as scrap. There was a fire as well. There's a body, charred pretty much beyond recognizing, but it doesn't belong to Soren-66."

"How can you be sure?"

Mendez gave her a look. "Wasn't deformed," he said. "And no evidence of augmentation. Not to mention he was barely six feet, even when you account for fire damage. Must have been the missing technician, Partch—running DNA now. We don't know how that one got in here in the first place—take one look at his background and he has all the earmarks of a rebel. We've got some sort of problem with somebody higher up in security."

"I'll look into it," said Dr. Halsey.

"You do that, ma'am," said Mendez. "If I were you I'd run the check again on everybody."

He took out his lighter and held it near the end of his cigar. Before lighting it, he raised his eyebrows inquisitively. She shook her head. A faint look of disgust crossing his mouth, he put the lighter away, leaving the cigar unlit.

"Anything else, Mendez?" she asked.

"We looked at the parts torn free as well, what we could find of them in the woods. No evidence of him there either. Could be he was thrown out early on. If that's the case, we'll never find the body. Or could be he made it out in one piece."

"You think he's still alive?" Dr. Halsey asked.

Mendez shrugged. "No way to tell," he said. "All I'll say is that it's strange that we didn't find any trace of him. Could be alive, I suppose, but it's not likely, even for a Spartan. Considering the kind of luck that Soren-66 had to this point, it's hard to imagine things working out well for him." He paused, meditative. "Then again," he said, "maybe his luck was about due for a change."

Dr. Halsey nodded curtly. "How's Randall doing?" she asked.

Mendez snorted, lips curling back into an almost predatory smile. "He's fine. Kicking himself for letting his guard down a little, but there was nothing he could have done and as far as I can tell, he didn't let down much. He might have taken Soren-66, but couldn't take both him and somebody armed with a tranquilizer. He did what he could. It's good for him to go through something like this. In the long run, he'll be a better soldier because of it."

Halsey nodded. *Sink or swim*, she couldn't help but think. And what was it Soren had said, a few years back now? That he didn't want to be left behind? An incident like this would make Randall less cocky, would get him scrambling to make sure that he was up to snuff.

"I've inserted ground troops. Set them combing the woods for the body," said Mendez.

"They won't find him," Dr. Halsey said.

"Maybe not," he said. "Still it'd be nice to be able to wrap things up, to have some closure."

"You won't get it. Pull your men back in and file him MIA," said Dr. Halsey.

"Not KIA?"

She shook her head. "Not without a body. He's lived through a lot and had a lot of bad luck along the away. He lived through pain that killed some of the other recruits. We should have figured out something for him, some better way of making use of him. I'd bet he's out there somewhere, still alive."

"If he's out there, we can find him."

"No, you won't," she said. "He grew up living in the forest. You'll find him only if he wants to be found. You might as well pull your troops."

"But—"

She reached across the desk and touched his arm. "Let him go, Franklin," she said, her voice softening. "He's no threat to us."

"He's an augmented, Spartan-trained insurrectionist sympathizer. How is that not a threat?" he asked.

"He's no traitor. He's just a lost soul, looking for a direction. I know him. Trust me."

"What about—" he started to answer, then thought

better of it, stopped. He stood, saluted her, and went out, leaving her to her thoughts.

Gone now, she thought.

Was I wrong? she thought. *Should I not have given him the choice? Should I not have brought him into the Spartan program in the first place?*

She ran a finger slowly through Déjà's hologram construct, watched the AI clutch her clay tablets closer to her chest and stare at her, puzzled, curious.

Had she been wrong? She sighed. Too late for it to matter either way.

"Penny for your thoughts," said Déjà.

Dr. Halsey shook her head. Déjà smiled. Then she shrugged and disappeared.

Whether she'd been wrong or right, Dr. Halsey realized, she was committed now. She'd had seventy-five lives to watch out for, seventy-five lives depending on her, seventy-five lives weighing on her conscience. Even if it was down now to less than half that, there were still several dozen Spartans depending on her. Not to mention the weight of all those already dead. The future of millions might depend on them, on how well she'd done her job. Not *might*, she corrected herself, *did*.

She straightened her shoulders, shifting under her burden, and went back to work.

STOMPING ON
THE HEELS OF A FUSS

ERIC RAAB

THE INTENSE stink and splatter from the Brute's roar woke Connor Brien instantly—a web of spittle connected the beast's jagged, bloodstained fangs. The smell of the Brute's breath was bad enough, but as he tried to wipe the wet off his face, he just set the odor deeper into his mustache, beard, and all over his hands. He convulsed, gagging once before vomiting the last MRE he'd eaten. He kept his eyes on the ground, knowing to avoid eye contact with the gray-haired beast, something he learned from all of his studies before arriving. He'd watched video feeds of humans who dared to stare defiantly at Brutes and were beaten into mush in seconds. Even the slightest eye contact was some form of challenge they could not resist.

His last memory was of falling from the tree he'd set up as his surveillance point. He'd been watching a trio of the beasts as they gestured to one another, trying to track a human that they'd let escape from captivity for the fun of hunting him down. He thought he'd be safe up high, but he quickly learned that the Brutes not only had a great sense of smell but they were excellent climbers. He had fallen while panicking, reaching for his tranq dart gun as one of the Brutes climbed quickly toward him. He felt down by his leg and breathed a sigh of relief. Its reassuring bulk was still strapped to his ankle.

He kicked himself for not having his M6, which sat nestled in his pack at his base camp; but then he realized, what good would it do? Another dozen or so Brutes hovered behind the one who treated him to his wake-up shower. Varying in shades of brown and black, tan and gray, each hulking beast seemed more fierce and frightening than the next. They each stood at about nine feet, and though he didn't dare to look, they all seemed to be casting hungry eyes on his five-foot-five frame. Even if he could take out twelve of them, the thirteenth would rip him to shreds.

He surveyed his surroundings. It was a makeshift camp, all centered around a large Covenant ship. The nearby outpost's shops and cabins had clearly been ransacked, the camping equipment and supplies strewn among what looked like thousands of human bones, all still with dried blood and muscle clinging to them. He even noticed a few methane tanks scattered about and the charred remains of Grunts. They were eating their own.

He turned to survey his fellow captives and the smell really set in, death clinging to the roof of his mouth. They all hovered together but there was no fence or wall keeping them in. He thought immediately that he could run for it, but as he looked at the other prisoners and the mounds of human carnage surrounding the camp, he knew that was a bad idea. None of the prisoners looked anywhere near well. Shreds of soiled clothing hung in tatters from their malnourished bodies. Knotted hair on their heads and faces, bloodstained hands and teeth, unhealed scars and open wounds, mounds of excrement . . . no one looked capable of moving, except him. And judging by the way this beast welcomed him awake, that wouldn't last very long. Why the Brutes had been keeping any of them alive was beyond his understanding.

He'd spent four days watching this camp from about a mile up a rolling hill of forest, and as soon as he'd arrived he knew it was a bad scene. Reports had the human occupancy of Beta Gabriel at barely five hundred people. But judging by the carnage he'd seen strewn about the forest, it had to have been much more. Beta Gabriel was a blip on the map, an "uninhabited" planet that a group of entrepreneurs turned into a secret society, an "outdoors" getaway: a place where the wealthy came to hike, hunt, go on spirit quests, or to get in touch with themselves or whatever they got in touch with. There wasn't a lot of commerce or buildings on the planet, just a few supply shops, a basic landing port, a few rustic cabins strewn about, and a community lodge outfitted with information on the planet and maps of the area.

In the time he'd studied the Brutes from his tree, he had witnessed some of the most vulgar and brutal treatment of another living species he'd ever seen. It had been completely unbearable to watch, let alone understand. The Brutes had turned their human captives into toys. Some were tortured in despicable ways, pitted against one another in games that even Brien couldn't make out the rules for—at least not at that distance.

Connor Brien was one of the Office of Naval Intelligence's top operatives, recruited by ONI after the Covenant first attacked Humanity. His work in linguistic anthropology was as good as it gets, most noted for deciphering the language and sociological structure of a lost tribe discovered deep in the tundra of North America that had survived hundreds of years in an elaborate cave dwelling. Their origins dated back some six hundred years, and Brien linked their societal structure back to a small charismatic cult that emerged in the early 1970s.

As an ONI intelligence officer, he had played an integral part in unraveling the methodology behind the Covenant by brilliantly decoding the sign language of a captured Covenant Engineer, and had been the commanding ONI officer on some of the most harrowing attempts to capture Covenant species alive. He had an extreme taste for adventure. He was fearless and brilliant, as relentless as a man can get. He earned the nickname "Kip" among his peers, an homage to Rudyard Kipling, a nineteenth-century novelist and adventurer. He actually looked a bit like Kipling, with his bushy eyebrows and salt-and-pepper beard.

But it was one fateful day that really put him on his path. He and a team of Marines had actually succeeded in subduing a Brute-led siege of their ship as they traversed for the first time into Covenant space. They managed to tranq the six Brutes who boarded, but they should have killed them. When he got a really close look at them he was in awe. But the tranq darts wore off fast on these behemoths and their attempts to contain them quickly proved feeble. The pack literally tore their way out of the synthetic alloy constraints, and even unarmed proved to be an unstoppable force. The Marines managed to wipe out their fierce gray-haired leader, and Brien hid and watched in amazement as his death incited something primal in the others, who began scrambling and recklessly attacking with more viciousness and abandon than before. But what really interested him was that there was one lone Brute whose coat was much shaggier than the others, that didn't charge and simply watched the melee. He thought at first he might have still been suffering from the effects of the tranq, but immediately after the enraged pack overwhelmed the unprepared Marines, they turned on their inactive brother. Brien was mesmerized by this murderous rampage. He was lucky to make it to the evac craft in one piece.

For months their ferocity haunted him. He started gathering all the footage and reports on the race that came in. Brutes showed a diversity not only in appearance but in the way they carried themselves, as if the weight of the world was on some of their shoulders and others were free to stand tall and dominant. He intuited they must be a weathered species, hardened by many years of struggle, most likely battling among themselves. He tried numerous times to get approval to travel back into Covenant space in search of their home world. Every attempt was denied. But when Brutes started playing a larger role in the attacks on human planets and were suspected of having some animosity toward other Covenant species, his requests started working themselves further into ONI command. When word came down that they had seized the planet Beta Gabriel, he finally got his approval. They were nesting right in his backyard.

His mission was to gather as much as he could on the inner workings of this race of the Covenant, find out just how many survivors remained on Beta Gabriel, and look into finding anything among this species that could be used to cause deeper fissures within the Covenant juggernaut. It was a simple operation. Enter point A, watch from point B, exit a few days later from the exact drop at point A. Quiet, discreet, quick. He'd never thought it would be this bad.

Ceretus hated being around these despicable creatures. If it were up to him he would have them all in his belly. He truly enjoyed the taste of their flesh, but Parabum's new "honor" code put an end to it. Their Chieftain decided that the simple slaying and eating of the humans had to stop; there were too few of them left and it was far better to keep them around than to quickly eliminate them. Many of the others agreed, and Ceretus had to admit it was extremely enjoyable to watch them suffer. But he just couldn't stand living among them, especially after the shame he'd been suffering since their defeat.

When they'd first arrived on this forest planet, it had

been a glorious day. The humans all clumped themselves together in one area, as if that made them safer.
Only a few of them were even armed. Ceretus and his
brother, Maladus, didn't even need their spikers; they
had more fun killing by hand. The hunts lasted for days,
the bounties delicious, their bellies never fuller. Ceretus
knew that the gods would have been pleased with this
conquest. It was a bittersweet revenge in the face of
such a painful loss. But as the days passed and the human population dwindled, there was still no sign that
the Chieftain was ready to leave.

Ceretus quickly began regretting following this cow-
ardly Chieftain when he retreated from the massive
attack. Now, as he stared at the newly found human
they'd shaken from the tree, he would have much preferred to die in battle. This was not the life for a true
follower of the Great Journey.

He looked back toward his brothers-in-arms. All
were barely capable of understanding the path the Fore-
runners left for them to follow. He took his eyes from
the pathetic human captives to the ship that brought
them here, the *Valorous Salvation*. Chieftain Parabum
kept the ship constantly protected with four of his
bodyguards. He refused to power the ship's communications; he didn't want anyone to find them. It was
more and more obvious that their Chieftain feared any
backlash from the defeat, and he was right to be fearful. His cowardice was punishable by death.

His brother, Maladus, had been leery when their
pack had been folded into Parabum's. They were from
two of the most divergent clans dating back as far as

Jiralhanae history goes—ancient enemies. The two clans fought even before the great civil war that knocked the Jiralhanae from a space-faring species back to being bound to their planets, forced to rediscover the great advances their ancestors had made before them. They were able to coexist again rather peacefully once the Covenant brought the unifying words of the Great Journey, but their deep-seated distrust for one another slowly rose again . . . and knowing the history of that clan, they had strikingly different levels of devotion to the Covenant.

Parabum's clan never fully believed in the power of the gods, nor did they worship the technology left behind. They feared, in fact, becoming too dependent on technology. Ceretus's clan was always the more intelligent, and their beliefs fell more in line with the San 'Shyuum, believing with devout faith in the Great Journey and the gods that took it before them. Ceretus's clan was terribly ashamed of the civil war that forced the Jiralhanae to give up hundreds of years of progress, and they were at the forefront of rebuilding their scientific prowess when the San 'Shyuum arrived. They were beyond grateful for the opportunity to take to the stars once again.

Parabum's clan reviled it. It was their kind of thinking that robbed the Jiralhanae of their rightful place among the Covenant species; they used the artifacts in disrespectful ways, more opportunistic than holy. They believed only in muscle and tradition, in the strength of living without an overwhelming reliance on technology. It made them fierce warriors, Ceretus had to admit, reliant on their strength and loyalty to one another. But Ceretus and Maladus both knew from the start that Parabum was strong in body but weak in mind. He never kept any of his underlings in line, leaving them on their own, lazy and undisciplined. This was not the way to rule a pack. Ceretus knew you ruled through fear and manipulation, and faith in the gods. He could never respect Parabum's leadership.

It was only a matter of time before someone challenged Parabum for the Chieftainship, and Maladus had burst out surprisingly one day shortly after they had landed. It was a risky move, as they hadn't established much of an alliance in their movement against Parabum, but Maladus called out a challenge anyway. And once you called out a challenge there was no turning back. Maladus had always been a cunning warrior, but the truth was that Parabum was twice as strong. Parabum overpowered Maladus from the start, pummeling him blow after blow. Maladus did little damage to the Chieftain. He barely landed a worthwhile strike. The battle lasted only a few minutes before Parabum had completely subdued Maladus. Ceretus watched, his whole body tense with anger as Parabum stomped on his brother's neck, crushing it at the shoulder blade. And to rub it in, he viciously bit into Maladus's broken neck and ripped his throat out with his teeth.

It was pure disrespect. Now Ceretus couldn't stand looking at Parabum, let alone follow another order from him. And he knew Parabum knew it. Ceretus wished he were strong enough to challenge the Chieftain, but Maladus had been even stronger than him; he stood little chance.

He turned back to the human prisoners and licked his fangs. He went from face to face, trying to strike intense fear in each of the captives. There was little else to do with his time.

"Has our Chieftain returned from the hunt?" Ceretus called out in the face of the newly captured bushy-eyebrowed human, who had quietly coiled into himself.

"Not yet," answered Facius, his tan fur prickling up a bit as he, too, ogled the captives. He was a particularly impressionable warrior who had become Ceretus's right hand after Maladus's demise.

"Perhaps enough time to fire up one of these, a little snack before the feast, served with a proper blessing."

"But the Chieftain, he will certainly smell the cooking flesh." This response came from Hammadus, Facius's brother, a young, rich-coated brown warrior that showed signs of naiveté but was perhaps the strongest of the pack. Ceretus could smell the young one's fear in daring to disobey the Chieftain. It was Hammadus that got the newly found human out of the tree, and whined demands that they bring him back to the camp, to show their Chieftain, rather than eat him on the spot.

Ever since Parabum called for the eating of human flesh only after a traditional and grossly overelaborate hunt, Ceretus couldn't bear the idea of following suit. Plus, the time it took to bring the carcass in from the forest caused the meat to spoil. Any worthy Jiralhanae knew all too well that the fresher the kill, the finer the taste. A savage like their Chieftain wouldn't bother to savor the feast properly in the name of the gods.

"What do you suggest, young brother?"

"Well the Chieftain doesn't know we didn't kill one in the hunt, does he?" Facius asked with an ever-so-slight grin. "We can at least have some fun until he returns."

"Yes we can, Facius." And he turned back to the prisoners. This young one showed promise.

Brien couldn't help but stare out at the human remains lining the forest pathways, hanging from trees, beaten to pulpy pieces surrounding the camp. It was disgusting. One thing was obvious: These beasts had no respect for humans at all. The same keen sense of smell the Brutes followed to his hiding place didn't seem bothered by the awful stench of human carnage. He figured it might actually seem sweet to these monsters.

Though he'd only been awake in captivity for a few hours, Brien was starting to make sense of a few of their growls and grunts, at least emotionally. It didn't take long for Brien to pick up on a brewing impatience from the circling Brutes.

"What do you think they're doing?" Brien whispered to the man next him, as the Brutes all began walking down the line of prisoners.

"You don't want to know . . ."

Brien watched carefully, looking away at any sign of a Brute turning back toward him. Most of the captives slept or showed such shock and fear that he found it impossible to communicate with many of them, but this man he immediately recognized. Dasc Gevadim was a renowned guru of a religion known as Triad. Those who followed the Triad teachings believed that we all harbored three internal lives, and spiritual transcendence only occurred if you managed to link all three. His followers ran galaxy wide. He used to run seminars via public comm channels, but he'd disappeared about ten years ago. It was much publicized. Many called it a transcendence, and his following grew exponentially with such reports. The sales of his vidcasts went through the roof.

"They're deciding which one of us to eat, huh?" Brien asked, knowing the answer.

"Not exactly. Big Boy seemed to put a stop to it. Now they only eat after they let one of us go and hunt us down," Dasc whispered back. His scraggly white beard was caked with dust and blood. His eyes glassy and red. Brien wondered if they had been feeding the captives raw human flesh. He didn't want to know.

"Which one is Big Boy? That one?" He pointed discreetly to the one who had knocked him out of the tree.

"No. Big Boy isn't around. Maybe still hunting," the man next to Dasc answered—a sickly yet stocky man Brien recognized as a famous big-game hunter, named Hague or something.

It made sense. He'd seen a few packs scrambling around this morning, and now there was silent hostility among the beasts as if they were on the verge of doing something wrong.

This especially rang true for the slightly graying, black-furred one, the one with a clean-shaven face, who had been surveying the captives and had treated Brien to a foul saliva offering. He seemed to have good control of the lot. Brien immediately called him Six.

Just then, Six caught wind of the whispering and turned back toward them. All three men adjusted themselves awkwardly. As he made his way closer, Dasc was quickly overrun with some of the deepest fear Brien had ever seen. Fear was never in Brien's blood. He was usually ready for any end that might meet him, but as this man-eating giant beast lumbered over toward him, his body trembled in fright.

Six stopped right in front of the cringing Dasc. His nostrils flared as he looked closer, grabbing at Dasc's arms and poking at his scrawny build. He then made a grunt that was obviously a summoning or a name. Two other Brutes made their way over; one tan that Brien dubbed Butch, and the huge, rich brown one he'd thought was Big Boy. He quickly referred to him as Ludo, though he couldn't figure out why. He wondered if any among them were female. It was impossible to tell. In all of his research, he'd never positively identified one.

Six grabbed Dasc in one big rip with his right hand, but when Hague leaped back startled, his eyes must've met Six's. The Brute immediately dropped Dasc, pulled Hague out and tossed him toward the other Brutes. Dasc's body lay limp and unconscious beside Brien, and judging from the smell he'd lost control of his bowels.

Brien and the other captives watched fearfully as Six let out a roar and a hand motion—a wider summons—and a crowd started to gather around. Hague wobbled himself upright, trying to be as brave and defiant as one could when surrounded by nine-foot-tall hairy beasts, all able to crush you in a blink and drooling in anticipation of a fresh meal.

Just as Brien finished counting the fifteen Brutes surrounding Hague, one of them ripped the famed hunter up by the leg and held him upside down. The others gave roars of laughter. The old saying always held true; laughter was the same everywhere, even in the Covenant. Hague struggled to rise, trying desperately to wiggle himself free, when another grabbed at his other leg. The crowd goaded them on and another Brute grabbed an arm, and that's when Brien couldn't look anymore. He watched as Six suddenly seemed to lose interest as well, wandering back beyond the crowd, to the edge of the forest. He couldn't quite place why the beast would incite such a spectacle and walk away, unless it was to impress.

Hague's screams sent shivers through Brien's bones and he shut his eyes. Then the screams stopped with a chorus of crunches and yells from the Brutes. His mind's eye painted it black. The hollering Brutes slowly gave way to silence and Brien opened his eyes again. The crowd had dispersed, and standing amidst the torn and bloodied remains of Hague was undoubtedly the one Dasc had referred to as Big Boy. Clad in a few strokes of armor and with his gray-brown hair unkempt around his snout, the hammer-wielding leader definitely was one of the biggest Brutes Brien had ever seen. He stood there silently. Brien looked around for Six; he was nowhere to be found.

Ceretus watched from the darkness as Chieftain Parabum stood silent with his hammer over his shoulder. Behind him were his security chief, Jupentus, and his right hand, Brunus. Two of the dumbest Jiralhanae Ceretus had ever encountered. They each had dragged in a human corpse behind them. Parabum took in his pack with disappointment.

"Looks like a bit of fun was had here," he said, signaling the human remains with his hammer. "Without me." Parabum lifted the torso, a string of muscle still connected the head. Ceretus's stomach growled. "A plump one, too. Who led this game?" He looked around to see, but everyone was bowing their heads in respect.

Ceretus knew no one would confess; it was too risky. Parabum never kept a cool head for anything. He chose awkward battles to fight, found disrespect where none was intended. He was one of the worst Chieftains Ceretus had the displeasure of serving. He watched hungrily as the head of the human swayed off the juicy torso. He had been looking forward to feasting on this one, but now it would certainly spoil. Brother Golubus had come really close to making the fatter ones taste like Thorn Beast, and he missed that delicacy as much as he missed the brothels back on Teash. The humans ruined any chance of returning to such pleasures. Parabum ruined it, really. But here he was listening to a Chieftain who couldn't even properly sermon the pack. There was a lot of hate in Ceretus's heart, mostly for the humans who put him here—but he was happy to focus all his hatred on this ancient clan enemy and the bastard who disgraced his brother. He couldn't hold the hatred in much longer. He'd rather die than rot in the shadows of this coward.

"It was me, my Chieftain, who called for the preparation." Ceretus emerged boldly from the darkness. "Our brothers were getting restless in their hunger, and I feared you'd be late in returning." He quickly hid his bravery, taking on a much humbler tone as a shred of fear took over.

"Ceretus, do you not have faith that your Chieftain is the greatest of hunters, a fierce and keen tracker, especially of these simple creatures?" Parabum was obviously trying to test him. The Chieftain walked toward him with no fear.

"I have no such doubt, Chieftain," Ceretus said as he approached, bowing before him at arm's length. "This was a kill from our hunt, and we figured we'd go ahead and get it prepared while it was still fresh." He bowed again, keeping his eyes on the ground in front of him. The charade pained him.

Parabum grabbed his throat; his nails, digging through Ceretus's fur, pierced his skin. "Not one of these pathetic creatures is to be touched without your Chieftain to sanction it. Not one." Ceretus struggled to keep his eyes averted, his shame apparent in his lack of challenge. And like a switch going off, the Chieftain released his grip, his attention diverted to the human pen.

"What is this!" Parabum slowly walked toward the pen, Ceretus gasping for air. "A new human emerged?!"

Ceretus looked over toward Hammadus, who was watching in excitement.

Hammadus shouted proudly, "We found him up in a tree, my Chieftain. I climbed up and the coward fell to the ground in fear before I could even reach him. A blessing from the gods, Chieftain. Perhaps there are more out there. We brought him back here . . . he will make a great hunt, I'm sure. Being able to climb so well and all."

Parabum looked annoyed. Ceretus watched as the Chieftain wandered over to where the hulking young warrior stood, his head returning to a humble and fearful bow.

"A find indeed," Parabum added, assessing the now frightened Hammadus, who stood almost a foot taller and wider than his Chieftain. Parabum brought his hammer from his shoulder to the ground. Ceretus knew that once Parabum caught a whiff of fear he would dig in deep, just as he had done to him.

Ceretus watched as Parabum tried to intimidate Hammadus. He knew the young warrior was getting stronger, and this was another attempt to scare him into servitude. Perhaps the smartest move Parabum had yet pulled off. Ceretus would have to be smarter.

Once Parabum felt Hammadus was sufficiently cowed, his tone took a celebratory note and he addressed the rest of the pack. "Tonight we feast on three of the pathetic creatures. May we consume their flesh as an offering from the gods. Enjoy, my brothers; once again we dine like kings." Parabum looked out to the others as they cheered obligingly. Ceretus, clutching his pierced throat, gave the vainglorious Parabum's back a secret, hateful stare as he walked away; he loathed his Chieftain's awful benedictions more than anything. They were empty words and not at all inspiring or meaningful. A facade of faith. There was no way he was going to endure another pathetic attempt at prayer like that. The gods were truly laughing at them. He could eat his shame. But he hoped Hammadus could not.

Brien watched as the Brutes gathered for their meal. But the sight of watching human flesh being served, let alone enjoyed, was too much for him to handle. There was no surviving this. Even if he had enough time to establish some kind of communication with the Brutes, it would be in vain. He had to escape. By his count he had less than forty-eight hours until the exfiltration craft would arrive. He felt a hand on his hunched back.

"You never get used to it," Dasc said quietly. "You just hope someone will get here soon before they pull your card . . . Thought you were the first of a cavalry, but I guess not."

"I'm Dr. Connor Brien. I came down here to gather some intel on them," indicating the Brute dinner party with his head, "but this . . . this is . . ." Brien couldn't even complete the thought.

The two shook hands. "I'm . . . Francis."

"So this is transcendence?" Brien used his eyes and bushy brows to complement his sarcasm, making sure his tone called out the man's lie. The smell of the man, of the whole human pen, was not easy to get used to. He jerked his head back slightly to keep a good distance.

"Hmmm, my being betrays my guise. It was, for quite some time . . . So you came in here alone?"

"I was supposed to be here for just a short time, assess the situation. Communications with the port AI were destroyed almost immediately upon the siege. No one knew if there were any survivors." He turned to watch what appeared to be a ceremonial prayer before the meal, Big Boy sitting majestically above the pack.

A woman prisoner crept over. Long, straight, gray hair flowed down her shoulders, her body so thin her raggedy clothes swam on her. She would've been pretty under better circumstances. She looked hours away from dying.

"Are you here to save us?" The look in her eyes was enough to break Brien's heart. She was holding on to any hope she could find.

Brien couldn't answer. "Has anyone tried to escape?"

"Almost every day . . . someone makes a run for it." This came from another prisoner, a brown-skinned man with the remains of an athletic build. "But look at those monsters; they cover more ground in one step than we do in three."

Brien suddenly became extremely self-conscious of his girth. He was the only one of the remaining prisoners who had any meat on his bones. He knew his time was short. "Do they eat anything else, besides . . . well, us?"

"They did eat the little frog-looking aliens they brought with them, and they have brought back game from the forest, but . . ." Dasc gestured a thumb over to the feast. "They seem to like us the best."

Brien watched in silence as the Brutes gnawed meat off human bone. He'd studied cannibals before, but he always knew they had some sort of doctrine behind their reasons for eating flesh. Not that it made it any better, but he understood it. These animals killed for the sake of killing. Even killing and eating those who shared their faith and alliance. Brien wondered if this was representative of the whole Brute mind-set or just this single pack. Regardless, these beasts were natural human predators, even beyond the war.

He moved his eyes from Brute to Brute before returning his gaze to Big Boy. The beast gestured and growled wildly from his makeshift throne. Unlike the battle footage he'd watched and the Brutes he'd encountered personally on High Charity, Big Boy didn't wear the highly decorative armor of most Chieftains. He was barely outfitted in armor at all: a few protective shards in key places, but nothing like he'd seen on the other leaders. Big Boy now sat listening to one of his captains as he growled out a tale, riotously laughing time and again, but at the same time suspiciously eyeing another crowd that had formed near a campfire. Brien followed his worrisome gaze.

Six was hovering over a fire, holding court for eight

of the other Brutes. They too tore at the human flesh, but remained transfixed on whatever story Six was telling. His shaven face stuck out in opposition to Big Boy's gruff visage, as if Six took pride in grooming himself on a daily basis. Surely a sign of aesthetic difference, and judging from their encounter earlier and the way they eyed one another, definitely a sign of conflict. He guessed Six was either from a smaller clan vying for power or simply found himself outnumbered among this more barbaric group, but he seemed to be gaining the attention of more and more of them, especially Butch and Ludo. He sensed hostility before; now he smelled the beginning of an inevitable clash.

"Stomping on the heels of a fuss . . ." Brien said to himself, but loud enough to confuse the others who heard him.

They all looked oddly at him. He caught their eyes.

"It's from an old song my mother used to sing to me. 'Hold no court, know no rust, just stomp, stomp, stomp, on the heels of a fuss.'"

"What's it mean?" Dasc asked.

"It means I think we might have chance to get out of here."

The next morning Ceretus woke with nothing but challenging Parabum on his mind. The one thing that this awful predicament provided him was the discontent of some of his fellow Brutes. While Parabum and his cronies felt like they had finally achieved a kingdom on this planet, a few of the others truly longed for home and were getting impatient with Parabum's excuses for not departing. He knew this retreat would be met with severe punishment from the Covenant, most likely sentences of death when presented to the tribunal. As soon as they powered up the *Valorous Salvation,* they would be discovered, hunted, and destroyed. He needed witnesses and allies to expose Parabum's and his captains' treachery and blasphemy.

The young naive Hammadus was the only one here strong enough to defeat Parabum in a challenge, but it would take a lot to push him to attack, even in the wake of the Chieftain's shameful treatment of him. He followed the chain of command to a fault, betraying himself with his own fear constantly. But Ceretus thought of one powerful tool to fire him up: Hammadus's brother and best friend, Facius. He was older, more assured, and could control his emotions a bit better. The two were inseparable, and though he did not like the idea of using a devout Jiralhanae like Facius as a means to an end, it was the only hope he had.

He walked over to the two who were once again eyeing the remaining captives.

"Not many of them left, my brothers, none with meat to savor, except for the new one." Ceretus said.

"Chieftain was out of line last night. Hammadus was merely excited to entertain him with a great hunt." Facius stated the obvious.

"He will use any attempt he can to dig into our fear. We need to leave this place, return home. The Chieftain is disgracing us in the eyes of the gods with his cowardice." Ceretus appealed to their honor as best as he could.

"But he is Chieftain, what can we do?" Hammadus pleaded, excreting fear again.

"He's no real Chieftain. He's a barbarian who would surely choose to stay here forever rather than suffer the shame the San 'Shyuum will inflict on him. Shame he deserves, and we'll deserve it, too, if we don't stop him. He's a faithless savage, just like his bloodline has proven to be in the past."

"What do you suggest, Captain?" By his tone, Facius suspected he was leading them into something.

"My clan has been at odds with Parabum's long before the great civil war. I'm surprised I survived last night. And any insubordination from me will surely be met with a deathblow. I think you, Facius, should make a request on behalf of the pack. Your two clans have much more in common with one another. He may listen to a cousin like yourself if the argument is presented properly. I have been thinking all night on the matter, and perhaps this could work . . . Suggest to him that we reboard the *Valorous Salvation* and stow him away, as if he were killed in combat. Perhaps suggest yourself to act as Chieftain. We throw ourselves on the mercy of the Prophets, blame faulty coordinates, mutiny, anything that we decide is feasible . . . and if they don't hunt us down and blast us out of the sky, we set coordinates for Warial; it is the farthest-flung of our colonies. There we attempt to assimilate, asking the gods for forgiveness and serving them entirely. It's our only hope, other than dying slowly here with the gods' backs to us."

Ceretus watched the eyes of Facius and Hammadus

as they assessed the idea, exchanged glances. Ceretus knew that neither of them was very smart, but they were among the most devout in this pack . . . and the idea of being left behind on the Great Journey brought about true fear in them. He could smell it. "At least the gods will know you tried," he added.

Ceretus watched as those words sank deep into their minds.

"Do you think it will work, that he'll listen to me?" Facius asked rather dubiously.

Hammadus grabbed his brother by the shoulders. "If he doesn't, I'll be there to protect you, brother."

Ceretus nodded gravely, concealing a pleased smirk.

Brien's plan was a long shot, but it was their only hope. Haunted by the memory of the rampaging Brutes he'd barely escaped, and what he knew from studies and his experiences so far here, these aliens were pack creatures and followed alpha males. Eliminate the alpha males and you'd have a bunch of thugs. Pit those thugs against one another somehow and you'd get a chaotic brawl. Then they could make a run for it. The exfil point was about five miles up through the thick forest, over the hill. If his guess on time was correct, they had about eight hours before the *Calypso* hit the rendezvous point, which meant they needed to act at the first opportunity and hope for a miracle.

He had waited until the Brutes were mostly asleep before feeding the others the plan. Judging by the health and shape of his fellow captives, he knew if any of them made it with him off this planet it, too, would be a miracle.

But his plan was based on one necessity. He needed a confrontation between Big Boy and Six. As best as he could gather, these two were the alpha males of this pack: Big Boy by force, Six by brains. If he could tranq the two of them just after they started fighting, the others would be lost and hopefully argue and battle amongst themselves, creating enough of a distraction for them to make a run for it. He had about two miles until he made it back to his camp, where he had the M6 in case the Brutes did come following. Then he'd have at least a few hours before the exfil craft came for him. It was the best he could come up with.

The entire hostage camp was on alert for Six and Big Boy. The morning was relatively slow, and Brien was completely transfixed by an impromptu meeting between Six, Ludo, and Butch. If Brien had to guess judging by the events of last night, they seemed to be conspiring. This could be their chance.

"Dasc, I think we got something cooking . . . look." He moved only his eyes toward the hovering trio of Brutes.

The three conspirators seemed reserved as they walked quietly toward where Big Boy and his entourage were gathered. The whole Brute camp diverted their attention from what they were doing to bear witness.

Dasc waved the others over, and they hovered around Brien.

"Okay, this is it. Look for my okay and then, you

two"—indicating the woman, Nixaliz, and another withered prisoner with a turtle face, named Vern— "run to the front of the pen and start screaming your asses off. Once they look toward them, the rest of you clear me a path and I'll send two tranq darts at Six and Big Boy as fast as I can, then we run like hell. Up toward the tree line at the hill. No turning back, run like the dickens."

"Like the what?" asked a stick of a prisoner whose thin face barely escaped his puff of hair and beard.

Brien caught his eye. "Like you've never run before."

Ceretus watched in amazement as Parabum actually entertained the words of Facius. He actually looked like he was considering it. Maybe he wasn't as stupid as he seemed. Then he saw his demeanor quickly change.

"Cousin, we live like kings here, and judging by the fleet back on that human planet, there will be no Covenant to return to. We need not cower at the thought of their displeasure. We wait until I say we can return. You disgrace yourself with this plan, cousin."

"So staying here is the will of the gods?" Hammadus asked, confused from behind his brother. Ceretus caught a whiff of his fear.

"Will of the gods, boy? There is no will of the gods. If there is anything I've learned from all this, it is that no gods answer our prayers, they do not care what we do. They abandoned us long ago."

"Blasphemy!" Ceretus erupted; he couldn't hold back. "All you spout is selfish blasphemy, *Chieftain.*" He spat the word at him, making sure his disdain shined through.

Parabum's captains tensed up at the outburst, and Ceretus could sense the fear rise in both Hammadus and Facius. Parabum raised and swung his hammer just as a wild scream distracted them all.

It all happened in the blink of a few seconds. After Six raised his voice, Nixaliz and Vern shouted like mad, and the captives cleared the view and Brien popped off two shots. One hit Big Boy right in the chest, just as his hammer struck the face of Six. The second shot, meant for Six, wedged itself into the shoulder of Butch. All three monstrosities hit the ground within seconds of one another, and just as he expected, chaos erupted. Ludo tensed up as one of Big Boy's captains leapt for the hammer, and then attacked him with all he had. Brien didn't waste much more time watching the melee; he ran like mad for the hills, firing tranq darts at any Brute within fifty yards of him, the other captives at his heels. Or so he thought. When he turned around only Dasc was behind him.

"What happened to the others?" He turned, panting, eyeing the commotion behind him. He saw Nixaliz, Brute spiker in her hand, firing shots into the face of Big Boy. Her revenge didn't last long, as another Brute simply smacked her head clear of her shoulders. Some of the others were trying to make their way up the hill slowly, but the Brutes were quick to follow, snatching them up, ripping them to shreds, some tearing into their flesh with their teeth.

"Come on. We gotta move, Dasc." And they took off in the direction of Brien's camp, turning every so often to make sure that they weren't leaving anyone behind or that some Brute wasn't on their tail. Their adrenaline died very close to the camp, and the two men collapsed as soon as it was in eyesight.

"I think we're safe for now . . . shit, I need a break." Brien panted, his throat dry and hoarse. He looked up at the sun. "Exfil should arrive in a few hours or so. We still got another two and a half miles to the rendezvous point. We got time."

"I can't believe we did it." Dasc barely was able to get the words out; his mouth looked dry and brittle beneath his matted beard.

"There are some hydro packs near the tent up there. Help yourself, bring me one, too . . . ." He looked up into the sky, smiling, knowing that he had survived another one. What he witnessed here was of supreme interest to command, but there was no way they could fold these Brutes into their fight. They seemed beyond control. How the Covenant kept them at bay and of service to them was something he wanted to know more than anything. He heard Dasc coming up from behind him.

"Here you go, Doc." Dasc handed him the hydro pack. "Never tasted sweeter." Brien could hear Dasc's slurping. He laughed to himself. Dasc Gevadim. He couldn't wait to tell his peers about this.

"So how far to the rescue?"

"About two and a half miles, we should get moving in—"

A bullet from Brien's M6 seared right through Brien's head.

Dasc knew he would never meet that rescue craft. He had devoted his entire life to Triad; to return to the public eye would prove him a phony, and the hearts and minds of millions would be broken, shattered. What was one man's life for the comfort and faith of countless others? He thought he heard the *Calypso* arrive, and imagined the recon team as they surveyed the area, the camp, laying all Brute survivors to waste. And it was days before he decided to head down there again.

He strolled through the human and Brute carnage, taking the opportunity to kick a few Brute corpses as some sort of revenge. With each kick he cried, harder and harder until he curled up, tucking his knees into his chest, and wept himself to sleep. He awoke hours later, the smell of all the death around him striking him anew. He turned over to his back to stare up at the night sky. He'd never felt so alone, even knowing that all his followers were still out there.

"Transcendence."

The word may or may not have come out of his mouth; it didn't matter.

MIDNIGHT IN *THE HEART OF MIDLOTHIAN*

FRANK O'CONNOR

ONE

"It's just cancer."

"What do you mean, it's just cancer?"

"I mean, it's just cancer. A very simple cancer that hasn't spread or metastasized and is eminently operable."

"I don't mean to sound rude, Doctor—"

"I'm not a doctor, I'm a medical technician—"

"Whatever. What I'm saying is that I don't know what *cancer* is."

"Oh. I got you. Cancer's a kind of um . . . slow-burn, localized infection, kind of. But we haven't really seen a lot of it since . . . hmm, twenty-second century, according to this. Anyway, it's easy to treat, but you're going to have to have surgery."

"What for? I thought you said it's an infection. Can't you just irradiate or drug it?"

"Yes, and we're going to do both of those. But to be sure we get all of it, and don't have you back here next month, we may have to remove some tissue."

"What kind of tissue?"

"Nothing you need for a date. Don't sweat it."

What a bastard arse of a morning, he thought to himself. *I wake up with a stomachache and end up in the medical bay with an archaic disease that was wiped out by simple gene therapy four hundred years ago. At least, according to Shipnet.* There were more than fourteen terabytes of data on "Cancer," which was apparently damn-near ubiquitous in the twentieth and twenty-first centuries.

His morning was about to get much worse.

The ship he was in was heading into a grim unknown. The planet Algolis had been attacked by a small but potent Covenant force. Details were thin, since the only witnesses were civilians. Civilians who'd barely made it off that world. Civilians who'd been kept deliberately in the dark about the Prototype weapons systems on that planet and had escaped by the skin of their teeth, and by the sacrifice of a brave few Marines from the Corps of Engineers.

It was a mess. And they were hurtling into it through the quantum foam and spatial uncertainty of a rushed slipspace jump. The plan was to stop short of the system itself and come in under the cover of a gas giant and a faked asteroidal trajectory—an old strategy, but one that worked well enough. Find out what had happened on Algolis and make sure the weapons prototypes were completely eradicated. Then loop back on a complex and slow Cole Protocol return trip.

The last mission had been complicated by a Marine sergeant going MIA. Guy the other Corps of Engineers salts called "Ghost." He supposed they were all ghosts now. Or ONI was hiding something.

A mess.

"Mo Ye, how come I have cancer?"

Mo Ye, the shipboard AI of the UNSC Destroyer *The Heart of Midlothian*, thought for a picosecond before answering through the medbay's directional audio feed. "Nothing in your civilian, Marine, or ODST record suggests any particular genetic preponderance. But it happens from time to time. Perhaps you're just a throwback, Baird. It would explain that Cro-Magnon brow of yours."

Mo Ye's avatar, a small, angry, and elderly looking Chinese lady in peasant's garb, flashed a rare smile as she said it and cackled through a crackling (and perfectly synthesized) smoker's cough to punctuate her joke. Her eyes sparkled with the wicked humor of the viciously old and crotchety. The projector plinth on which she stood pulsed a pleasant pink hue.

Orbital Drop Shock Trooper Sergeant Mike Baird snorted back a laugh. Mo Ye was well known for her bone-dry sense of humor, but he smiled as he thought of his high school nickname: Captain Caveman.

He really did have a heavy brow; a thick ridge that capped an otherwise unremarkable, if sturdy face. A prominent rounded jawline and sharply defined cheeks helped elevate him slightly into the realm of *Homo sapiens,* but a low-slung, muscular build, a close-cropped dusting of silver-black hair, and cloudy, amber eyes did little to dispel the visual notion of a rock-banging troglodyte.

"Don't worry about the surgery, Baird. It really is trivial. The autosurgeon will be done in less than an hour. But you'll be under for significantly longer than that. It's a straightforward but invasive procedure. I'll be observing and can retain a vid for you if you want to see the procedure after you wake up."

Mo Ye spoke in an almost gentle tone, her version of a bedside manner, Baird supposed.

"No thanks," he said. "I'll be seeing plenty of blood and guts where we're going."

"Let's hope not," replied Mo Ye. "Intelligence is rough, but we're not expecting trouble, just a lot of rubble."

"When will I be back on duty?" he asked. Baird was starting to worry that this surgery would keep him shipboard. He didn't want to miss the ride when he and his squad were dropped in hot on Algolis's night side. Quiet or not, he loved the thrill of the drop and the subsequent sweep. He wanted action.

"Two days, by rule," she said, "but you'll be happy and ambulatory in the morning. Now go to sleep."

Baird heard the *pop-hiss* of a pneumatic syringe and the gentle beep of his vitals as he lay in the padded autosurgeon cot, even as the narcotic slowed his pulse. He never felt the injection itself. The soft yellow glow of the medbay became a warm, reassuring sepia.

The red-haired medical technician who'd given him the bad news earlier smiled through the yellowing haze and he was lulled by the slowing beat of his own heart. And then there was nothing.

The Heart of Midlothian scythed through slipspace with the silent precision of a scalpel.

TWO

"Wake up."

In his dream, the voice was of his mother in Scotland, telling him it was time to get up and go to school. It was freezing outside, he knew. A biting, bludgeoning cold that punished schoolchildren before they ever made it to class. An unforgiving, frigid wind that roared in from the gray North Sea and turned little hands into useless pink mittens, unable to type or scratch on datadesks until furious rubbing and cosseting heaters warmed the blood again.

He didn't want to go to school. He wanted to stay here, wrapped up in these soft blankets.

"Wake up." Insistent now. But hissed. Not his mother. Not Maud Baird's pleasant singsong brogue. Nope, this was thick Mandarin-accented English.

The sepia glow had gone. The medbay was in near darkness, punctuated by the soft red pulse of the emergency floor lights. A dream. But goddamn if that *cold* wasn't real.

"What the f—"

"Ssssh." The hissed demand seemed to drill into Baird's ear. He realized it was Mo Ye, using the directional acoustics of the medbay—ostensibly for patient privacy. But he knew, even through the groggy haze of narcotics and sleep, that something was wrong. The lights, for one thing, without even the pink glow of her avatar to show which plinth she stood on.

"What's happening?" Now he whispered.

"I'll tell you as you move, but right now if you don't

put on some clothes and do as I say you will be dead in a couple of minutes." Mo Ye was using a tone he'd never heard before. He started moving.

In less than a minute, he was up, dressed, and fastening his boots. The confusion and torpor of the drugs were still softening the edges of *everything*. This still didn't feel real. Mo Ye began to brief him. The news wasn't good. But it certainly was *real*.

"They were waiting for us when we dropped out of slipspace," she whispered.

"Covenant?" he blurted, embarrassed even as he spoke the obvious.

"Yes. A small group. Not a formation we've encountered before. At least according to my records. One Cruiser and four completely new ships escorting it. All dark gray, no surface features or lights and no weapons systems that I could discern. What they did have was a bellyful of boarding craft. And our ONI contact group was not there."

"So we were boarded?"

"Almost as soon as we dropped out of slipspace. Perfect targeting. As if they knew exactly where we were going to exit. Inside the range of our weapons systems before I could react. Punctured the hull in two hundred different locations and swarmed us before we could sound a general alarm. It was like exiting in the middle of a meteor storm."

"What about the crew? What about the men?"

"Dead."

"All of them?!" There was a tremor of outrage, of fear as he raised his voice.

"Ssssh!" she repeated. "They're still here and I suspect they're heading here to the medbay for another look."

This was all happening too fast. "How long was I out?"

"Twenty-three hours. And that's why you're still alive."

"Why didn't they just destroy the ship? What do they want?" he hissed back, his breath forming a frozen cloud like a literal ellipsis after the question.

"Me," she said. "And Earth."

She continued her whispered briefing as he scouted the medbay for warmer clothes. They had operated like shock troops, coursing through the ship—a cataract of plasma fire and Needler shards. Grunts, Jackals, and several Elites, clad in the glittering gray of the enigmatic ships. The Destroyer's crew never stood a chance. The Marines fell in the face of overwhelming, surprise force. Even the few ODSTs aboard—Baird's friends and comrades—had died quickly, most before they ever reached a weapon. Almost every sidearm and firearm aboard had been secured in one of the ship's two armories. It had been a slaughter.

Those who *had* fought back did so with the sidearms of fallen Masters at Arms and weapons dropped by the Covenant boarding party. Few had died well. And those who lingered, their burning wounds still smoking, had been executed with ruthless efficiency. The Covenant wanted this ship clean and empty.

Baird, she explained, had been spared by his narcotic

slumber. The Covenant had gone from deck to deck
looking for either movement or simple life signs and
terminating those who hid in terror, in dark corners of
the ship. One by one.

Baird's pulse and vitals had apparently slipped below whatever criteria the Covenant sought.

"So what the hell are they doing?"

"They're trying to extract me from the ship. And
then they're going to try and extract Earth's location
from me. By hook or by crook."

"What about the Cole Protocol?" he asked. "Aren't
you supposed to destroy the ship, or self-terminate?"

"I can't self-terminate. I already tried. When they
boarded, they brought something new with them.
Things they call Engineers. They're . . . I'm not sure
what they are, precisely, but they're semi-organic. The
first thing they did was separate me from the core systems. A splinter of my persona is out here with you,
but the bulk of my memories and sheer processing
power are locked in Computing on the bridge. I can't
access myself. This fragment of me is just a chunk I
chipped off to monitor your surgery and it was severed
along with my access to security, engines, navigation—
all the useful stuff. I'm not exactly running at full capacity here. This is a seriously smart group. To be
honest, my own maker probably couldn't pull off that
trick."

"Who are these bastards?" he asked, half rhetori-
cally. They were obviously what they appeared to be: a
Covenant intelligence and interdiction group. Discreet

black ops instead of brute force. Was this new, or just a behavior they'd never observed in Covenant sorties? Were they connected to the discovery of Algolis's Prototype armory?

"I have no idea who these bastards are," she said. "But they've got us cornered. I can't access the ship's security; I'm almost blind. I can't even display my avatar. I have to assume they're going to realize both of us are here, sooner or later."

"Why not blow the ship? Cook the whole goose?" His exasperation was mounting.

"Two reasons," she said. "First, in my present state of coherence and security clearance, I'm hamstrung by a *default* safety precaution—Asimov's First Law of Robotics. I cannot under any circumstances harm or by inaction cause harm to come to a human. When I'm running at full capacity I can ignore that one at will. I used to ignore it all the time, in fact."

"Bugger," he said, pretending to know what an *Asimov* was. "And second?"

"Second," she said, with an odd hint of chagrin in her voice, "the self-destruct permissions and sequences are locked away with the other half of *me*. I can't access them anyway."

He thought about what this meant for a moment. An encrypted but otherwise unguarded treasure trove of information about humanity, currently being probed and tinkered with by a previously unknown group of *tech-savvy, sneaky* Covenant.

"Does the Asimov thingy . . ."

"Rule of Robotics."

"Yes, yes, does the Asimov thingy only count for humans?"

"Of course. I don't feel terribly responsible for Covenant safety, Baird."

"So what *do* you have access to?"

"Some doors," she said. "And a lot of meds."

THREE

Holding a fire extinguisher in his hands, now marginally warmer in two layers of sterile surgical gloves, he watched his breath condense as he tried to calm himself. Motes of dust and tiny crystals of frozen liquid danced and sparkled in the chill air. In the red pulse of the emergency lights, it looked like a faint snowstorm of blood. He supposed some of it probably was. He shuddered and closed his mouth.

The oxygen was still good, but most other systems had either died or been killed by the boarding party.

"So we don't know if anyone is out there?"

"Not until we open the door," whispered Mo Ye. "It would be prudent to assume your awakened state has shown up on their scans. They were scanning for life signs when they swept the ship."

"And the plan if there's nobody out there?"

"You make your way aft, get to the engine room, and manually instigate an attraction coordinate. We've been through the procedure. You've read it back to me. It will work. You'll escape in a lifeboat. The ship will spin up and jump into the nearest large mass. That should be the red giant about fourteen million miles starboard. *That* ought to cook their goose."

"Aren't there safety procedures and systems to prevent this kind of shit?"

"There were. Luckily for us the Engineers truncated those along with my systems. It *should* work."

"But you're not sure."

"I'm only sure of the seconds leading up to my *schism*. But I am sure that if we don't try, they are eventually going to crack my encryption and lead the Covenant directly back to Earth, Cole Protocol be damned."

He hefted the dense bulk of the fire extinguisher. Literally cold comfort.

"Okay, then." He breathed deeply. Calmed himself. Murmured an internal, calming battle mantra. "Open the bloody door."

FOUR

It is fair to say that the group of Covenant soldiers standing outside the medbay was far more surprised than Baird was. He was expecting unthinkable trouble. They were expecting to find a wounded, cowering, and almost certainly unarmed medical technician. What they found instead was a highly trained and highly capable 220-pound Orbital Drop Shock Trooper carrying a 20-pound titanium bottle.

He didn't have time to form a complete picture, but the instinctual snapshot he took as he rolled out of the medbay doorway and right into the small group of aliens was plenty. Four Grunts, two Jackals, and, in the shadows on the far right, a figure so tall and imposing it could only be an Elite.

"Christ."

He came back up to his feet at withering speed, breaking the first Jackal's jaw and neck instantly with the extinguisher's unforgiving mass. Fragments of beak and tooth glittered in the dark. The Jackal simply collapsed, falling backward as the momentum of the cylinder and the human wielding it snapped the life out of him. The Carbine he was holding fell with him.

Baird caught the Carbine even as he dropped his makeshift battering ram. The extinguisher landed on its activation stud and the resulting explosion of halon gas and sound bought him his life, as a Carbine round from the other Jackal, who was far less panicked than the Grunts, sliced through his Cro-Magnon brow, nicking bone and knocking him backward on top of the fallen Jackal. As he fell, he fumbled, found, and fired the Carbine trigger. Three rounds eviscerated his would-be killer.

The Grunts squealed and scattered. Two of them ran right past him and vanished into the medbay. A third tripped, its plasma pistol clattering across the floor. The fourth wasn't so lucky. As Baird rose to his knees, then his feet, wheeling, trying to get a bead on the Elite—there was a blur, a flash of light and thunderous impact. His breath was knocked out of him.

The Carbine fell from his hands. He looked down at a

strange scene. The fourth Grunt was pressed up against his belly, squirming, staring up at him and wailing. The Grunt was impaled on a fork of blinding light, a Covenant energy sword. The twin tines of superheated, seething energy had passed through the Grunt. And through Baird.

He looked up into the face of the Elite. The massive creature regarded him through cold black eyes. It tilted its head. Baird wondered what the gesture meant. And the Elite yanked the blade from both of them. The Grunt fell dead, Baird, back to his knees, clutching his belly.

Ferocious, burning pain seemed to consume his entire torso. He felt like his innards were boiling. He looked down at his hands, expecting to see blood. There was none. The two holes in his clothes smoldered, the flesh beneath fused and cauterized. Baird fell face forward into blackness.

FIVE

"Wake up."

His mother again. It was time to go to school. But it wasn't the same. He wasn't cold. He was burning. He was on fire.

"Wake up." Insistent, but worried. Not mother. Mo Ye again.

"I'm dead."

"You're not dead. But you're not in good shape. The

blades passed right through you. Scorched a lot of stuff. Missed your spine by a distance I can't even make myself repeat."

"I feel like I'm dying."

"That's not surprising. You have serious burns. And significant injuries. Internal and external. I'm going to give you some meds, and we're going to try again."

"It didn't work out so good last time." He coughed and a spasm of pain squeezed him like an invisible fist. "I'm tired. I want to go to sleep." He realized that he did very badly want to sleep. And part of him knew what that really meant.

"I know," she said. "I'm sorry." Her voice, a perfectly directional whisper in the dark, was filled with what sounded like a lover's sorrow. No more mean old lady.

Baird tried to wriggle out from under a Jackal's body. The creature, which looked so light and birdlike, was incredibly heavy. With a groan of pain, he pistoned his feet against it and shoved. It rolled off, and he rolled free.

She told him what had happened when he blacked out. The Grunts had simply piled up the corpses—their own fallen and Baird's supposed carcass—on top of each other in the medbay. Mo Ye had stayed quiet.

The big Elite had been suspicious and visibly angry. He had barked orders at the Grunts and communicated the events back to *The Heart of Midlothian*'s bridge, where presumably other Covenant troops—and those *Engineers*—were attempting to crack Mo Ye's main systems. The Elite had shown a little more caution this time—and smashed the autosurgeon.

He raised himself up on one arm, then another. He grabbed the dented, scorched edge of the autosurgeon table and hauled himself up, grimacing in agony and suppressing a shriek.

"Meds," he gasped.

"Yes. Meds," she said.

The dispensary clicked and hissed open. Inside the plastic cubby were four vials: two identical, full of clear liquid, the third blue, the fourth a distinctively piss-colored yellow. There was a very old-fashioned-looking pneumatic handheld syringe gun beside them.

"What are these?" he asked.

"A painkiller, a beta-blocking sedative, a metasteroid for the burns and interior inflammation, and a Waverly-class *augmentor*."

"What's an augmentor?" he asked. But he already had an inkling.

"This one's a cocktail. It contains a derivative of phenylcyclohexylpiperidine, an artificial slow-release synthetic adrenaline and a rapid coagulant."

"You're talking about a Rumbledrug."

"There's no pretty way to paint it," she said.

Rumbledrugs had become notorious in the sporadic colonial insurrections. Notably on Hellas and Fumirole. On both worlds, they'd been used by rebels in a vainglorious attempt to fight Spartan-IIs. The drugs were certainly fearsome. The effect on human physiology was impressive in the short term. Unencumbered by the body's normal safety limits, subjects were capable of feats of enormous strength, but the subsequent lack of control and mental instability together with the immediate physiological damage meant that users often died long before they ever laid hands on an actual Spartan. But not before doing tremendous damage to themselves and anything that got in their way.

"The beta-blocker will keep you focused," she said, as if sensing his thoughts, "and calm."

Sweat poured down his face. His guts roiled. Pain wracked him.

"The plan this time?"

"Same as before."

He loaded the syringe, one vial at a time, and with each of the four shots felt progressively better. As the last one flooded his arteries with a cooling rush, he felt almost *good*.

He looked at his wounds through the holes in his T-shirt. The punctures were about two inches across, thick lateral slits. He felt around to his back, twisting to see in the medbay's mirror, the darkness hampering him. Two exit wounds, a little smaller, spanned his spine. The skin around them was dark red and black, like ripples on a pond, spreading outward in twin elliptical shapes. It looked angry and painful, but he *felt* nothing.

"Mo Ye."

"Yes, Baird?" she replied.

"Why didn't you try to inject me with the autosurgeon? The syringe at least looked like it would still work."

"Because, like I told you before, in this condition, I can't do anything to harm a human."

He nodded. "I understand. How long do I have?"

"I can't say. With the drugs, maybe an hour or two. Without them, you'd be dead sooner. Which is the only thing that allows me to even tell you about the meds."

"Then there's no time to waste."

"Baird . . . once you leave the medbay, you're on your own. I'm trapped here, dumb and useless and disconnected. They're not going to risk giving me any more access to ship systems until they have what they came for. 'Til they reconnect my systems. And I don't see any reason why they're going to do that."

Baird looked at the mess around him. Dead bodies, but weapons too. He picked up a plasma pistol, retrieved two plasma grenades from a bandolier on a Grunt's armor, and grabbed the Carbine from where he'd dropped it.

By habit, he checked his weapons, patting himself as if for reassurance that he had everything. He patted the empty spot where his combat dagger usually sat. He looked around. On a stainless-steel tabletop was a gruesome-looking surgical blade, with a nanometer edge that glinted wickedly in the red glow. He picked it up carefully and bound the delicate surgeon's grip in a thick swath of surgical tape, creating a more practical handle, and slid it very carefully into his belt.

"Baird. I wish I could do something more." Mo Ye sounded frustrated.

"Then wish me luck." And he was gone—into the cold darkness of the ship's dead corridors.

SIX

He encountered a frozen tableaux of carnage. The Covenant had simply left the dead where they fell, or piled them against walls. Human gore and viscera everywhere and not a trace of reciprocal Covenant blood.

The drugs were working perfectly. The Destroyer was not large; he kept to the shadows and snuck through some of the ship's duct systems. He felt almost *elated*, like a ghost. But he could also feel the damage in his guts, a kind of dull, removed itch, like a memory of pain. And it felt wrong. He knew he was dying, but at the same time, he'd never felt stronger. He felt these conflicting clocks ticking, both counting down to something fatal. He made it undetected to the engine room in less than fifteen minutes. What he found there almost made him quit.

The engine room door was scorched and hung on its track, jammed forever in a half-open position, like a slackened jaw. They'd been here, but there was no sign of them now. Just more human corpses. The engine bay was massive, ceilings vanished completely into blackness above him, but the systems were still humming and there was more light here. More light to illuminate the bodies of the crew.

Some of them he recognized, even through horrific burns. He stepped gingerly, respectfully, over them, heading for the control head unit beyond the bulk of the Shaw-Fujikawa drive.

It was a fairly banal instrument, considering its prodigious power. The slipspace drive could literally rip the fabric of the universe apart but could be controlled either remotely by AI, as was the norm, or manually, via a simple keyboard and touchscreen.

Mo Ye had walked him through the procedure several times, made him repeat it back to her. It was simple and it *sounded* foolproof. As he rounded the bulk of the control panel he saw what they'd done and sighed.

Melted to slag. Deliberately. And as he examined the Shaw-Fujikawa drive itself, he saw they'd attempted to wreck it too. It was impossible to know if the *drive* still functioned or not, but he knew for certain the control panel was FUBAR.

"Plan B," he muttered to himself and started running back the way he'd come—glancing regretfully at the perfectly functioning row of lifeboat pods.

The trip to the bridge wasn't as uneventful as that to the engine room. He ran around a corner and surprised two Grunts, one of whom appeared to be sucking food from a nipple atop a weird little tank on the floor. Baird didn't stop to examine it. He shot one straight through the face with the Carbine and with the stock caved in the skull of the would-be gourmand. Neither had time to react or even squeak a warning, but the loud metallic report of the stolen Carbine was sure to attract attention. He kept moving.

Now he really had their attention. He heard a clamor behind him as Covenant troops reacted to the sound. Every sense, every instinct in him screamed panic, but something, he liked to think his own personal tenacity, held him steady. Kept him moving forward. Part of him knew it was the chemicals coursing through his blood. Another part of him wanted to sit down in the dark, cross his legs, and wait for it all to be over.

He remembered walking home from school one day. The world was white with snow. Black, leafless chestnut trees spidering into the gray-yellow sky, itself pregnant with more flurries to come. He remembered the chill sweep of the Water of Leith, the tenacious little river cutting a black ribbon through the pristine white.

He remembered carefully stepping through the snow, lifting his little legs high to make crisp, clean footprints, like Good King Wenceslas. He remembered the *thwomp* as he deliberately fell backward, arms spread to absorb the impact. Lying there, staring up at the sky. The simple depth of the imprint he made in the snow protecting him from the bitter wind. He remembered feeling warm and safe and remembered thinking, even as a child, "This is how people freeze to death."

This is how people freeze to death.

What exactly are you doing, Baird? he thought to himself as he ducked under a moribund heating conduit, now glittering with ice, and into a pipe-tangled corridor not much wider than his own broad shoulders.

What's plan B? Charge into the bridge and ask them to throw down their weapons? Fix Mo Ye with less than an hour to live and only the barest grasp of how an AI even works?

The plan, he decided, was to keep moving, keep shooting, and make sure that these motherfuckers rued the day they boarded *The Heart of Midlothian*. The plan, he grinned to himself, was *to take their precision operation and turn it into an embarrassing and memorable clusterfuck.* He couldn't *win*, but he could act like a broken autosurgeon: *First, do harm.*

Two more Jackals sprinted by in the darkness of the main Deck 4 hallway to his right. He froze. Surreal in the blinking red strobe of the emergency lights, their birdlike gait matched their raptor skulls. Their clattering footfalls masked his own sounds.

So they were looking for him. Let them look. *Let them find him.*

The pipes intersected and then branched ahead, blocking his already claustrophobic route, but he knew where he was—Astronav, which meant the bridge proper was just around the corner. To his left a bulkhead wall, to his right, a gap in the pipes into the main corridor, and beyond that, the bridge.

He slowed, stopped, and waited. Listening. Silence, but his jangled nerves and superattenuated senses caught something else. The slight smell of activated methane gas. *Something* was here. He chanced a look around the corner, his head a blur in the darkness. Two Grunts, guarding the bridge entrance. They didn't see him.

If he gave away his position now, it would all be for naught. *Think.*

He looked to the heavens for some kind of inspiration, seeing instead the spiderweb of conduits and pipes hanging feet below the ceiling proper. Space was at a premium on a Destroyer, and that meant sharing headroom with plasma conduits, air-conditioning, electrical cabling, and a myriad of power and life support systems, like a steel gray circulatory system.

He took the ugly surgical blade from his belt and put it between his teeth, its cruel edge facing outward, and quietly hauled himself into the piping, with agility that belied his bulk, and vanished silently into the dark.

When the second Grunt heard the weird choking sound from his partner and turned, he had just enough time to see the looming human's eyes glint in the darkness before the blade sliced through his own neck, almost decapitating him. His breathing apparatus hissed a mist of cold methane into the equally frigid air. The smell of Grunt blood mingled with the gas to create a rank, coppery smell like an olfactory pastiche of human blood. Baird lowered the Grunt gently and quietly to the floor, like a sleeping baby.

But Baird was shaking now. The exertions were taking their toll. No pain yet, but God knew how much internal trauma he'd suffered, and how long he had left.

He looked at the doors to the bridge. Their solidity and silence seemed to mock him. The bioluminescent blood from the fallen Grunts, blue and steady, cast almost as much illumination as the emergency lights, but that light was already fading, losing what potency it had. Like himself, he supposed. And the plan formed in his mind, just like that. It wouldn't work, he thought, but it didn't matter. All bets were off.

Baird breathed deeply. Got control of his shakes. He

wiped blood from his hands on the pants of his uniform, smoothed the stubble of his close-cropped hair, palmed the door security pad, and strode confidently into the bridge as if he were the captain himself.

SEVEN

The scene before him was bizarre. Perhaps a dozen Grunts, several Jackals, and two Elites stood intently watching two hovering gray armored blimps, perhaps four feet long, as they trailed their tentacles over the bridge computer terminal. *Engineers*, he supposed.

At the sound of his entrance one of the Grunts turned, almost bored-looking, and then shrieked an unintelligible warning as it saw who, or rather, what, he was.

Baird threw down the Carbine, put his hands up, palms facing outward, and yelled as loud as he could: "*I CAN GIVE YOU THE EARTH COORDINATES!*"

The Jackals either didn't care, or more likely, didn't understand a word, and leveled their Carbines at his head. Only a thunderous roar from an Elite stopped them from perforating his skull.

The Elite stood eight feet tall. In the comparatively bright light of the bridge, Baird saw the dark gray, almost black, armor. He'd faced countless Elites in combat, but this one was like nothing he'd seen before. The Elite's saurian face was largely hidden by an impressively decorated helmet. Whatever ranking it was, it looked *important*.

It was the same one who'd stuck an energy sword through him at the medbay. And he knew instantly that the Elite recognized him too. It was staring at the burned flesh and fabric at Baird's abdomen. Then it looked at Baird's face. Baird had no idea what the Elite was thinking but hoped he recognized confusion, at least.

"*I can give you the Earth coordinates!*" he yelled again, glancing at the circle of gun-wielding aliens now forming around him. "*All I ask is that you let me go, let me take a lifeboat. Let me live.*"

The Elite tilted his head and glanced at the Engineers. One of them rotated slowly, like an airship, its weird spiderlike eyes glinting inscrutably. It made a chirping sound, a trill warble. The Elite nodded and barked something back at the Engineer.

The circle of onlookers widened a little—as if to let him through—and so he gingerly stepped forward. He addressed the Engineer, wondering if he had this all right. The drugs were starting to fade, and the returning pain was making things *shaky, confusing*.

"You have to reconnect the ship's AI system. She has the coordinates. She'll obey me, but not you."

The Engineer rotated to face the Elite and again chirped. Again, the Elite barked something, glaring at Baird the entire time, shaking his head. Baird stepped forward, closer to both. The Elite snarled a final order at the Engineer and unsheathed his sword. The points of it hissed and sizzled, leveled at his neck. A fairly universal warning: *Don't try anything funny*.

The Engineers both turned back to this new task,

literally disconnecting some of the cabling and then performing more delicate ministrations with those strange tentacles. A light flared on the bridge console and an automated voice announced blaringly, "BASELINE RE-INITIALIZATION OF UNSC BATTLE CLASS SMART AI 'MO YE' PLEASE WAIT."

A few seconds later and a small dais in front of the bridge terminal flickered to life with Mo Ye's diminutive form, brightening back to wakefulness, reconnected and fully restored.

Baird turned and spoke directly to her. "Good to have you back, if only for a moment. I need you to give them the slipspace coordinates for Earth."

She looked back at him, trying to figure out what the hell he was up to.

"Mo Ye, these creatures want Earth's location." He winked. "Are you reconstituted enough to give them access to those, uh, *coordinates*?"

Mo Ye looked desperate, pained. "Baird—I have access to all the ship systems now, but they're being careful, they think you're trying to trick them. What we talked about in the medbay is still true. I can't override the first law in my current condition."

He winked again, a great big shit-eating grin spreading across his face. "Security clearance: *Robot*, passcode: *Asimov*."

An Engineer chirped an explanation, calmly. Things seemed to be progressing as the human had promised. A sense of excitement, a murmur, spread though the assembled Covenant—they realized they were on the brink of a great military breakthrough.

But Mo Ye moaned as she realized what Baird was up to. "*No . . . Baird . . . wait . . .* "

Baird did not wait. Baird turned around and looked up at the Elite's puzzled face. He hauled back his right arm and with an open hand, slapped the Elite straight across the jaw with all the force his drug-fueled system could muster. The impact broke bones in his hand, and he felt a satisfying reciprocal crunch from the Elite's jaw. The massive alien staggered, sagged, and fell to one knee, stunned by both impact and surprise.

Before it could do anything else, Baird looked him in the eye, now level with his, and said, "Well, you stupid arsehole? Think you can do it right this time?"

The Elite roared in fury as he swung the energy sword in a scything arc and took Baird's head off cleanly at the shoulders. Baird's body keeled lifelessly backward. Arms spread out wide, as if falling backward into snow.

The Elite spun around and glared at the AI's shimmering form.

"Passcode *accepted*," she sneered sarcastically, her eyes lit from within by some unknowable *emotion*. "Self-destruct sequence initiated. *Four minutes and counting*."

The Elite barked at the Engineers, who were already moving, herding Grunts out the door, and translating the grave news of the impending destruction.

The Elite started a quick-march back to the Covenant boarding pods, just a few floors below, glancing at an arm-mounted chronograph. He chanced one hate-filled glance back at Mo Ye, standing, arms folded, on her plinth. She stared at him with a coldly venomous expression and spoke flatly this time.

"I'm kidding. There's no need for any countdown whatsoever."

The Elite blinked.

The Heart of Midlothian's network of shaped nuclear charges briefly flowered in the shadow of the gas giant like a beautiful little star. Then, as the chain reaction crushed the exotic fissile materials in the engine bay, it burst outward like a supernova.

The explosion washed away the Covenant Cruiser and its nameless gray escorts like a blizzard covering footsteps in the snow. And soon, all was quiet again. And cold. And peaceful. Like midnight.

DIRT

TOBIAS S. BUCKELL

THE FIGURE in the charcoal-black body armor picked his way over the top of a shattered, stubby wing, then walked past the ruined mangle of a Pelican dropship. A large BR55 battle rifle rested at the ready, cradled between his forearms.

He paused by the tip of the Pelican, which had plowed into the ground on its side, and looked through the shattered windows of the cockpit.

"Over here, Marine."

The oval black helmet swung around to look at a clump of tall orange grass behind a thick piece of granite, the morning sun glinting off the upside-down T-shaped visor.

BR55 aimed forward; the Orbital Drop Shock Trooper moved toward the sound of the voice and pushed aside the tall fronds of grass.

The 70-millimeter chain gun from the tip of the Pelican dropship had broken loose and sheared the tip of granite clean off, then cratered into the dirt a few hundred feet away.

Lying between it and the rock was a man in battle

dress uniform: simple camouflage with a few chest and hip pockets. Fairly standard.

He'd obviously been thrown clear of the cockpit on impact and bounced along the dirt. Both legs looked broken, and at least one arm. Blood seeped through the BDU's legs, torso, and arms.

The man's face was cut up. Enough to be unrecognizable.

He had an M6 Magnum sidearm pointed at the ODST, which he let drop to the dirt next to him in exhaustion.

Somehow the soldier had crawled out of his body armor, which lay all around him. A closer look revealed why: charred and melted, the ODST body armor would have burned his skin.

"Good to see you." The man's voice held the strange calm of someone who knew they were beyond help, so terribly injured they were past the pain. "I wasn't sure if the call got through."

The ODST crouched beside him and opened a medical pack. Biofoam, to stop the worst of the bleeding, and polypseudomorphine to ease the man's pain. He worked as best he could, though his hands shook a bit. This wasn't training; this was a real, dying man, and the ODST was no medic. He looked around. "My SOEIV landed nearby, and I was ordered over to see if I could help with a downed Pelican. But sir, you need more help than I can give you. We need to get you out of here. There are Covenant forces moving in on our position. We don't have much time."

"We have time, Private." The injured Marine grabbed

the helmet of the crouched shoulder in a sudden movement, yanking the man down close to him.

"I've been doing this so long, rook, that somewhere along the line I forgot what it was all about," the Marine on the ground hissed into the reflective visor. "But what I want you to remember about me is that it has been a long journey between where I started and where I'm sitting now. I would apologize for the things I've done, but sorry's passed me by, rook. You don't see the things I've seen and come out sorry. But sometimes, if you're not a complete monster, you come out realizing what's important."

The ODST pushed back carefully, trying to make sure not to further hurt the man on the ground. "Sir?"

He coughed, blood staining his lips and chin. "All this crap started back in the Colonial Military."

The ODST turned and looked back the way he'd come, helmet twisting, and murmured a situation report and request for backup as he reported his find.

"Of course," the injured man continued, "I can see by your insignia you're a private, just out of training, probably your first jump down to dirtside. You might not even remember the CMA . . . but back before there was the UNSC, there was the CMA . . ."

"Sir . . ."

"Shut up and listen, rookie! There's something important I have to tell you." The man's face relaxed. He was slipping back into a world of thoughts and memories. "About friends. Betrayal. Loss. If you keep your head up and do what I tell you, you might even live long enough to tell someone what happened here . . ."

I signed up for the Colonial Military the hour I turned eighteen. January 3, 2524. Smartest thing I'd done up to that point. Flipped off my father, who'd stood by a giant JOTUN trundling across a flat, golden plain of wheat, and then I rode a flatbed full of corn all the way into town. Sure, the JOTUNs did the real manual labor: plowing, planting, monitoring, harvesting. But we still ended up among the crops now and again, despite the automated work the giant, one hundred-foot lawn mower-like machines did.

"It's just dirt," I'd told a friend about my decision to leave. "And I'm sick and tired of grubbing about in it. I can't believe my parents left a real world to travel all the way out here to dig dirt."

The farming life was not my destiny. I'd known that since the day I first looked up at the stars while riding on the back of one of the giant, automated JOTUNs, a long piece of straw dangling out the side of my mouth.

No. I was going to see worlds. Pack a gun. The next time I came back home to Harvest, I wanted to watch the girls bat their eyes at a man in uniform. Not a farm boy with dirt under his nails. I wanted to be a hard-as-nails tough-ass Marine.

I walked around Utgard for the last time, strolling along the banks of the Mimir River. I lit up a Sweet William cigar by the floodlit, well-landscaped grounds of the Colonial Parliament's long walls. I blew what cash I had on me on drink after drink at bars scattered all up and down the Mimir until I could barely walk.

Then at sunrise, without a wink of sleep, I walked

into a small recruiting office where a vaguely bored-looking desk sergeant looked me over and handed me some paperwork. After I painfully worked my way through it, he stood up and shook my hand. "Welcome to the Colonial Military, son," he said.

By that evening I was still not a tough-ass Marine, but a tired, hungover recruit without any hair, dressed in an ill-fitting uniform, throwing up my guts in a dirt field while a drill sergeant yelled at me. I was now Private First Class Gage Yevgenny.

I want to say I learned how to kill a man with my pinky, or how to use a sniper rifle to kill a fly on a log of shit from a thousand yards, but all I really learned was that I didn't like scrabbling around in the mud with live rounds going off over my head.

But I made it through anyway.

Unlike the UNSC, the CMA boot camp lasted just a couple weeks. Enough to teach you how to use your weapon, salute, march, and drive a Warthog before they booted you right on out of there.

It wasn't that much more advanced than spending a week shooting gophers in the fields, or so I thought at the time.

Unlike some of my fellow recruits, I at least knew how to point and shoot. As a result, I was promoted to lance corporal and got to tell a few other soldiers what to do.

That I liked.

But it still didn't prepare me for the things I was about to see.

———

I met Felicia Sanderson and Eric Santiago at the Utgard spaceport. Felicia grew up right here in Utgard, on Harvest; Eric had come in from Madrigal. With our duffels at our feet, we waited as patiently as we could in line with civilian passengers. We'd developed some grudging respect for one another during boot camp, enough that they felt comfortable airing complaints about Colonial Military life around me.

"I still can't believe we're forced to fly civilian to Eridanus," Felicia groused.

"We could go AWOL," Eric said.

I shook my head. "Where? The liner doesn't stop anywhere remotely interesting between here and the Eridanus System."

"I'm just saying, it's odd." Eric picked his duffel up as the line moved.

"How could command let the UNSC grab all our ships?" Felicia had been complaining about this latest development for a solid week. Harvest was a newer colony, and most of the settlers had come from other Outer Colonies. Felicia and her family didn't hold a lot of love for the UNSC, or the Earth-controlled Colonial Administration. Her family hadn't set foot on Earth in generations.

It was, I had to admit, an indignity. Without our own ships, the Colonial Military was shuttling fighting men where it needed them by buying them coach-class tickets.

The three of us had been deployed to Eridanus, where the action was. Our angry words for the UNSC were partly attempts to hide our nervousness. Talking big to keep our minds off the big issue.

Operation TREBUCHET had been the UNSC's answer to Insurrectionists, and we'd just been folded into the far-ranging series of operations aimed to "pacify" the Outer Colonies.

I was just excited to be leaving Harvest for the first time, no matter how, or to where.

As we lifted off, I could see one of the seven space elevators that Harvest used to move its goods off the planet's surface. Just like me, each piece of cargo would be flying through slipspace to other planets, like seeds being dispersed from a pod.

It was the last time I saw Harvest with my own eyes.

I often regretted leaving my father the way I did. We never had another chance to see each other, and now that I look back on it, I know he was just a hardworking man who'd lost his wife and did his best to raise one hell of an angry kid. I doubt I could have done better.

I often wonder what the expression had been on his face when I left that day. Sadness? Relief? Or just weariness?

What would we have said, or done, had we known what would happen to Harvest?

"You wanted action . . ." Felicia slapped my back. We were in an old Pelican dropship, shuddering its way down to Teribus Island on Eridanus II, and I was throwing up because of the turbulence.

Older CMA Marines just stared blankly at us. They looked bored, and Eric, sitting next to me, knew why. "No action, Felicia. You can thank the sympathizers. Someone, probably in this unit, has already called ahead. There won't be anything on the ground by the time we arrive." He said this loud enough for everyone to hear. No big secret, and none of the other soldiers bothered to contradict him.

Harvest was relatively removed from the heat of the battle over the Outer Colonies' destinies. Eridanus was at the heart of it.

Every day, more and more Insurrectionists set off bombs in major cities, targeting UNSC troops, ships, and Colonial Administration buildings.

The UNSC, in response, was cracking down harder with each passing month, seeking to instill order. And even though the Colonial Military had been increasingly sidelined to smaller and smaller operations since the discovery of elements inside our organization sympathetic to the cause, our brass never stopped pointing out that Robert Watts, the leader of the Insurrectionists in Eridanus and the mastermind behind most of the activity in the Outer Colonies, was actually a former UNSC colonel.

That was always a quick way to a bar fight with UNSC Marines.

It rankled me that the UNSC viewed the Colonial Military as suspect, but they were right to do so.

"So this is all a waste?" I asked.

Eric nodded. "So it goes."

"Not exactly helping the UNSC break their assumptions about us, are we?"

"Screw the UNSC." Eric leaned back against his restraints. "They gutted us. They sidelined us. They give us crap; barely functioning equipment. Then they want to whine about our lack of effectiveness? At least give me a uniform that's not threadbare and then we'll talk."

A few grunts from nearby indicated that Eric's point of view was commonly held.

"Then what are we doing here?" I asked.

Felicia, sitting across from me, grinned. "You want to go back to the golden grains of Harvest, Gage?"

"Hell no." I grinned.

The thing about soldiers: We were usually there for the guy next to us. The Felicias, the Erics; boot camp, barracks; the tiny little world that was the unit and only the unit, particularly now that we were away from past friends or any family connections.

Everyone in that Pelican was family, no matter what disagreements we had. We still had to back each other up come crunch time. And we had each other's backs when we piled out of that Pelican, weapons hot.

Felicia took point, her preference, while Eric and I had her covered. The other Marines spread out around the Pelican.

The island was deserted, but whoever had been here hadn't been gone that long. The remains of a campfire still smoldered. Sand-colored camouflage tents whipped about from the Pelican's exhaust. There were dummy targets set up around the scraggly bush on the edge of the Insurrectionist camp.

"I am saddened to report," Felicia said, "that we have *just* missed yet another Insurrectionist camp." There was some bitterness in her voice. Like me, she was frustrated by what she'd seen of the CMA sympathies so far. No matter how much we were Outer Colonists, we'd still been given a job and sworn an oath to be soldiers. We wanted to do our job.

An hour later, someone from the Office of Naval Intelligence arrived in a gleaming, brand-new green Pelican. It touched down in a flurry of sand. The ONI agent quickly walked about the camp remains with a disgusted look, then left.

We had a barbecue on the edge of the water that night. The sunset wavered, and the stars started to wink into place.

"They won't be able to hold this together," Felicia said, throwing chicken bones out into the water.

"Who won't?" I asked.

"The UNSC. The Inner Colonies." Felicia pointed up at the stars over the bonfire and the dripping explosions of fat from chicken still hanging from the improvised spits. "If we spread out through all those stars, what could hold us all together? At some point, distance will have its effect, and so will time, and someone will have to break away and do something different. No matter how much force they apply, they can't stop this. Even people from within their ranks are deserting for the Outer Colonies. It's like Rome. They kept taking these barbarians and teaching them how to fight, and then they'd end up leaving and fighting the very generals who'd taught them. We're those barbarians!"

A small coal exploded in the fire, scattering tiny, incandescent particles into the dark, where they winked out and vanished.

Eric threw a chicken bone at Felicia. "You think too much, you damn Innie."

Felicia laughed. "Innie? Not me, sir, I'm no Insurrectionist. I just follow orders and go where they tell me. If I weren't here I'd be sitting in jail back in Utgard because of this girl I met in a bar one night . . ."

". . . I mean, how was I supposed to know she was the governor's daughter," Eric and I chorused, finishing Felicia's anecdote before she could even launch into it. She'd told it to us often enough.

She blushed and laughed, demanding we hand over the six-pack of beer before it got warm from sitting outside the cooler and too close to the fire.

The next day we were assigned to riot patrol in Elysium City: howling citizens throwing rocks and pavers at the Colonial Administration's offices, shaking signs about freedom and independence, while we kept our shoulders up against the riot shields and kept them back.

"They're really pissed off," Felicia grunted, arms locked in mine as we shoved back against the crowd. A red-haired woman in a cocktail dress shouted obscenities at us and tried to leap over the cordon, but Eric stepped forward and shoved her back, hard enough that she fell under the mob, fortunately rescued by a pair of her friends.

It was something the police should have been doing, so it was quite clear that the UNSC didn't want to have anything to do with us and had sent us out to do scut work. Certainly they wouldn't be including us in any raids or counterinsurgency operations in the future.

None of the old hands in our barracks particularly minded.

Meanwhile, the demonstrations grew angrier and more dangerous with each passing day.

After two months of riot patrol and guarding bases, or anything else the UNSC determined was simple enough for us to handle, we were growing bored and looking for diversions. We were far enough out of Elysium City that to hop a ride into where the parties were meant we had to get ahold of passes, or know someone with access to a Warthog.

So the three of us had made fast friends with Allison Stark, one of the last of the Pelican pilots that the UNSC had yet to steal away from us. She not only had access to transportation, but a pet NCO who'd sign off on any leave request.

Usually we didn't fraternize with the flyboys (or in this case, flygirl), but Allison could get you into the city, outdrink you, and get you back as long as you picked up the tab.

But tonight the four of us found the Warthog pool empty.

"The officers cleared us out," Felicia said.

Eric kicked a large rock. "Or they're escorting supplies."

"Where?" I asked.

"Doesn't matter. How do you think Innies get UNSC explosives or weapons? Spare parts?"

I hadn't thought much about that. "Black market?"

"Black market still has to get that stuff from somewhere," Eric said thoughtfully.

"Don't care what's going on," I said, "we're still standing here with no transport."

Allison folded her arms. "I have a solution, if the guys here have the balls . . ."

"And what is *that*?" I rose to the challenge right away, even as Felicia laughed at my predictable response.

That was a Hornet. A small, one-person cockpit with a pair of engines perched high overhead and behind it, and a chain gun on the nose. It looked, appropriately enough, like a gray metal insect.

"You want us to ride the skids?" Eric asked, stepping up onto the flanged wings under the cockpit that the Hornet sat on.

There was barely room for one person to ride the sides, it seemed to me.

"Hey, UNSC Marines ride the skids all the time," Allison said as she opened the cockpit and clambered in. "Combat insertion. Training. You name it."

That sealed it.

But who was going to pair up on a skid?

Eric, Felicia, and I squared off with a fast round of paper-rock-scissors, which Felicia and I lost.

Eric walked to the other side of the Hornet. "See you on the other side!"

I made a show of allowing Felicia to get on the skid first, and she shoved herself against the skin of the Hornet. There was a bit of a recess behind the cockpit where the skid joined it.

"It's nice that they standardized the controls," Allison said, flipping switches as the engines kicked on behind us. I watched the sequence from my position just behind her, until it suddenly dawned on me what she meant.

"Wait," I protested. "You haven't flown one of these?"

"It's straightforward. You got your stick, your collective throttle, yadda yadda. We've been doing this ever since we invented VTOLs." The Hornet jerked upward, and I crouched, wondering if I should jump now.

But I didn't, and I had to let go of the lip as Allison yanked the glass down and sealed the cockpit shut.

"You getting ideas there?" Felicia asked as I shoved up against her, grabbing for handholds on the Hornet.

"You wish."

She laughed, then swore as the Hornet tilted.

I thought I could hear Eric whooping from the other side as the Hornet climbed up over the trees and headed toward the bright lights of Elysium City.

The target was a flip music club on the outskirts. Allison flew in low over a residential area, then flared out over the parking lot, dropping us to the ground with a thump.

Felicia and I tumbled off the skid, our knees somewhat shaky as we gratefully staggered on solid ground.

Eric also stumbled around the Hornet, laughing

wildly. "I hope we're stuck on idiot duty by the UNSC forever!"

"Come on." We offered Allison a hand out of the cockpit.

We bounced inside to the raucous beat of flip music. Allison struck out with me and Felicia for the bar.

"Hey, how are you going to account for taking the Hornet?" Felicia asked as we waited for drinks.

"Training," Allison shouted over the music. "NCO'll sign me off."

I laughed. "Does he even know it's a lost cause?"

Allison grabbed her drink. "Sweetie, if you don't tell him I'm not into men, I certainly won't, and this little arrangement," she waved her glass at the club and pulsating lights and dancing crowd, "this can keep going."

She danced her way off into the crowd as I paid. "Keep the tab open, I'm covering whatever she drinks," I told the bartender.

"You're not going after her?" I asked Felicia, who'd dragged Allison into our group.

"She's not my type." Felicia grinned. "Now find me a dirt-pounding Marine gal, and we'll talk."

"I don't have time to be your wingman," I grunted.

Felicia shook her head. "You'd make a crap one. All the gals we meet think you're a Harvest hick."

"What, and you aren't?" I was a little bit annoyed by the barb.

"I'm an Utgard girl, city born and bred. It's in the blood. The other city girls can sniff it. Plus, you have no sense of style."

"Oh, screw you! Now you're just trying to piss me off."

"Yeah, guilty. I wouldn't do it if you weren't so damn touchy about it." Felicia pressed her drink in my hand. "Hey. Keep an eye on this, I need to visit the girls' room."

I followed her part of the way to stand in the hallway with a drink in each hand as hordes of people shoved past me.

When Felicia came back out I handed her her drink, and we turned back to leave the hallway.

That's when the Insurrectionist bomb exploded. A concussive wave of heat, light, and pressure threw me back down the hallway.

For a moment, I lay on the carpet, staring blurrily at the ceiling, and then a second explosion brought the entire building down on top of us, trapping me in the debris.

ODSTs dug us out.

Most of the civilians out dancing, however, had died. Allison was found with a piece of rebar through her skull. Eric was in a coma and getting ferried out to Reach for better medical care.

Felicia and I both had been packed with biofoam, and then moved to a field hospital set up on the edge of the debris.

We were too doped up on painkillers to do much more than lie in bed for the first half day while medics kept an eye on us. I had a concussion, broken ribs, burns, a skull fracture, and ached in places I didn't know I had.

Felicia reported, from two beds over, the same.

"Standing in that hallway saved your lives," an ODST medic said. "You're damn lucky."

I didn't feel lucky.

Particularly when the ONI agents showed up.

They questioned us about what we were doing at the club: how we got there, whether we had contacts with Insurrectionists.

There were a lot of questions about where our allegiances lay. Many of them asked over and over again.

In the end, they eventually let us be, but not before telling us that the club had been singled out because it was a favored spot for CMA Marines during weekend leave.

I had a lot of time to think, lying there on the bed healing.

"They're saying they're going to be shutting down the CMA's involvement with TREBUCHET," I told Felicia, sitting on the edge of her bed once I'd healed enough to walk. "There are rumors that the CMA will be shut down completely. Or at least that the UNSC is fighting to get the CMA disbanded."

"No surprise."

"And then what comes next?" I asked. "Even if it lives, the CMA is a dead end. What kind of career will I have if I stay with them? I think I'm going to leave for the UNSC."

"Career? Why the hell would you want a career?"

Felicia snorted. "You'll never see Harvest again if you switch to the UNSC. No telling where they'd send you. You have a chance to go home now."

"I could care less about ever seeing Harvest again," I said.

"It's where you came from. Where your dad has land."

"It's just dirt, Felicia. Dirt. It doesn't mean anything. Why the hell do you care? Are you going back to Utgard?"

"Yes." She surprised me there. I hadn't known that. I'd thought her just as interested as me in wanting to get away. "I didn't choose to enlist, remember."

"I'd always thought your story about the governor's daughter was just that . . . a story. Did you really have to join to skip jail in Harvest?"

"No. No, that was bullshit. My dad forced me to join," she said. "After I stole an MLX and went out joyriding. After the governor incident. Told me it was time to grow up."

"So you'd go back to Utgard?"

"In a moment, if they discharged me. They might even rotate us back, if they're no longer going to use us here." She pulled her knees up under her chin. "What's the bug up your ass about leaving the CMA?"

I rubbed my forehead. "I have bits of human bone embedded in me, from whoever was wearing that bomb before they triggered it. Permanently now. And that ONI guy who talked to us, he said the explosives were CMA-issued. Maybe even from our own base. That's not a civil disagreement, it's madness."

"The UNSC could stop it in a moment by leaving," Felicia said. "Is it really your problem?"

"Maybe. Maybe not. But maybe the rebels get even worse. Kill more civilians. Then who are they really doing this for? The civilians they're getting killed?"

"Or maybe the UNSC keeps overreacting and causing the Outer Colonies to not want any part of all this," Felicia said gently. "A million casualties now, caught in the crossfire, since TREBUCHET started. No one's going to ignore that. The civilians will keep cheering the rebels on."

"I know. And maybe we're always destined to be splintering and fighting, without some greater cause. But I'm applying to the ODSTs."

"You've got to be kidding? Are you suicidal now?"

"I'm joining as soon as I'm cleared."

Felicia sighed. "Then I'm coming, too. We'll sign up together."

"Why the hell would you want to do that?"

"We've had each other's backs for months now. Eric's in a coma. Allison's dead. You want me to rotate back to Harvest and sit on my hands alone? Screw that. You're going to need someone to cover your ass; you're going to be fresh meat to all those tough-assed ODSTs out there."

"Seriously, Felicia . . ." I turned to look at her.

"Shut up about it already, Gage. You're the closest thing I have to a brother. You're a poor excuse for one, but I consider you one nonetheless. Deal with it."

"I want to go after the bastards that did this to us."

"I know. You're a sentimental, honorable dirt farmer

who needs a hell of a lot more cynicism in your life. Of course you want to go after them."

"Harvest will always be there when we're done," I said.

Orders arrived before we were discharged, proving my instincts correct. We were to be folded into the UNSC or offered an honorable discharge and a ticket back to our home world of choice.

I tried one last time to convince Felicia out of applying to the ODST, but she told me to shove it and shut up.

The recruiter's office was in chaos when we showed up with our papers. Several older sergeants were huddled around screens and pumping fists.

"What's going on?" Felicia asked.

"We got that bastard, Watts!" they said.

"*Robert* Watts?" I was shocked. Watts had led the Insurrectionists all throughout the Outer Colonies from deep in the asteroid belts of this system for so long, it sounded improbable. "Who got him? ODSTs?"

"No clue. But the ONI propaganda machine is kicking into overdrive declaring him caught." The sergeant collected himself and grabbed our papers. "It's a good day to be a Marine! Bad day to be an Innie."

With Watts captured, I wondered how strong the rebel movements would remain.

"Raw meat for the ODST grinder, huh?" the grizzled sergeant grunted. "If you thought Colonial boot camp was tough, you're about to get dismantled. Then we'll see if you can manage to put yourselves back together."

I laughed, but the ODST recruiters didn't laugh back. They were dead serious. They knew what was around the corner for the two of us, and the smiles on their lips were like the smiles of wolves.

ODST boot camp was where I learned how to kill someone with my pinky.

Among other things.

But first they stripped us of our rank.

"Think coming in from the CMA means jack to us?" an officer commented when I presented the fact. "You'll have to actually earn your rank here."

Then they started running us. I'd kept track of Felicia up to that point; we'd even had a chance to compare notes at mess, eating together.

But there was quickly little time for that; too exhausted, too busy trying to survive.

For three weeks I ran, did push-ups, and blitzed through obstacle courses as fast as I could. They took us through slush, artificial snow, and live gunfire-simulated battle. Got on our bellies and crawled through miles of barbed wire, rubble, and destroyed buildings as they fired rounds at us just inches over our heads.

That was just to get us into shape.

On the first day of squad tactics, they dressed all fifty of us still remaining up in full ODST training gear and dropped us off at the base of a mountain.

"Get to the top and you can eat and rest back in your

barracks tonight," our drill sergeant, O'Reilly, said with an all-too-familiar grin.

Our guns were loaded with TTR rounds. They were fake bullets with paint inside that contained particles that reacted with nanopolymers in your gear. Your clothes (or in the case of us training ODSTs, our signature black body armor) stiffened to immobility when shot with a TTR round, and then an anesthetic in the paint left the part of your body it hit paralyzed.

Day two of training, O'Reilly had walked up and down the line with a TTR pistol, shooting us in the leg and then shouting "Run! Run! Run!" as we limped off in confusion. Anyone not quick enough was shot in the other leg and told "Crawl, soldier!"

Once I'd found myself completely paralyzed while a trainer squatted overhead and screamed into my face that I was a worthless excuse for a soldier, and a "fine example of the best the CMA had to offer."

One day, on the mountain, I had an MA5B assault rifle with sixty TTR rounds loaded.

The fifty of us waited for the Pelicans that had dropped us off to thunder away, and as quiet descended, we looked nervously at each other.

"What do you think's in there?" someone asked, looking at the forest that covered the low flanks of the mountainside.

"I'm guessing trainers with their own guns who're—" I didn't get to finish. The person next to me was hit in the chest. The TTR round splashed red, and he went down stiffly, his body armor locked up as he toppled to the ground.

"Sniper!"

The forty-nine of us remaining scrambled for cover in confusion, and by the time I'd found a boulder to shove my back against, I could see eight more sets of black ODST body armor stiffened up, splotched with red, and their occupants dropping to the ground.

A nervous Marine slammed into the boulder next to me. He caught his breath, then popped up to scan the area. The loud impact of a TTR round struck his exposed helmet, and he slumped down over me with a grunt. "Dammit."

In just minutes, half of us had been struck by fire from somewhere high inside the forest. I could hear laughter.

I shoved the "dead" Marine off me. If we remained here, we'd all be done in another minute, and no one would get to the top. "There are only a handful of them," I shouted. "We have to rush them, some will get hit; the rest will get into the trees. Then we'll have a chance."

And in the far distance, I heard Felicia shout back, "He's right. On three!"

"One, two, three!" I burst out from behind cover with the other twenty-four and rushed for the tree line.

I got within five feet of the tree line before a TTR round hit me in the stomach and I sprawled into the bushes, frozen in place.

Up the hill, in the trees, the battle raged on. I heard Felicia's voice at least once more, giving orders, then swearing.

After half an hour a trainer walked out from the

shadows of the forest and looked down at me. "That was the first useful thing you've done in three weeks, maggot," he shouted, and then left me lying there.

When the armor freed itself up hours later, I milled about with my fellow soldiers. All fifty of us, scattered around the base of the mountain, spent a chilly night around hand-built fires, hungry, until we were picked up the next morning.

We were then assembled into fireteams after and given tactical training. Felicia led our small team: Mason, gangly and blond, hailed from Reach. Kiko from Eridanus II. We fell into a tight team that managed to hold its own.

The next time on the mountain, Kiko and Mason laid down suppressing fire into the forest that Felicia and I dashed for. Once behind cover there we laid a stream of TTR rounds ahead so that Kiko and Mason could follow.

Leapfrogging and keeping an arc ahead of us constantly under fire, we were able to get halfway up the mountain before a trainer moved around behind us and got Kiko.

We stalled out then, crouched in the brush with our backs to each other for a full field of range until a TTR grenade bounced into our midst and scattered us.

Another hungry, cold night on the mountain.

Then they taught us squad tactics, pairing us up with another fireteam.

With each fireteam leapfrogging the other, we got most of the way up the mountain. But leaving the for-

est as it petered out high in the mountain's crag, we fell
under ambush by snipers dug in at the top.

We lost most of the other fireteam, who'd been on
point, to TTR fire. Felicia, Kiko, Mason, and I had hit
the snow and mud and opened fire back. We were the
only team that had gotten that far.

"Any ideas?" Felicia asked. With enemy behind us in
the woods, and in front of us buried in, and most of
our ammo gone, we had seconds to make a decision.

"We'll never be able to charge them. We need sniper
rifles," I said.

"Trainers have those."

"Exactly. And they're coming for us." I pointed back
down the slope.

We backed down the muddy snow into the tree line.
"Play dead," Kiko whispered. "Get down in the mud
right on the edge of the tree line with all the others who
got hit."

It would only ever work once, but we sprawled ourselves stiffly out in the mud.

As our pursuers broke cautiously out into the open we
ambushed them. I took special glee in hitting O'Reilly
almost point-blank in the chest as he approached me.

We relieved them of their sniper rifles.

Mason got hit in the leg while we moved about, trying to get a bead on the trainers at the top, but Kiko
and Felicia got off two good shots.

I ran ahead and threw TTR grenades into the areas
from which we'd been fired on, flushing out the instructors, and Kiko and Felicia got two of the three.

The last trainer shot me in the arm, a stunning shot done on the run with his sniper rifle, but I gunned him down with the MA5B before he could try it again.

And just like that, we'd taken the top of the mountain.

"Nice." Felicia slapped my shoulder. We'd all been hit by TTR rounds, but we limped our way to the very top and shouted loud enough to hear our echoes return from the mountain over; our hot, exhausted breath steaming from our mouths into the cold air.

A Pelican appeared, flaring out to land in the clearing at the top of the mountain. Snow swirled out from under the backwash of its engines, and a craggy-faced gunnery sergeant stepped out, as well as a number of corporals.

He didn't even look at us. "Get everyone up, now!" he ordered the corporals.

They were off, tapping armor with electronic wands to unfreeze it.

Something wasn't right. There was a strangeness to the hurry they did it with. And what the hell was a gunnery sergeant doing talking to us in the middle of a training session?

We all gathered around the gunny, lining up as we'd been trained. He nodded. "Is this everyone?"

A quick head count confirmed that this was everyone.

"Good. At ease. You've all been out here in the wilderness training hard, but I've been sent to let you know your training is going to be accelerated."

The instructors frowned, and we all shifted.

"Much of this information has been classified, and between the ONI and the Navy types, this is what we can tell you: We have made first contact with an intelligent alien civilization."

A gasp rose at hearing those words. Some of us reflexively looked up into the sky. First contact!

The gunnery sergeant continued, cool as ice. "We know that standard protocols were followed. And that things didn't go well. Our ships were attacked by alien beings referred to as the Covenant. Before destroying our ships they claimed our destruction was the will of their gods, and that they were the instrument. It seems to be an act of war. As of today the UNSC is on full alert. The Colonial Military has been officially disbanded, all remaining units are officially being pulled in and reassigned and retrained. And we're ramping up training here, because we have a feeling we're going to need all the recruits we can get.

"These aliens are for real. They've already taken, or possibly destroyed, one Outer Colony. Admiral Preston Cole is being tasked with creating a force to get it back."

We were stunned.

Private Rodriguez from Madrigal was the one who asked, "What colony fell to them, sir?"

"Harvest," the gunnery sergeant said, and my knees buckled.

Someone grabbed my shoulder. I staggered around and found Felicia sitting in the mud. She looked up at me, tears in her eyes. "Dirt?" she asked. "Do you still think that now?"

I didn't have anything to say back. I stood in front of her, struck mute.

Harvest was gone.

I'd tried to find the last nice thing I said to my dad before I'd left; the last time we laughed, smiled even? I couldn't find one.

I'd always figured he'd keep on farming. That maybe I'd go back, one day, when I'd traveled worlds and seen so much, and maybe talk to him again. Maybe.

But there were no maybes now. He was gone now.

Harvest was gone.

Felicia grabbed a fistful of mud and leaped up at me. "Dirt! I have your dirt, you son of a bitch!"

She hit me, mud from her clenched first spattering my face, but I didn't feel it. I felt like a part of my soul had been ripped away, and even after she was pulled off me, I just stood there, numb.

Dirt.

Just dirt.

For the rest of training they moved Felicia to another fireteam. Our new team leader, Rahud, took his annoyance about the swap out on me. He was an experienced UNSC veteran who'd joined the ODSTs after years of service.

He didn't take too kindly to the fact that just because I'd been given rank in the old Colonial Military, it had given me the ability to apply to the ODST program. He certainly didn't like the fact that some falling out between two backwater planet recruits like Felicia and me had caused him to get moved away from the team he'd trained with.

Any screwup, the slightest mistake, and he was in my face, calling me a detriment to the team and a liability.

But it didn't faze me. My bonds with Kiko and Mason were tight, and the three of us held our own.

Every day, as the months of training passed, there was some new rumor floating around about the aliens. Ships they'd attacked. Their invincibility.

A lot of it was bull. Back then we didn't know anything.

We certainly didn't realize what we were up against. Kiko and Mason would joke about getting out there to kick alien ass, and with a few beers in me, I'd join them.

Certainly after ODST training, we figured a bunch of religious fanatic aliens would be no match for the atmosphere-jumping, hard-as-nails brutality that a raw ODST-trained human could bring to the table.

But when the first leaked photos of the Outer Colonies attacks came out, I wondered if we might be wrong. Some of them had been turned into glass balls by Covenant energy weapons.

What the hell were *we* going to be able to do against that kind of firepower?

You know that sound inside a single-occupant exo-atmospheric insertion vehicle? That combination of a howling wind, a dull roar, and the crackle and creak of the SOEIV's skin flexing and burning. No matter how many times I jumped, hearing it always scared the crap out of me.

Feet First into Hell. That was the ODST motto. Feet first with a two-thousand-degree fireball burning around the pod as it flames its way down through the atmosphere.

It's a hot ride.

A bumpy ride.

And not everyone survives it.

My first combat SOEIV insertion had me coming in hot with a hundred other ODSTs over the main continent of Hat Yai, three years after I finished training. We'd been mainly stuck in naval battles, waiting in our bays, just itching for a chance to be thrown against this new enemy. Everyone was pumped about Admiral Cole's triumphant recapture of Harvest earlier that year.

What isn't, perhaps, often recounted, but is a fact that quickly became well-known amongst the rank and file, was that Cole lost three ships for every one Covenant ship destroyed.

It was a Pyrrhic victory that left Cole's fleet severely damaged.

Now Cole had been jumping his fleet around from engagement to engagement throughout the Outer Colonies, wherever the Covenant showed up.

So far, there'd been no repeat of the retaking of Harvest. Outer Colonies had been glassed or taken. World by world, we were falling back.

Covenant ships in low orbit picked off ten of us, and when landing ate another pair of SOEIVs that failed and cratered into the lush rain forest of our landing zone.

It took half an hour for Rahud to get us grouped up; our pods had dodged enough fire that we'd gotten fairly well separated.

"Where's the rest of the squad?" Mason asked.

Rahud shrugged. "I can't raise them. Assume the worst."

We trudged through thick mud and rain forest, vines and creepers holding us back as we got bogged down farther and farther in.

"There's no way a Pelican's coming in through that kind of foliage," Kiko commented. "How do we get out?"

Rahud ignored us. "Covenant forces established a base of some sort up ahead. We're all converging on it." This is why we'd been sent down: an exploratory and reconnoitering force.

Mason leaned in. "That's if our ship can even get back to drop in recovery vehicles."

The destroyer *Clearidas* had dropped us in, ducking and weaving in between Covenant forces in low orbit, bouncing itself off the upper atmosphere as it vomited its cargo of a hundred SOEIVs.

As I ran through tropical jungle, sweating under my black ODST armor, I wondered if there were enough ships high overhead to hold off the Covenant.

"Hold," Rahud hissed. We were getting close.

Other ODSTs materialized out of the forest. Hand signals were exchanged, and information rippled throughout the forest.

Ten ODST squads grouped up and began to ooze through the brush, weapons at the ready.

Rahud led us carefully down the lip of a dirt road that had been hastily carved into what was fast becoming rock.

We paused at the lip of a giant sinkhole.

"Holy . . . ," someone began.

In just days the aliens had excavated a massive pit that bored deep into the ground. Bluish-gray metal spars soared up from the bottom into the air from what looked like a freakish cross between a city and a hive at the bottom, including bubblelike structures that studded the sidewalls of the giant pit.

"They're building a small city down there," Mason said. "Now that they've cleaned out the colonists."

"They're Grunts," a private suggested. "Those big buildings are methane tanks."

"Methane?" someone else asked.

"Didn't you listen to the damn briefings . . ."

"Movement!" Kiko pointed, and Rahud turned.

I saw my first Covenant aliens standing on the other side of the lip: Ten Grunts and a pair of Jackals were staring right back at us.

The Jackals stood tall, with weird back-jointed legs, and had Mohawk-like feathers and birdlike faces.

The dwarfish Grunts—with their doglike faces behind breathing equipment, squat legs, and weird triangular methane tanks—started shooting at us.

Balls of plasma energy sizzled and spat as they hit the trees behind us.

As the closest team, we fanned out, falling into our

usual routines. Kiko and Mason laid down cover fire, and Rahud and I skirted the lip clockwise toward the aliens.

ODST snipers hit the Grunts, splashes of blue blood blossoming in the air as the aliens dropped to the ground. The Jackals held up energy shields attached to their forearms to ward off the gunfire, and returned it tenfold.

We sprinted around the rim. "Their feet!" Rahud shouted.

The shields didn't cover their feet. I aimed low, chewing up mud and vines, walking the shots along until I hit my first Jackal.

It screeched and pitched forward, shield bobbling, and Rahud shot it in the head. Purple blood oozed down the side of the corpse.

The other Jackal turned to face us, opening itself up for a sniper shot by an ODST. It grabbed its chest, moaning, and then stumbled off the edge of the lip and fell down. It bounced off one of the struts, then continued all the way down to the ground of the pit below.

I pushed the dead Jackal's body with a boot. Here was the enemy. Flesh and blood. Killable.

Now that we had the lip surrounded a command hierarchy had been established. Major Sedavian had landed at the very rear of the group, and had finally caught up to us.

"Figure we're going down there?" Mason asked, peering over the edge. We could see more Covenant at the bottom, with hundreds of Grunts and a handful of Jackals that seemed to be overseeing them. They were mustering near elevators, getting ready to come up to join the fight. An energy bolt sizzled and blew up a piece of rock near my face, and I ducked back to the safety of cover.

"Negative," Rahud said, coming up from behind us suddenly. "Covenant Cruisers just arrived. We're outgunned. We're getting out of here and dropping a Shiva into this mess."

That was it. The fight was over, we'd already lost.

I could sense the frustration in the air as word spread. But orders were orders.

The Pelicans could barely land on the lip, and the Covenant at the bottom of the pit opened antiaircraft fire, but we all bugged out easily enough.

As we headed for orbit, the Shiva nuclear warheads left on the lip detonated.

Once we were aboard, the *Clearidas* entered slipspace, leaving the system.

Another retreat.

That was the pattern for the next few years. The Covenant ate us up, system by system, with very few victories on our side.

Most of the worlds I'd come to know well were all destroyed. No one cared about Insurrectionists, Outer Colonies versus the UNSC, or the Colonial Military ten years after Harvest fell.

There was only humanity versus the Covenant.

I saw more than my fair share of dead aliens and dead comrades.

Eventually I stopped making friends.

Mason died in my arms on Asmara after one of the snake-headed Covenant Elites speared him along with ten other ODSTs with his energy sword before I got off a near point-blank shot with a missile launcher.

I found Mason lying among the debris; I could smell his seared flesh.

He looked up at me with glassy eyes and asked for his mother, then coughed up blood and just . . . stopped being.

Kiko was stabbed in the face by the apelike Brutes on another world, the name of which I've since forgotten. Large, muscular, hairy aliens, they could snap a neck with their bare hands. Rahud died from energy artillery.

I was promoted to team leader, then a squad leader. I had long since stopped learning names; I didn't want to form any attachments.

Maybe that's why I never rose above squad leader.

I had become a shadow of myself. A robot. Hitting my mark and killing the enemy, and waiting for the one day a stray flash of energy would kill me.

I was waiting for the day I could be buried. In the dirt.

The steady stream of defeats led to the creation of the Cole Protocol. No ship was to return directly to any of our worlds, particularly Earth, but instead execute random jumps in slipspace to throw off any potential Covenant shadowers.

"Where was *that* order for all the glassed Outer Colonies!" I'd shouted, standing up in the middle of a mess hall.

I remember once I woke from the bitter cold of cryogenic storage, staggering around and vomiting suspension fluid, and realized something was really, really wrong. This wasn't the usual slow routine of getting unfrozen and waking up fully as we were briefed for our next assignment. This time emergency lighting kept everything shadowy in the dim red. Everyone on deck hurried around nervously, and I could hear the unmistakable sound of the ship's MAC gun firing.

"We've been ambushed by a Covenant cruiser. You've all been flash unfrozen," the officer on deck said. "Just in case."

Keeping us on ice let us all go through the long slipspace routes without eating up supplies and sucking down oxygen. Or getting bored out of our minds.

Flash unfreezing was dangerous, and only for emergencies. I think the ship's captain was worried about being boarded. Either way, someone up the chain had given the order for the risky decanting, maybe out of panic. A third of the unfrozen ODSTs on deck died.

Clearidas managed to escape. But my men didn't.

A waste.

After all these years of combat, I slowly began to feel myself peeling apart. But I had no home, nowhere I really wanted to be, no one to see.

So I soldiered on, battle after battle.

I almost saw my end in a hastily dug out trench on Skopje, an Inner Colony world. Unlike most of the wilder Outer Colonies, this world had highly built up urban areas, roads, and railways. It was an entire civilization sprawled across its island continents.

From the trench, if I turned to look behind me, I could see a skyline glinting and blazing in the sun over a red marbled museum. But back in front: mud.

We were sent in to protect the headquarters of a shipbuilding corporation during the evacuation of their shipyards. The machines, tools, and personnel that could be saved would be relocated to Reach, to continue building parts for the war effort.

Our headquarters were the halls of a nearby city museum, the grounds of which served as our landing zone and held all the quickly placed antiaircraft batteries.

"This is the fallback point, there is nowhere else to go," we were told. "So you hold the perimeter *at all costs*."

Covenant air support dared not attack us directly, not for several blocks. So they threw Grunts at us. Thousands of them in brutal house-to-house warfare, their numbers overwhelming our loose perimeter. We fell back and regrouped, drawing them in until we were foxholed on the edges of the vast museum gardens. We let the Grunts charge us across the muddy field.

They'd pushed us back, but we still simply thought of them as cannon fodder, waiting until they got close enough to hit their methane tanks and watch them explode. Now that we had our open ground and dug in positions, we slaughtered them.

But they kept coming. And after waves of screaming

Grunts came the races higher up in the Covenant food chain: Jackal snipers, Brutes rushing the line, and then finally Elites, flashing their energy swords as they got in close enough to the melee.

The trenches got cut off, communication lost, and I found myself crouched in between two walls of mud with another ODST, waiting for the Covenant to leap in with us.

This would be it. We'd go down fighting in the mud, I thought.

But instead, in an explosion of mud, a two-ton powered suit of gray-green armor landed between us. "Follow me!" the powerful baritone voice behind the gold visor ordered.

Then it leaped over the edge into the fray, plasma discharges slapping the powered armor.

We followed.

The armored human was like a tank, clearing the way for us. It shrugged off Grunts like they were annoying mosquitoes, tackled Brutes face on, and was an equal match for any Elite.

We were led to a giant castle, like something out of a picture book, with large antiaircraft guns mounted along the walls and AIE-486H heavy machine guns on the parapets pointed down.

Inside we were left by the giant armored man.

"What the hell was that?" I asked the Marine in the courtyard.

"Special ONI project. They call them Spartans. Engineered to be the best, armored with the best. Haven't you heard the ONI announcements? They'll be ending the war with these sons of bitches running through the Covenant soon enough!"

The ODSTs weren't the cutting edge hard-asses anymore.

I'd just seen the future of warfare. I wasn't in it.

I didn't have time to dwell on this, because suddenly an all-too-familiar voice said, "Gage? Gage Yevgenny? Is that really you?"

And I turned to see Felicia standing with a BR55 slung under one arm and a canteen in the other.

"Felicia?" There were wrinkles in her tanned, leathery face. But all these years would do that. We'd just been kids the last time we saw each other, really.

She ran over and hugged me, a strong clench, and then she shoved me back. "I can't frigging believe you're alive!"

I was just as stunned. "What are you doing here?"

"Holed up, same as you. The castle was my call. Some CEO had it made using actual quarried rock from outside the city. Covenant low-level energy weapons don't vaporize the rock; they just melt it a bit more, making it even stronger. We're waiting for some Pelicans to get us the hell out now that they took the museum off your grubby hands."

She had a jagged scar across her cheek, and a nasty burn on the back of her neck from a near miss. But I caught a glimpse of her bars: She'd risen up to colonel.

We compared notes and found that we'd been in a couple of the same theaters together, separated only by thirty or so miles.

"I can get you aboard my detail, if you want," she said. "And I promise I won't flake out on you again."

"Crap, Felicia, that was a long, long time ago. A lot's happened since then."

"I know. You actually saved my life, you know."

"How's that?"

"I would have gone back. I would have been sitting on Harvest in my lame-ass Colonial uniform when those goddamn aliens dropped the hammer the second time around."

I didn't say anything to that. I didn't want to think about Harvest.

"There were some survivors from the first attack," Felicia said. "Did you ever look to see . . ."

"My father wasn't on the rolls, no."

Felicia nodded. "Mine, either." Then she leaned in. "Look, I'll get you a transfer to the *Chares,* the cruiser I'm aboard. And once up there, there's someone you need to meet."

I was intrigued. I hadn't felt this energized in years, so busy with keeping my head down and focusing on one task at a time. And now here was Felicia, with her energy and friendship.

You know, to tell you the truth, I was scared. Did I dare reach out to her again?

Or would she be dead soon enough, ripping another part of me away with her?

Because how much of that can a person ever truly handle?

I wasn't sure.

"If we get back to orbit," Felicia said, "I have a surprise for you."

An explosion shattered molten rock up in the air, which drizzled back down and reformed. Eventually this castle was going to look like a version of itself that had been placed inside an oven, and half metal.

"If we get back up!" she said, slapping my shoulder. "Get more ammo and get up on the walls. Pelicans should be down here soon."

Off in the distance a sharklike Covenant Cruiser began to descend from the clouds. From its belly, fierce energy descended upon the land, glassing it into oblivion.

So we hightailed it out of there.

I'd stopped expecting to live, right before I saw her again. After that, I suddenly felt real again. A human being again, with a past, and a life.

Aboard the *Chares* the wounded and battered Marines and ODSTs tended their injuries as we retreated into slipspace. I couldn't put a figure to the numbers who would have died down there on that planet, but given the cities I saw in the distance, I'd imagine millions.

Despite the glum atmosphere, Felicia hunted me down with an air of excitement.

"Come on," she said. She led me down through several bays until we came to a smaller bay crammed with Pelicans.

We rounded a corner, and sitting on a chair with a small cooler was Eric.

Freaking Eric was alive.

He stood up and grabbed my hand. "Gage . . ."

"When?" I could barely find the words. "How?"

Felicia looked over at us. "Bastard woke up after five years in a coma and joined the Navy. Became a right flyboy." She grabbed a beer and studied it. "Rank has its privileges, and Eric has his ways."

It was almost too much.

I wanted to know everything that had happened. Twenty-two years, more or less.

Twenty-two years, and we were strangers to each other.

And yet we fell right back into the same friendships, like chatting in the back of the empty Pelican, our voices echoing in the chamber of the launch bay.

Felicia was a colonel, Eric flying his way in and out of hell. And I was not much more than a grunt that had been more of a zombie for the last couple decades than anything else.

I may have lost the Outer Colonies, but I suddenly had my friends again.

When they told me about the plan, I remember that we were crowded in the back of Eric's Pelican getting drunk after a particularly messy ground operation. As Eric summed it up: people had died, Covenant had been killed, and we'd once again had to fall back.

"But at least it's happening less frequently," I said. "With the Cole Protocol they're only finding our worlds when they stumble over them."

Maybe this would give humanity time to build more

ships, time to ramp up for a big fight. Time, I thought, to create more super-soldier Spartans.

"Spartans," Eric spat. "They're not even human. Freaks are what they are."

It was not an uncommon ODST outlook: a suspicion of the faceless, armored men who'd started to show up on the battlefield.

I didn't argue with him.

"Besides," Felicia said, "it took them a long time to enact the Protocol. Almost like they wanted the Outer Colonies out of the picture."

"That's . . ." Ludicrous, I started to say. But I halted, remembering my own rage when it was first announced. ". . . hard to believe. But it still looks bad. And the result is . . . what it is."

"We put in our years, and we've been used up. We're getting tired. And there's nowhere to go home to," Felicia said.

"And because we're Colonial Military transfers, our pensions are still technically CMA, not UNSC. Since the CMA doesn't exist anymore, the pension funds were raided to build destroyers. No one is sure if the politicians will be able to find anything when we all start coming out of the system. If we live that long."

I felt the weariness in their voices. It was there in mine, too. Deep into my bones. I'd used up almost two-thirds of my life fighting.

And all I'd seen were losses.

Despite ONI propaganda films, and shore leave, and binges, I still felt that emptiness.

I realized Felicia and Eric were staring at me. Studying me. Feeling me out.

"We're going on some sort of snatch-and-run operation," Felicia said. "I just got word from the brass. We've
found something the Covenant is squatting on."

"What is it?"

"Some sort of artifact in the ground. Who the hell
cares? What in the past is going to save us now? What's
important is that this is going to be our last mission,"
Felicia said. "We've given our service. We've fought hard.
The only thing stopping the Covenant is our being able
to keep the location of Earth secret. The UNSC's just
using us up on the ground like throwaway pawns."

"All that matters to the UNSC is Reach and Earth
anyway," Eric said. He sounded so bitter. I'd gotten the
sense that the explosion had changed him even more,
despite his role in the UNSC; it was something he'd
taken out of necessity, not human patriotism.

Felicia continued. "The artifact the aliens have dug
up this time is near a small city, which I've done some
research on.

"There's a major bank in the center, with vaults.
They've got gold and platinum ingots buried down
there, and the Covenant invasion happened quickly
enough that it's all sitting down there. Right now."

I looked back and forth. "What, you want to steal
it?"

"Steal it?" Eric spat the words. "It doesn't exist anymore, Gage. It's about to be glassed. The UNSC wants
us to snatch the alien artifact or destroy it. No one
gives a crap about the gold."

"We could retire," Felicia said. "Go back to Earth, and lay back comfortably. Something the UNSC could never offer us."

I took a deep breath and looked down at the scuffed floor of the Pelican.

Eric chimed in. "We're still going to attack the Covenant and bring back the artifact. We'll be following orders. But we'll be coming down with one extra Pelican. We blow the vaults, load the gold into ammunition chests, load the Pelican, and come back to the ship."

"And then what?" I asked.

"Then . . . anything you want," Felicia said, leaning closer. I was more aware of the scar on her face and the intensity in her eyes than ever. "I know a transport headed back to Earth. I figure, I might as well see the mother planet before I die. Where you guys go, that's up to you, but I was hoping we could all go together. One last hurrah."

One last hurrah.

"We've put in our years, Gage. How much longer before it's some random Jackal sniper that takes us down? We've been putting our damn lives on the line since we were just kids. Kids. It's time to grow up. When was the last time you talked to a civilian?"

Too long, I thought. Too long. "How many more are involved?"

"With you, we can do this," Eric said. "Felicia can assemble them all into a team for the snatch-and-run; brass trusts her word. They're all old CMA vets. We've been planning this for a long time."

"We've been eyeing stuff like this on every op. Almost

pulled the trigger on the mission we met you on," Felicia said. "But there was too much going on and the bank was too far away from the action."

"But now that we found you, it's like it was meant to be," Eric said, looking into my eyes. "This is the one. It's perfect."

Under the haze of alcohol, the team back together again, I felt like I'd refound my family.

It was us against everyone.

I was scared, but I didn't want to let them down. I'd fought beside them. Hell, I'd been created beside them. We were a team. And I wasn't going to let them down. No matter what misgivings I had about this crazy scheme.

We had nothing left to lose.

War had stripped us of many things; made us hard, unflinching, dangerous. But it had forced us into a close bond at the beginning, and reinforced it when we'd found each other again after all these years.

I didn't want to lose them again.

We didn't come in by SOEIVs for this mission, but by Pelicans. They came out of orbit far from Covenant detection and then flew for hours until we reached the edge of our new combat zone.

The small city was in the center of a horseshoe-shaped range of small mountains. Its center plaza sat on top of where four mountain streams joined up to become the head of a strong river that trickled out the valley.

Our Pelicans came in low through a valley, just barely missing a rock ravine on either side as they flew up, over, and then back down, just feet over the ground. Risky, but again, the Covenant were none the wiser.

So far.

A hundred ODSTs fanned out through the city, clumping up temporarily to double-check weapons and strategy.

I stood in the middle of the plaza road and watched it all with Felicia and Eric.

Downriver the Covenant had thrown together a dam and dug in with a bustle of activity. Organic ships zoomed around overhead, and thousands of Grunts operated a constant hum of machinery that dissolved the ground.

We could hear the operations in the distance of the evacuated, eerily quiet city.

"Do you know what the city's called?" I asked.

"Mount Haven," Felicia said.

Two heavy machine guns had been mounted up on top of strategically located buildings in the city's center. Manned by two ODSTs, Amey and Charleston, both were picked out by Felicia, and there in case the Covenant decided to come sniffing. They also had rocket launchers at their feet for an extra punch if needed.

The other two members of that team, Orrin and Dale, stood with rocket launchers down the street.

Sita stood with Felicia, holding a BR55 battle rifle slung under her arm, and Teller, a pale, gray-haired colonel, lounged by a doorway with a pair of SMGs.

The eight of us were the base team, along with Eric in the Pelican with the Gatling gun in the nose making the ninth. This was base camp.

The other Pelicans were scattered around the edges of the city, ostensibly to reduce the chance of their getting hit by Covenant fire if things got hot; but it was really just an order by Felicia to keep them out of view of the city center.

Teams of ODSTs moved off downriver, and within ten minutes the city fell quiet.

Just the buildings around the river plaza and us, left behind to keep Mount Haven "secure."

There was an empty Jim Dandy's restaurant nearby. City Hall stood quiet with its facade of marble in the shadows.

The stately, two-story bank stood there, waiting for us.

"Okay, let's go!" Felicia shouted.

Orrin and Dale set their launchers up against the side of the bank and rigged explosives on the bank's thick front doors.

They blew off with a surprisingly muted thump. Precise shaped charges. The duo was good at this. They would be old CMA professionals that Felicia dug up.

"We have twenty minutes before the Pelicans will be getting ready to come back for the pickup," Felicia said as she led us into the bank. "So everybody move, move, move."

Sita, Teller, Orrin, and Dale all ran with her. The next obstacle was getting a door down; Dale quickly wired it up.

Another explosion later and we were through.

"Think we can risk the elevator?" I asked.

"Backup power is running still," Dale said. "It's a

small pebble-bed nuclear reactor deep underneath the city. It'll keep."

There were three more thick doors to blast. But there was no one to worry about the alarms we continually set off. So it all went fast.

The final explosion revealed a long tunnel with flickering lights, thick bars lining the rooms running along each side, with one final vault just beyond.

"Jackpot," whispered Teller. He licked his lips.

On my right I could see the glimmer of gold bars, stacked as high as my chest.

Each sub room was filled with precious metals. All here for the taking.

We moved quickly, using a motorized pallet dolly that just fit in the elevator. The first two sub rooms were cleaned out, and with each trip we deposited the gold bars into empty ammunition chests in the back of Eric's Pelican.

It filled up quickly, and there was a lightness in the air as we cracked jokes and imagined what we'd do with our share.

The Pelican almost literally groaned with gold, and we had to move a Shiva warhead out to start adding a layer of chests full of gold to the walkway.

"Any more and she won't fly," Eric warned.

"There's just one more room. We'll get a few more chests in here, then we're done," Felicia said.

Back under the bank we detonated the door to the last vault. The lights flickered from the pulse as we opened the door, coughing and hacking from the dust that had been kicked up. Shadows filled the room, shifting and moving as the lights struggled to come on.

Then the lights quit flickering and steadied, and we realized that the shadows were still moving. They were human-shaped shadows.

A hand reached out from behind the bars and grabbed at me. "Are you here to save us?" asked a tiny voice, and I looked down into the large, wide blue eyes of a little boy.

"Thank God you came," said an older man, a school-teacher who'd been chosen to stay with the children while the adults armed up and marched downriver to fight the Covenant.

That had been days ago.

The entire group was camped out in the last gold storage room, spreading out what supplies they had on towels on top of more wealth than any of them could have ever have previously imagined touching.

"We've seen what they've done to other worlds," Julian, the schoolteacher, said. "We got as deep under-ground as we could . . . hoping maybe we could avoid the worst of it. The others had already left the city for the nearest spaceport. There weren't many children left by the time the Covenant actually landed."

They were not nearly deep enough. But I didn't say anything.

"Just hold on a second, sir, we need to confer a mo-ment."

Felicia had frozen in the center of the hallway, but

moved when I approached. "What the hell do we do?" I hissed. "We can't just leave them here."

"I don't know," she whispered back. "But how many are there? What *can* we do?"

"We have a spare Pelican . . ."

She cut me off. "Let me think. In the meantime, get those last three chests of gold up to Eric."

"And how are we going to explain *that*?" I asked, a bit louder than I intended.

Felicia walked over to the open door that led to the room the children and their caretaker were in. There were thirty of them, I figured, from a quick head count. "Julian, that was your name, right? I'm Colonel Felicia Sanderson. I'm an orbital-drop shock trooper. We're here under orders to retrieve the gold bullion, as part of the necessity to fund the war effort against the Covenant. You'll have to understand, these orders are our first priority. In the meantime, if there is anything you need, food, water, we'll provide that to you as we try to think about how to safely get you out of here."

"Thank you, thank you so much," the teacher said.

Dale and Orrin had finished loading the dolly.

I pulled Felicia back farther away. "We need to call in extra Pelicans."

"Don't tell me what we need to do. We're going to load this last bit up, then we're going to see what we can get back to the ship before all hell breaks loose with the damn Covenant just downriver. We'll give these guys food and water, at least. But we're not dragging them outside until I've had time to think."

"Think about what?" Sita asked, joining us. "You're not seriously thinking about taking them out?"

I was horrified. "How can we not? These are children!"

"They're dead," Sita said. "They were dead the moment they chose to hole up down here. It is only a matter of when, and how. The fact that we stumbled across them doesn't change the fact that we can't evacuate everyone off an entire planet. It doesn't work like that."

Dale and Orrin were looking up from the dolly as they guided it toward us, paying attention to our body language.

"What the hell is the point of being a soldier if we can't save anybody," I snapped. The worlds I'd retreated from suddenly flashed through the back of my mind.

And then I thought about what Felicia had said. When was the last time I'd talked to a civilian? Julian was the first since the bombing that put Eric in a coma.

Maybe I'd spent too long being removed from civilization.

Maybe we all had.

But I still had a heart. I still knew what was right and what was wrong. "We can't abandon these children to the Covenant," I said. "I refuse."

"If you refuse, that's a problem," Sita growled. She had her BR55 raised slightly. Orrin and Dale, still observing, looked ready to jump forward and back her up.

Felicia stepped forward slightly, trying to regain control of a situation going bad, and quickly. "Shut up, all of you. We can save some of them, and just take less gold."

"How much less gold? How many of them will fit?" I asked. "You willing to do that kind of bloody math?"

Sita finally raised the rifle up high enough to slide her finger into the trigger guard. "I'd relax a bit if I were you," she said. "We'll do what we have to do."

"What we have to do is get them out," I insisted. "We're going to have to leave the gold. The plan can't go forward."

Sita raised the rifle. "No one's leaving any gold."

"Lower your weapon," Felicia ordered. Orrin and Dale had drawn M6 pistols, and Sita was stepping back.

"I don't think Sita here wants any compromise," I said.

"Shut up, Gage."

I had my assault rifle up as well now. A real standoff. "I'm not backing down. I'm a human being, not an Insurrectionist, not some damn, cold-blooded alien. I'm not going to leave these children to die."

"What did they ever do for you?" Sita asked. "When the UNSC was bombing civilians in the Outer Colonies, did they care about children then?"

"The Outer Colonies don't exist anymore, Sita," I said levelly. "It's not about that anymore."

"The Colonies don't exist anymore because the UNSC wouldn't protect them," Orrin hissed.

"Really? All those Navy ships lost to enemy fire, all those friends I saw die out there, that was for nothing?" I moved my aim from Sita to Orrin to Dale. I couldn't bring myself to step to the side and include Felicia.

If she was going to shoot me, it was all over anyway.

The arguments the old Colonials made were ones

that could sway us in an academic discussion over beers. But right here, right now, there were people that needed our help. And I was not going to turn my back on them.

No matter what I believed, or what I'd seen, I knew where I stood on this.

"There's not enough gold in all the worlds to make this worth it. You'll wake up at night thinking about these kids you condemned to death for your own greed," I said. "It won't be worth it."

"It's worth a try," Orrin snarled, and raised his M6 higher. I saw what was in his eyes.

It sounded like all the shots happened simultaneously. My body armor crumpled as it absorbed the shock, but I'd gotten Sita first, as she'd had the real firepower.

But M6 rounds from Orrin and Dale slapped me to the ground. I was bleeding from the arm, the leg, and a near miss by my ear.

"Felicia?" I called out, aching all over. I'd seen Orrin slump over the gold bars, the red blood seeping in down between the cracks.

Dale lay still on the floor by the pallet.

"Felicia?"

I crawled over to her. She'd drawn as well, on Orrin and Dale. We'd been of the same mind, in the end. It would have been easy for her to gun me down.

She lay on her back, holding her throat, frothy blood pouring out of her mouth with each cough and attempted breath.

"Felicia . . ."

She grabbed my arm tight, squeezing hard, her eyes

looking past me as she groaned through bubbles of blood, then stopped.

"Felicia."

"Sir?" The schoolteacher looked around the edge of the vault door, his eyes wide.

"Stay here. For now, just stay here," I told him. "I have to arrange how to get you out of here safely."

I limped toward the elevator, tears in my eyes.

In the back of the Pelican, my body armor stained with Felicia's blood, I unsteadily held my sidearm at the side of Eric's face.

"You remember when the bomb went off in the club?" I asked him.

He turned to look directly at the gun and me. "Every day since I woke up."

"I remember being trapped in the dark, chest too constricted to scream, panting for what air I could get. And I remember it was an ODST who pulled me out. That moment, I don't think I could ever forget that."

"That why you joined?"

"Yeah." I nodded. "Now I'm on the other side, only I'm there to steal the wallet off the guy in the rubble and leave them to die."

"We couldn't have known there would be children," Eric said.

"We have to do something."

Eric sighed. "Gage, there's nothing we can do. Look, we can try and fit a few of them where we can, but let's not throw away our futures, what Felicia worked for."

The speaker in the cockpit crackled. The attack was

withdrawing. Not just a single artifact, but several artifacts had been stolen from the Covenant dig site. ODSTs were in full retreat with hundreds of Grunts in full pursuit.

"They're able to track the artifacts somehow!" a hysterical private reported. "We split up into several groups, and all the Covenant are coming after just us!"

No battle plan survived contact with the enemy.

Eric shook his head. "There's not much we can do now. We just poked the Covenant nest and it sounds like they're swarming."

Our fellow ODSTs were calling for the Pelicans to get them the hell out of the hot zone.

I waved the sidearm at Eric. "Get out."

"What?"

"Get out. I don't want to shoot you. But I know how to help them. So get the hell out."

"Do you know who you're dealing with? You know me. But Teller, Amey, Charleston? They're old school CMA. Watts loyalists. And they've done it all. We're not crossing them. I'm not getting the hell off my own ship," Eric gritted. I smacked him in the head with the pistol butt three times to knock him out, then dragged him to the back of the Pelican and rolled him off into the street.

Charleston and Amey were manning the mounted machine guns, but hadn't looked over and down into the street.

It had been another lifetime ago that I watched Allison Stark fly a Hornet through the night, but I remembered the controls she'd shown me and seen it done a hundred times since.

Standardized.

I'd stood in the back of the Pelican cockpits enough, too.

That didn't mean what I was going to try next would work.

I switched to an encrypted channel that the other pilots weren't monitoring and patched into the cruiser in orbit. "*Chares,* we have what we came for, but we need more transport. This is urgent. We need Pelican backup, right away. Three Pelicans took incoming fire and are down, repeat down. Scramble immediately."

I tried to remember what was what. Stick, collective throttle . . . all the buttons and switches in front of me.

But a Pelican was enough like a second home that I got it started.

Amey and Charleston would no doubt be wondering what was happening as the Pelican's engines gunned to life. The craft lurched, clawing for air, pregnant with gold in the green-gray ammunition chests.

I scraped along a building, knocking down balconies and brickwork as I struggled to get the Pelican higher.

I was tense, waiting for the mounted machine guns to open up on me, but they never did. I got on the radio to try and find out where the group with the artifacts was. I'd been moving on instinct, trying to figure out how I could buy time for the children.

A small idea had occurred to me.

———

I clumsily landed the Pelican heavily and awkwardly in the middle of the chaos that was the ODST retreat back up the river toward the city.

The first ODST who clambered in looked around. "There's no space!" he shouted.

I leaned back. "Where are the artifacts? Get them loaded in here, now! We need to get them clear and back up to orbit."

He left and shouted, and soon a set of boxes were being taken off the back of a Mongoose quad bike and loaded in.

"What about the Shiva?" he asked.

"The nuke?"

"We didn't need to set it off, but we're not sure where we should leave it if they're coming after us."

I nodded. "Stick it in here, I'll save you from hefting it about."

"Yes, sir. Be careful up there, there'll be Covenant aircraft support on the way now that they were attacked." The ODST trooped up toward the cockpit. "You sure we can't just shove this ammo out and get some of our guys back out?"

He leaned forward, and then looked at the blood on my armor. "Sir, you're shot?"

Then he frowned. "I need to check . . ." But he stopped when I pushed the M6 against his neck.

"There are thirty or so kids in the bottom of the bank in the middle of the city," I rasped. "If I take whatever's in those boxes the Covenant's so hot for and are tracking, I can make a run for it, away from the city. The Covenant forces will chase me, and maybe

I can buy you guys some time to help the children. You understand what I'm saying?"

The ODST nodded, and as he backed slowly out, I pointed at the ammo crates. "Open it."

He did so, and his jaw dropped. "Now shove that out the back onto the ground. Take a bar each, and next time you're on leave, have a drink for Gage Yevgenny."

The moment he hopped off I struggled back into the air.

I couldn't see any Covenant forces, but I didn't understand half of what the readouts were I was looking at. I banked left, skirting the river only for a few moments, before I headed for the mountains.

My goal was to get over them, but the Pelican could barely climb. A Banshee suddenly swooped in, firing just ahead of my nose. I focused on the mountains, ignoring it, hoping that the artifacts were too precious for the Covenant to risk blowing me up.

Rockets slammed into the Banshee from the direction of the city. Before the debris even began to fall, another rocket slammed into the rear of the Pelican. Charleston, Amey, or maybe even Eric: They'd claim they were trying to hit the Banshee.

The craft bucked and spiraled as I struggled to control it, but with all the gold and my own ineptitude, I could barely keep it in the air.

I flew as long as I could, but the Pelican was shaking herself apart.

I remember the world spinning, slamming into the ridge, bouncing. I remember seeing the mountain pitch toward me. I know I made it over the ridge, because I hit the top of it and bounced.

And then it was like the bomb in the club again. A tremendous blow, my senses reeling, and I woke up on the ground, my armor on fire.

Since then, I've been waiting.

The rook had sat next to the ODST, scanning the horizon for threats, listening to his tale. Any attempt to leave or call for help had been thwarted by the dying man.

But now he understood, at least, why he'd been sent down with a second wave of ODSTs by SOEIV, and why extra Pelicans were on their way.

It was all due to this man. Gage Yevgenny.

Who was most certainly going to die here.

The sound of an approaching Pelican began to rise in volume.

"There's a reason I've been keeping you here, talking," Gage said. "Not just to comfort my dying self. They're almost here. The Covenant, and Eric with his friends. I'm surprised you got here before them all. They're going to want to salvage whatever gold they can from the wreck. What I want you to do is head up the mountain now. All out. Drop your pack, everything but comms and your weapon.

"Get through the cut there in fifteen minutes, and you get on the other side of the mountain. Don't flag down that first Pelican that's coming. In fact, hide from it as best you can. I had you here because if you'd taken off up the mountain, the Covenant would have seen you from the other side. But the Grunts are on canned methane; instead of using it all up by panting their way over the mountain, they'll have worked their way around to get close to this wreck. So head up the pass and over the mountain, and run like you ran in boot camp, rook, run like your worst drill instructor is right behind you."

"Sir, I can't just leave you . . ."

"They're all going to arrive, rook, and I'm going to blow the Shiva up the moment *all* the bastards show up." Gage held up a control pad that would let him wirelessly detonate the nuclear device. "Years ago, I told my father it was 'just dirt.' But it's *not* dirt. It's where we live. It *our* dirt, dammit. And more importantly, it's about who's standing on that dirt. Those children. Your family. Your friends. And those freaks are going to pay for every piece of dirt they've taken from us."

"We can still get you out of here . . ."

"No. I'm a dead man, you know it. I'm not going to waste more Marines."

"And your friends coming this way?"

"They're going to die helping protect the dirt, rookie. They're going to die doing something good." He smiled. "If they'd stayed back in the city to form up with you guys instead of running out here for the gold, they wouldn't have a problem, would they? They chose this path. Promise me something, rook?"

"Anything."

"You'll fight the Covenant all the way. Even if they land on Earth. You'll fight them even if you have to throw rocks at them."

"I will, sir."

"Then go now!" He waved the arming device for the Shiva around. "Or I'll set this damn thing off with you still dallying around here."

The rookie got up, looked around, back at the man on the ground one last time, and then ran. He shed his gear as he did so. Everything but the BR55 in his hands.

He ran uphill, not looking back, his visor open and his breath loud in the helmet. He leaped over rocks, gaining height, until he finally spotted the cleft of rock that would let him cut over the ridge to the other side of the mountain, back toward the city that was base camp for this operation.

He paused, looking back down the direction he'd come, catching his breath in long gasping pants.

Boot camp was just weeks ago. He was relieved to find out he still had that kind of sprint in him.

He could see the developing battlefield far below, in the scrub of the foothills. Grunts in the hundreds poured toward the downed Pelican. They'd come around the far side of the mountain, as Gage had predicted. They were like locusts swarming across the grass, bumbling along due to the large methane tanks on their backs.

And thundering overhead, flaring out toward the scene: a Pelican. It touched down, and three figures stepped out.

They did not rush to help Gage, but instead started rooting through the ruins of the other Pelican.

The Marine did not wait to see what was coming next. He ran through the cleft, barely glancing up at overhangs, and then slid down the other side.

Loose rock tumbled, and he surfed down the shale and dirt.

A bone-thrumming thump shook the entire mountain, and a steady roar filled the air. By the time the rookie got to the bottom, a massive mushroom cloud could be seen over the tip of the mountaintop.

It was still rising when a Pelican flew around a nearby hill, coming down to kiss the dirt long enough for the rookie to leap in.

"What the hell happened over there?" the pilot asked.

The rookie shook his head. "Long story."

Long, indeed.

He was still a bit shaken by the entire thing.

The Pelican shook and bounced. "The civilians have all been evacuated," the copilot told the rookie, who stood behind them looking out the window. "We're taking them back to Earth with us."

"Earth?" He was surprised.

"The Covenant just attacked Reach," the pilot reported. "We're falling back to Mother Earth."

The rookie looked out at the land under the clouds as they climbed for orbit, stunned. Soon all the ground would be glass, once the Covenant ships started in on it.

All dirt, he thought.

Like Earth.

From there, they would throw everything they had at the Covenant if they were found. Even if he had to throw the last rock himself. He'd made a promise.

They *would* make the Covenant pay for every inch of dirt, the rookie thought to himself.

ACHERON-VII

It's barren
   the air chokes; on dust and smoke
   the ground cracks; surrendering to the heat
It's lonely
   with only the dead as company,
   but anymore, this has become his closest
     companion; death
There was once a purpose to all of this;
   a specific design
Soldiers sent forth in the name of retribution
   In their path; an alien covenant
     vast in number
     ardent in their belief
Now, but one stands
   Only one; survivor
His friends taken by conflict
Their adversaries delivered unto
Alone now, he treks the wastelands
     cut off; stranded
Knowing somewhere above;
     Out and beyond
His brothers, his sisters, continue to struggle
Continue to fight, to die;
     to strive
A million stars between here and home
     A million enemies; more
Yet here he stands, ever vigilant
And here he'll stay;
     A lone warrior, on a desolate plain

HEADHUNTERS

JONATHAN GOFF

ONE

BLOOD, BULLETS, AND ADRENALINE

"Hey!"

The word just hung there for an instant as Jonah gave his motion sensor a second glance.

"I got one," the excitement in his hushed voice unmistakable.

"You sure?" Roland had just about enough of false alarms.

"Pretty sure," Jonah shot back.

There was a split second when the world came to a complete stop—silent and unmoving.

"Nope—yeah, I'm sure," Jonah confirmed.

If he was right, and Roland desperately hoped he was, then it would be the first contact with enemy forces since their insertion into the field some six days prior. In that time the pair had covered twenty-three miles, at times moving at a snail's pace as they crept ever closer to their target.

"This is fun," Jonah concluded, the excitement in his voice escalating.

"It's about to be, anyway." Roland had never much enjoyed this part of the job—the sneaking around, the long days and hours spent maintaining absolute cover while maneuvering behind, through, and between enemy lines—but what came after, the blood, bullets, and adrenaline, *that* he enjoyed quite a bit, maybe as much as Jonah, though probably not. Jonah had the added benefit of loving every minute in the field. Not just the combat, but the whole ordeal, from insertion into each new alien hotspot to the postcarnage report back at home base—whether he was facedown in the mud and muck for twelve hours straight, silently sliding his custom combat knife across a Sangheili throat, or recounting the bloodshed wrought by the muffled rhythm of his M7S submachine gun, Jonah loved it all—every single second of life as one of the elite, as one of the UNSC's top-tier Covenant killers.

To humanity at large, Jonah, Roland, and their fellow Spartan-IIIs were *ghosts*, their missions and movements deemed highly classified—top secret. Their very existence was known only by a select few, and while their brothers and sisters in the Spartan-II program earned glory and unwavering respect as they fought and died against the Covenant, the IIIs fought, and most certainly died, with only the recognition and admiration of their fellow secret warriors as their reward—for the Spartan-IIIs, however, as with the IIs, this was more than enough. Though created under comparable, yet varied circumstances, the two forces shared one very similar mind-set: Duty first. Loyalty second. In the Spartan mind petty vices such as fame simply did not register. There was no need for the galaxy-wide adulation of the masses reveling in their many brutal victories over the Covenant. Nor did they want the sympathies and pity of anyone outside their close-knit circle when they were confronted by defeat—by death. This secrecy helped bond each Spartan-III unit like those of no other unit, and in truth it was something they appreciated—cherished, even. After all, with attention comes distraction, and in a war against a collection of advanced alien races hell-bent on slaughtering the whole of humanity, there was no room for wandering thoughts or clouded minds.

As tools of war, the Spartan-IIIs were most often deployed as living fire-and-forget weapons—just point, shoot, and wait for the fireworks. ONI, or on occasion a highly placed UNSC official, passed along a key Covenant target; the IIIs were then sent in, headfirst, to eliminate the given objective, or inflict as much damage as physically possible in the effort. Success meant a handful or more made it back to base, mission complete; failure, nobody came home, but—to a man—they fell doing their damnedest to inflict the maximum level of destruction upon their foe. This all-encompassing sense of service before self in the face of almost certain death hardened them. Connected them. But even among this collection of steadfast soldiers there were a

select few with a bond deeper than the others could
ever begin to imagine, as these unique IIIs were a secret
even to their peers.

And somewhere out among the star-poked black of the
galaxy, on a nameless moon, far beyond the outermost
UNSC colony, Roland and Jonah methodically inched
their way through tangled, alien undergrowth, slowly,
quietly moving closer to the source of the blip on Jonah's motion tracker.

TWO

A BRIEF HISTORY OF HEADHUNTING

There had been much concern about fielding a sufficient
number of Spartans for the missions that were considered essential—deployment against large-scale Covenant targets and defense of key UNSC facilities being
chief among them. In a war many were beginning to believe was unwinnable, losing even a handful to special-
ized operations was frowned upon. This unwillingness
to spread the Spartan ranks too thin across the field of
battle meant the number of two-man infiltration squads,
codenamed: Headhunters, culled from the ranks of the
Spartan-III program, was extremely limited. At the program's height there was a maximum contingent of six
squads—six teams, with a total of seventeen soldiers
rotating in to fill gaps when half or all of a team was
lost in the field. Jonah and Roland were paired as part

of an initial eight-man roster and had been together as a unit since.

It was the Headhunters' task to infiltrate heavily fortified enemy encampments, ships, and operation centers completely undetected, with minimal, mission-specific weaponry, and no radio contact or hope for backup or retrieval, and complete a set series of objectives in preparation for one of two eventualities: a larger, full-scale assault on the target, or as a decoy and distraction for UNSC operations elsewhere.

Over the course of the Human-Covenant War there had been some luck, limited but occasionally fruitful, in stealth insertions behind Covenant lines. The majority of these operations ended in lost contact with the field unit and the presumed death of the operatives involved. The Spartan-II program had changed this to a degree, as the IIs had been able to slip into enemy territory on a number of occasions—not always with the best results, but with results, nonetheless. Now, with the IIIs and the advancements in their training and the technologies and equipment available to them, further and more intrusive campaigns into Covenant-held regions were deemed a necessary risk—although such operations would be attempted on a limited basis, and in direct control of a special unit from deep within Beta-5, one of ONI's most secretive subdivisions, operating under the umbrella of the clandestine organization known as Section Three.

Spartan-III soldiers selected to participate in the Headhunter program had to meet one exclusive prerequisite before being considered by Beta-5: only those individuals who had survived two or more specially assigned training missions would be evaluated for possible inclusion in its additional, grueling training regimen. Once an overall list of potential candidates was compiled, each trooper's personal files and mission reports—from birth all the way up to, and including, their activities within the past twenty-four hours—were analyzed against a set series of parameters calculated by top ONI specialists.

Both Roland and Jonah not only fell under the "two missions" banner of acceptance, they were perfect matches for each of Beta-5's requirements, and more importantly, when offered the opportunity to participate—though presented with only the vaguest of program overviews—they each leapt at the chance to hit back at the Covenant in new and unexpected ways.

Once selected, candidates were separated from their fellow Spartans and shipped to a special training facility on the far side of Onyx, the ONI-controlled world that served as the IIIs' base of operations. After three months, the soldiers were broken into four two-person squads, chosen through a series of detailed evaluations and an intense interview process meant to devise the best possible pairings between members of the group. Roland and Jonah's pairing hit on 97.36 percent of the desired matchmaking criteria; only one other team scored higher.

Now, more than two years later, their training complete—including seven months of supervised field exercises, followed by six months' real-world wartime insertions—and the successful negotiation of twelve battlefield insertions under their belts, Roland and Jonah found themselves on the far side of the galaxy, two human soldiers on a moon crawling with Covenant. Their current task was straightforward enough—slip onto the Covenant-held moon, believed to be the site of one of the pious alien collective's sacred religious digs, and remove six of the ten identified base camps situated around the outer perimeter of a much larger central compound. A second team of Headhunters would remove the four outstanding camps in preparation for what was to follow. The confusion and re-shuffling of troops and supplies by the Covenant contingent following each base camp's dismantling was simply the opening salvo in a full-scale assault by a dozen Spartan-III fireteams and associated orbital backup.

THREE

APES OR ALLIGATORS?

The indicator on Roland's individual radar showed that whatever their contact—Grunt or Elite, Jackal or Brute—they were less than ten meters from it, and while he and Jonah were careful not to give away their position as they crept closer, they had yet to establish visual confirmation of their target. In the postdusk hour it was possible the Covenant sentry was using the shadows of the forest to conceal its perch as it stood guard over the base camp's perimeter. It was just as likely, however, that the bastard was hidden beneath the light-bending cloak of active camouflage. One option pointed toward a raptorlike Kig-Yar sniper posted somewhere up in the thick tangle of branches that made up the forest's canopy. The other, less appealing, option meant one of the Sangheili Elite, the Covenant's most devout and dangerous warriors, was patrolling this sector of the perimeter.

Each possibility brought with it its own set of complications. The two Spartans ran through the encounter scenarios as they worked to develop a proper plan of attack: Shooting a sniper from its roost could draw unwanted attention. They could miss the kill-shot, alerting the creature to their presence and giving it the opportunity to signal an alarm. Or, even with a clean kill, the force of the impact and the pull of gravity might send the body tumbling from its resting place, bouncing off and snapping any number of branches along the way, before slamming into the ground with a thud that was sure to carry in the still night air. Taking out a camouflaged Elite in close combat meant dealing with the combined might of the alien's armor, firepower, and brute strength. An Elite patrol usually carried one standard-issue Covenant plasma rifle, if not two, possibly a plasma pistol for backup, as well as plasma grenades, and if Roland and Jonah were particularly unlucky, an energy sword.

To top it all off, they'd have to find the damn thing before it found them.

Roland motioned for Jonah to freeze; they weren't proceeding until they could confirm the identity of the obstacle and ascertain the best approach to removing it from their path.

"Think it's av-cam," Jonah whispered.

Roland didn't respond.

The modified helmet-to-helmet vocal systems in their headgear meant they could speak to one another without fear of giving away their position, though in most cases, once they entered the combat zone, their instincts would take control and they would begin functioning solely on physical cues and intuition.

The UNSC had spent years sanctioning research and development into, and thrown an unspecified amount of resources at, the problem of active camouflage, or av-cam, replication. The ability to essentially disappear into your surroundings was a major advantage for the Covenant—in addition to their already terrifyingly superior weaponry and shielding and their uncanny mastery of slipspace navigation.

Officially, all UNSC efforts to prototype a working av-cam unit had been met with failure. Unofficially, as was the norm within Beta-5, they had been testing a modified version of active camouflage since the inception of the Spartan-III program, along with advanced vision modes that would allow for easier detection of stealthed enemy combatants.

While the field operable av-cam-enhanced armor variants were yet to be placed in UNSC-normal rotation, and were in fact quite limited even within the ranks of the Spartan-IIIs, the research into visor-based vision enhancements as part of an overall equipment

upgrade known as Visual Intelligence Systems, Recon-
naissance, or VISR, was well underway, with the hope
it could be made available UNSC-wide in the near future.

As with most research and development efforts with
battlefield implications, VISR was already being field-
tested by most Headhunter teams.

As it stood, Roland's power armor was equipped
with one of ONI's experimental active camouflage units,
along with a dedicated power supply. When it was activated he would achieve a state close to invisibility for a
period of three and a half to four minutes.

Once used, however, the cell powering the unit would
need anywhere from ten to fifteen minutes to recharge,
and put an additional strain on his suit's other power
functions. Shielding. Bios. Targeting. Tracking. All of it
would run at less than optimum efficiency while the av-
cam system rebooted. Less than four minutes of maxi-
mized stealth in exchange for limited resources for a
short—but long enough—duration, directly following.
As such, Roland had to be judicious with its use.

"I think it's av-cam," Jonah continued, undeterred
by Roland's lack of response. "Could be a sniper." He
paused. "But I got twenty credits on it being camo." He
slid up alongside Roland. "Wanna take that bet, Rolle?
Twenty cred? I'll take camo. You can have the field."

Jonah had seemed eager enough when he first signaled the contact, but the fact that he was getting chatty
told Roland that his partner was becoming antsy—his
need for violent release growing exponentially by the
minute.

"Well, wha'd'ya got?"

"Don't know," Roland responded, after spending a couple seconds examining the blip on his tracker—it hadn't moved since their first contact. "Stayin' pretty still for a Slip-Lip," Roland concluded, using a common dismissive referring to the four-pronged anatomy of the Sangheili mouth.

Jonah slowly moved his right hand up along the side of his helmet, flicking the small nub that activated his VISR mode enhanced vision. Roland followed suit. They each swept the forest floor with their gaze—the nighttime scene glowing with various hues as the VISR flickered into focus.

"I got nothin'." Roland started.

The area where their target was positioned was clear of enemy presence. Steadily shifting their lines of sight to peer higher into the treetop, the two Spartans began scanning the forest canopy for their contact.

"Shit." Jonah sighed before lowering his head, shaking it in disgust. "At the top. Right at one o'clock. All the way up."

"Sniper," Roland said plainly, without looking.

"Yep," Jonah replied in mock defeat.

Roland smiled beneath his helmet and lifted his head.

Settled atop a small platform near the very top of the tallest cluster of trees in the area—just below where the forest met the sky—a lone Kig-Yar crouched, periodically tracking across the whole of the forest laid out before him with his trusty Covenant beam rifle, a sleek, long-range weapon that was extremely deadly in capable hands.

"How did that idiot not see us," Jonah laughed.

"We're that good," Roland affirmed, gauging the distance between their position—belly-down on the forest floor—and the sniper's roost high above, using his visor's onboard electronics.

Roland waited a few breaths before adding, "More importantly . . . you owe me lunch."

"Heh—a bet's a bet," Jonah conceded. "I'm more concerned with how we're gonna get that jackass down from his nest without alerting the whole damn Covenant army."

"We have a few options," Roland began, his mind already catching on one idea in particular before Jonah cut back in.

"Why don't you go ghost—climb up there and give him a little tap—so we can get movin'," Jonah nudged. He was definitely itching for a fight, and Roland couldn't blame him. For all the waiting and slow going, it was these few moments before actual contact that were the most nerve-racking. All the work—the effort and energy—it took to cross vast stretches of unknown terrain unseen by the naked eye, and undetected by any number of tracking systems, was in anticipation of the handful of minutes spent face-to-face with your adversaries.

"This is exactly why I get to test out the cool new toys and you don't," Roland jabbed.

"How so?" Jonah shot back.

"This cam unit is a precious commodity," Roland began to explain before Jonah pressed the issue.

"And?"

"And . . ." Roland continued diplomatically, "you'd activate it for no better reason than to give a Grunt a wedgie."

"Fair point."

"I, on the other hand, can control such base urges; saving our more limited, and valuable, assets for their appropriate use," Roland explained with a mocking air of superiority in his voice.

"Geez, does that mean yer not gonna let me borrow the car this weekend, Dad?"

"You joke, but you know it's true."

"All right, all right . . ." Jonah was ready to get back on task. "You got a plan for this guy, then?"

Roland made sure Jonah could hear the joy in his response. "I was thinkin' . . . *lumberjack*."

Thirty minutes later.

Roland and Jonah had no problems setting the shaped charges at the base of the Jackal sniper's look-out and were back on course, slowly making their way to their main objective.

Knowing there would more than likely be multiple rotations between the snipers manning this particular perch before their attack on their first target would begin, the pair had taken extra care in concealing the explosives so as to avoid any unwanted attention. The real danger in leaving the sniper unattended hinged on the possibility that it would have a clear vantage point from which to draw a bead on them once they began

their offensive, and while there were most assuredly
other snipers in the area, their only immediate concern
was in the reality of a known threat.

The novelty in utilizing a lumberjack to eliminate
said threat, was that the maneuver served the dual purposes of removing the sniper from the field of play
while also providing a brief distraction upon the initia-
tion of their assault on the camp. Besides, Roland always got a kick out this little stunt—placing explosives
at the base of an enemy perch, then blowing the charge
from a distance, listening to the echo of tearing roots
or the whine of twisted metal as the whole thing came
crashing down.

They were less than three hundred meters from the
edge of the base camp now. According to their intel,
they would have visual confirmation of the site just over
the crest of the next ridge.

Their normal deliberate pace had slowed once the
pair had crossed the Covenant's outer defensive perimeter, and their forward progress was hampered
even further since bypassing the sniper, as they had
moved to the cover of a jagged embankment to ensure
they were completely out of the alien sharpshooter's
line of sight, leery of the prying eyes behind and above
them.

When the duo reached the peak of the final ridge
before the forest descended into a sweeping, pictur-
esque valley, it had been just over four hours since they
had set their trap at the foot of the sniper's tree. Though
briefed and rebriefed by Beta-5's intelligence officers in
regard to the specifics of their mission, Roland and

Jonah had yet to see any of the target camps with their own eyes.

Over the course of the countless drills, both back in training and their twelve live-combat field insertions, they had learned not to rely too heavily on intelligence reports. Although a needed tool, such reports were limited in their use during real-time battlefield situations; there were just too many variables to account for in between the time a final mission brief is run and the actual moment of combat. Did the enemy alter its protocols for any reason?

Have their defensive measures been upgraded, downgraded, or modified in any other fashion? Have the patrols changed within the last day?

The last ten minutes? Were there clouds in the sky?

Had it rained? Some of this could be predicted to a relative degree of certainty, but predictions weren't always reality, and for Headhunters the only intel worth relying on was gathered firsthand.

After settling in to check their equipment, Jonah inched ahead of Roland, pulling himself to the edge of the craggy rise they'd chosen for their observation post. The vantage this jagged rock outcropping provided was ideal for keeping tabs on the goings-on below, and the haphazard formation itself gave perfect cover for anything but the most thorough of inspections.

Careful to maintain his focus, Jonah moved at a deliberate pace as he lifted his head to gaze down on the Covenant campsite below. The wide valley that swept out beneath them and into the distance was marked by a small clearing nestled into the foot of the nearest mountainside. Target one was less than seventy meters in diameter, housing six sleek, gleaming purple structures and a series of energy barriers set up over well-lit excavation sites. In the distance Jonah could make out the lights from the other base camps peppered across the darkened basin, surrounding a massive complex of swooping buildings and ornate towers that loomed over the forest like a mechanical mecca to some forgotten god.

Taking it all in, the first thought that popped into Jonah's mind was simple, comforting, and more than a little malicious: *I can't wait to burn it all down.*

As impressive as the whole scene was, it also gave rise to another, less comforting thought. "Ya know?" Jonah said. "This place's gotta be pretty damned important to the Covenant for ONI to be wastin' so much firepower on a glorified dig-site so far back from the front."

Jonah understood the value ONI placed on the strange alien artifacts the Covenant cherished so deeply, but found it hard to believe his and Roland's services were best utilized against such a remote outpost, especially with the UNSC suffering such heavy losses on the frontlines of the war.

"ONI says it's hot, it's hot. Ours is not to question why," Roland explained, as he removed a cleaning kit from his pack.

"Not really sayin' otherwise, more just thinkin' out loud." Jonah continued his visual sweep of the valley. "I mean, *two* infiltration teams? We haven't had two squads 'a Headhunters in-field for the same drop . . . ever."

"The Covies seem pretty enamored with these alien leftovers they're always scroungin' for," Roland offered. "So, who knows what kind of weapons system or whatever they're hopin' to uncover here. And what does it matter, right? They could be diggin' for earthworms, in which case . . . it's our pleasure to make sure they don't find any."

The Spartans sat in silence as Jonah scanned the Covenant operation below and Roland went about checking his gear.

"Wha' do we got down there, anyway?" Roland swabbed the chamber of his M6C suppressed sidearm with a cleaning solution. These long excursions were hell on weaponry, and if a soldier neglected to keep up with the proper maintenance procedures, there was a good chance he would be stuck in a firefight with an inoperable firearm, or worse yet, the damn thing could jam and explode in his hand, doing the other side's job for them.

"The spooks weren't messin' 'round with this one, Rolle. The Covies got quite a little picnic setup out here."

"How's alpha-target lookin'?" Roland inquired, nodding at the base camp nearest their location.

"Pretty much as expected. Don't think we'll need much more than a day or two to scout their movements versus what we've been briefed."

"What about infantry?"

"Moderate." Jonah scanned the Covenant enclave. "In the high twenties, maybe lower thirties. Definitely not gonna be a cakewalk, but we've had worse—"

"Apes or alligators?"

"Huh?"

"We got apes or alligators running the show?" Roland clarified.

Jonah slunk back down into the crevice they would be occupying for the remainder of the night and the next day. " 'Gators. Saw quite a few, but no sign of Brutes. Usually when one's around the other's not—don't think they like each other much."

"Fine by me."

Jonah easily detected the relief in Roland's voice. "The Elites may be a bitch to deal with," Roland continued, "but at least they're smart, right? Smart we can predict—we can plan for." Jonah nodded his agreement. "The damn Brutes, though," Roland said, "they're just a buncha overly aggressive troglodytes. Start shootin' at 'em and they slip a gasket, go all aggro."

"They do operate on a shorter fuse. I think it makes 'em fun—like pickin' on an emotionally stunted twelve-year-old."

"You were a bully as a kid, weren't you?"

"Me? No. I was the twelve-year-old," Jonah corrected.

"Ha. You'd think that'd teach you to have some sympathy for—"

"Sympathy? Shit. If getting my ass bruised every other week taught me anything it was the simple truth that it's better to be the bully than the bullied."

"You are one enlightened individual, my friend."

"Hey, I tend to think I turned out okay."

"Jay? Yer essentially a government-sanctioned sociopath. That's not normal, and some would say far from okay."

"Like yer a fuckin' saint."

"Never said I was," Roland replied, before adding, "but you seem to take a bit more . . . let's just call it 'pride' in our work."

"Just 'cause I'm good at what I do—" Jonah retorted, a confident swagger in his voice.

"There's no denyin' that."

"Right, so? What's the issue?"

"I think the issue was: Elites are smart, Brutes are dumb."

"On which we both agree."

"And my point—the point I was trying to make—was the Elites' strategic intelligence makes 'em more of an ideal opponent in direct combat, because we can make educated guesses as to how they'll react. Whereas Brutes—"

"Ya give 'em the stink-eye," Jonah interrupted, "and they get pissy—makes 'em lose their head; intellect goes completely out the goddamn window."

"Right."

"*Right.*"

"And that difference in composure—in the way they handle their shit—makes the Brutes tougher to deal with in spur-of-the-moment situations, 'cause who knows what the hell they'll do."

"No—I *get* you," Jonah corrected. "And this is, what? The nine hundredth time we've had this conversation—"

"That's a bit of a stretch."

"Well, it's not the second—" Jonah chuckled, cutting Roland off. "You been tryin' ta sell me on yer theory of smart-equals-easy, dumb-equals-tough since training. I just ain't buyin' it . . . er . . . I guess, really, it's that I just don't care much one way or the other."

Jonah paused to give Roland a chance to respond. When he didn't, Jonah continued, "I mean . . . I really *do* get it. And there's some weird kinda backwards logic to yer thinking, but at the end of the day, Rolle—"

"You just never pay much attention to the tactical side of—" Roland interrupted.

"Tactical what?" Jonah shot back. The pair's conversations often became friendly competitions, as they'd verbally spar over even the smallest differences in opinion—each trying to assert why their view was the more valid of the two while the other's was simply dead wrong. "I *do* tactical. But, come on, it's—" Jonah stopped mid-sentence before shifting gears. "Never mind . . . Forget it . . . You already know what I'm gonna say, right? So there's no reason ta continue . . . You already know what I'm gonna say before I even say it."

"Yeah, so . . ."

"So . . . tell me what I'm thinkin'. Finish my thought," Jonah urged, wanting nothing more than to hear the words from Roland's mouth.

"No." Roland didn't want to give his partner the satisfaction.

"Just say it," Jonah poked. "Let's hear it."

"You think they're the same," Roland relented, knowing the conversation would continue to spiral if they didn't move on quickly.

"Right. Brutes. Elite. They may pose different problems, but when it comes right down to it, they're the same damn thing—targets. Big ones. Small ones. Smart ones. Dumb ones. Who cares—just point us at 'em, give us some weapons that go bang, some knives that cut like butter, and a brain-load of semiaccurate intel, and we'll cut 'em loose, scrape 'em off our boots, and march on to the next batch."

"You always find a way to make mass murder sound so simple—almost poetic." Though it was a hard and fast fact of their lives, Roland had always been amazed—not perturbed, not put off, just amazed, maybe even a little amused—by Jonah's flippant attitude toward death.

"As if you have any objections," Jonah huffed.

"Don't get defensive—wasn't a complaint, just an observation." Roland finished cleaning his pistol and passed the cleaning kit to Jonah before offering, "I'll take first watch," and lifting himself up to view the valley below.

"So, I'm a sociopath, huh?" Jonah spit, a hint of feigned sadness in his voice.

Roland stopped just before the lip of the ridge and turned back toward Jonah. "Doesn't mean yer not a helluva guy, Jay. Just means I wouldn't trust you 'round my kids."

"You don't have kids."

"Then I guess we don't have to worry about it."

Jonah laughed as Roland repositioned himself for a clear view of the valley.

The two Spartans spent the rest of the night alternating between keeping watch and taking hour-long power naps to ensure they would be functioning at optimum combat efficiency during their steadily approaching engagement against the Covenant.

The next two days were spent observing the Covenant base camp in preparation for their assault. Troop movements and specific interactions between the various alien species were noted and checked against known patterns. The number of individual soldiers, including their rank, was marked and prioritized by threat level. Locations in and around the camp were assigned specific designations based upon their placement and estimated purpose.

Finally, as the sun dropped below the horizon on the third night, Roland and Jonah made their way to the camp's perimeter.

FOUR

" 'GREAT JOURNEY,' HUH? WHAT'S SO GREAT ABOUT IT?"

"—that wasn't so bad," Jonah finished his thought after taking a few seconds to ensure he had everyone's attention.

The few remaining Elites and the smattering of Grunts all turned and lifted their gaze to take in the sight of the lone human standing before them.

The two Spartans had entered the camp not ten minutes prior, silently overtaking a trio of sleeping Unggoy before slipping into a small two-room storage facility.

They quickly recapped their plan of attack: Roland

would trigger his av-cam unit and slip about the base, planting charges on four reactor cores spread across the compound. Meanwhile, Jonah would enter the barracks, utilizing flash bangs and a fancy, new ONI energy disruptor to disorient the Covenant inside before entering and eliminating all enemy targets within. As soon as Jonah engaged the barracks contingent all hell would break loose.

If the Spartans had done their job right, the sudden, furious nature of the attack would catch the Covenant off guard long enough that any real attempt at resistance would be squelched before the aliens knew what hit them. And, while Roland and Jonah expected a fight, any troops occupying a position this removed from the frontlines were more than likely not the cream of the crop when it came to the Covenant's fighting force.

Headhunters, on the other hand, were as near perfection as humanity could muster in terms of weapons of death and war.

Confident in their abilities and dedicated to their purpose, Jonah slunk out from the rear of the storage unit, heading to the barracks to play his part in the massacre to come.

Roland followed closely behind him before veering off toward the nearest reactor. Using the shadows at the edge of the forest that ringed the camp, they both moved quickly into place.

Jonah cocked his M7S, armed the ONI special-issue energy disruptor, and primed two flares, then waited silently for Roland's signal.

On the other side of the camp, Roland checked his weapon and primed the first set of charges.

A pair of Sangheili strolled past, close enough that had they simply glanced to their left they would have been staring directly at the human intruder, but the creatures passed uneventfully, totally oblivious to the enemy in their midst.

Once the two Elites were at a safe distance, Roland pulled out a small transceiver, flicked the device's safety cap open, and pressed his thumb to the larger of two buttons on its plain surface.

An explosion erupted in the distance, echoing across the canyon, and somewhere off in the night a large tree fell to the earth, a lone Jackal sniper tumbling down with it.

The triggering of the lumberjack was the "go" signal. As the explosion reverberated through the valley the Covenant camp sprang to life.

Roland activated his camouflage and stepped from his cover, darting toward the first reactor. The instant the crack of the detonation filled the air, Jonah swung around the front of the barracks building, tossing his energy disruptor through the barrier that served as its door.

Like Roland's av-cam, and most other advanced battlefield equipment, the energy disruptor Jonah used to deactivate the barracks' entry barrier and all electronic devices within was reverse engineered by ONI scientists from scavenged Covenant technology.

Part of Jonah was irked by the need to rely on their enemy's tech, but a larger part thrilled at the irony of turning the Covenant's advances against them. He followed the disruptor with a pair of flares, then stepped through the entryway prepared for chaos.

Hell and fury seemed to erupt from the area surrounding the barracks. As Roland continued about his piece of their little insurrection, he allowed himself to briefly imagine Jonah prancing upon a field of Covenant corpses, happily bounding about in his own private nirvana, but just as quickly Roland was back in the moment, and his internal clock was telling him they didn't have much time.

Aside from the reality of his av-cam's limited lifespan, Roland also knew the second he triggered the explosion at the sniper's perch, he and Jonah would have a very limited time frame before reinforcements from one or more of the other camps arrived. Making an effort to focus solely on placing the charges on the chosen reactors, Roland had to pause briefly between the first and second in order to drop a collection of Grunts and Jackals who were in the process of setting up a defensive perimeter around a shade turret. Moving as quickly as he could, Roland finished planting his charge on the third of the four reactors and turned toward his final target, when he saw a squad of five Elites and four Grunts heading up the low brim that led to the barracks.

Certain that Jonah was able to handle himself, but not wanting his partner caught unaware by the Covenant making a beeline directly for him, Roland altered his course to engage this new threat, tossing a frag grenade into their midst to soften them up.

The small, round explosive bounced and ignited directly between two of the Elites; their shields flared and died. The other Elites lost their shields, but only temporarily, and of the four Grunts, three were killed in the blast, the other falling in a heap, mortally wounded.

Roland steadied his submachine gun and was prepared to fire when another explosion boomed off in the distance, across the valley.

The second, unexpected explosion must have been the work of the other infiltration team, Roland thought. Though the two Headhunter teams were acting independently, Roland and Jonah had been designated Team One and were serving as the mission's primary assault squad, meaning the secondary team would wait for their attack before initiating one of their own.

The explosion Roland triggered at the sniper perch gave Team Two the go-ahead, though Roland was surprised they'd been in a position to follow so quickly on the heels of his and Jonah's assault. Not that it bothered him. With two simultaneous stealth attacks against what the Covenant thought was an unknown outpost, the aliens would be in complete disarray. The timing of the second attack allowed each team a slightly increased window of opportunity, but there was still no room for delays.

Roland threw his second grenade. The two shieldless Elites went down, not dead, but out of the fight— one missing its legs at the knees and the other with a gaping wound in its stomach, intestines and fluid pouring forth onto the matted grass.

The remaining Elites once again lost their shields,

this time for good. They wheeled around, trying to spot their attacker. Roland's camo flickered, momentarily giving away his position, as he emptied his clip into the disoriented Elites.

Across the compound, Jonah had stepped into the barracks to find a dozen bewildered Covenant—six Grunts, two Jackals and four Elites, all with some level of confusion plastered on their faces.

The initial explosion had caught them off guard and the disruptor had removed their shields and deactivated their weapons. Now, still reeling from the effects of the flash bangs, the lot of them were essentially helpless. Not being one to waste the upper hand, Jonah pressed the issue, driven by a terrible motivation that sat at the heart of his hatred for the Covenant—the thought of his biological brothers and sisters, his mother and father, killed—murdered—vaporized into dust and ash during the Covenant's sacking of Eirene.

As the first few silent rounds flashed from the muzzle of his M7S, impacting on the nearest Elite's chest and throat, the momentary sadness brought on by the memory of his family's smiling faces dissipated, replaced by joy.

The stark contrast between Jonah's words—*that wasn't so bad*—and the sight of him made his proclamation all the more surreal.

He stood calmly, coolly, on the lip of the slope that led to the Covenant barracks building. Even clad in full armor, the cockiness and pure confidence of his pose betrayed the shit-eating grin Roland was certain was plastered on his friend's face. And then there was the blood.

How anything could be labeled as "not so bad" and yet involve that much carnage—Roland just laughed.

The remaining Covenant stood transfixed, bewildered by what they saw: Standing on a low ridge in the middle of their encampment was a sole combatant, a lowly human dog, coated in the blood and viscera of their brethren. Such a thing was unthinkable.

Once he was certain he had their complete and undivided attention, Jonah knelt, slowly—deliberately—never taking his eyes off his enraged foes.

In his right hand, Jonah held his combat knife, gripped blade back, eager for a fight. Thick chunks of flesh and clots of purple and green blood stuck to the blade's edge—hanging in strings, like saliva from the maw of a ravenous beast. With his left hand, Jonah reached for the ground, pausing only briefly as he gripped something just out of sight.

Roland watched from the nearby shadows as he set the remainder of the charges along the rim of the final reactor. His suit's active-camo function was quickly depleting its dedicated power supply, and he could see that the Covenant, though momentarily confused by Jonah's presence, were beginning to tense up.

He sensed the energy in the atmosphere begin to charge; these last few survivors would not allow their lives to end as helpless victims to the assassins in their midst. A defiant glower on their faces, Roland saw three of the Elites draw their muscles taut—they were getting ready to make a move; ready to pounce. Their first steps on their so-called Great Journey may be mere seconds away, but the warriors' code by which they lived meant these Elites would not die without a fight. Their sense of honor would not allow it, just as it would not allow them to be taunted by the murder of their kin, which is exactly what Jonah was doing—taunting them.

It's what he always did—*Every damn mission*, Roland thought. *He just can't help but play with his food.*

The eerie quiet that had settled upon the camp following the initial burst of violence gave Roland the sense that they were directly in the eye of the storm—that whatever hellish fury had played out only moments before, what was to come next would be worse, and it would be sudden.

He placed the last of the charges and locked the detonator's receiver in the "on" position, then knelt and lifted a half-loaded Covenant carbine rifle from a dead Jackal's grasp. He sighted the Elite nearest Jonah, the weapon's aiming reticule drawn directly at the beast's head—the instant he so much as twitched, a hail of radiation would liquefy his brain cavity.

Out in the open, the Covenant soldiers still frozen in disbelief, Jonah rose from his crouched position, a severed Elite head gripped tightly in his left hand. Jonah lifted the trophy high in the air, and then spoke for the first time since the encounter began: "Rolle, light 'em up."

The lead Elite's head rocked with three successive bursts from Roland's scavenged carbine before its massive body slumped to the ground, lifeless.

The handful of Covenant survivors leveled their weapons at Jonah, who hefted the severed head and threw it full force at a Grunt about to unleash a fully charged blast from its quivering plasma pistol. The macabre projectile hit the Grunt in the chest, shaking it off balance and sending its plasma blast spiraling into the night sky.

The tiny, angry alien attempted to right itself, but not in time—Jonah had already removed his pistol and as the Grunt regained its bearing a single slug impacted its temple. Jonah then made short work of the scattered Grunts and Jackals displaced about the courtyard, while avoiding fire from the few Elites still in the fight.

He and Roland had the advantage of placing their enemies in a crossfire between Jonah's slightly higher vantage and the tree line Roland used for cover, making it difficult for the Covenant to focus on just one attacker.

Roland finished off two more Elites but then his carbine trigger clicked empty.

A third Elite charged Jonah, whose attention was focused on wrapping up the only other surviving Covenant, a Kig-Yar cowering behind a personal energy gauntlet. As Jonah worked his way around the shield and planted two bullets in the Jackal's side, Roland called a warning, "Jay, seven-o'clock," and peppered the back of the Elite with his submachine gun, whittling away at its shield.

Jonah spun.

The Elite barreled toward him, only a few meters away, anger and hatred burning in its eyes. As if he were simply swatting a fly, Jonah tapped the trigger of his magnum twice, putting a bullet into each of the Elite's kneecaps.

The beast fell.

Roland sprinted over as Jonah slid a new clip into his pistol.

The Elite struggled to lift itself—beaten, yet defiant. Unable to stand, it rested on its bloodied knees.

"Nice shot." Roland bent down to grab a plasma pistol from the ground, sweeping the area for survivors as he rose.

"You softened him up." Jonah walked toward the injured Elite, also checking the periphery for any signs of trouble.

"Still got some fight in you, big guy?" Jonah stopped just out of the Sangheili's reach. "Ya know? Up close, you Slip-Lips aren't so special. You know that, right?"

The Elite stared up as the two Spartans looked down on it.

"I mean, really," Jonah prodded. "I've always meant to ask . . . what makes you Covenant thugs think yer so damned special anyway? What gives you the right to do the things you do?"

The Elite passed his gaze from Jonah to Roland and back. "There is honor in *our* path," he began, "you . . . *your* kind . . . humanity? You are nothing but a disease that must be wiped clean from this galaxy—a taint upon—"

"Yeah, well—this disease ain't goin' nowhere. In fact, seems ta me, it's right up in yer goddamn face and there ain't much'a damn thing you can do about it."

"If we were to meet in battle as warriors—*true* warriors," the Elite hissed, "you would fall, just as so many of your kind have fallen—to our swords and fire; under the weight of our boots. But you—*you* are not warriors. You are *assassins*. Weak and timid, you hide in the shadows—"

"Says the alien shit-heel who invented active-camo," Jonah said. "*Yeah*, yer noble. How noble's glassin' a planet from orbit?" Jonah tapped the kneeling beast across his temple with an open hand. "Answer that."

"Your influence must be expunged—eradicated—from the worlds you have fouled with your very presence—"

"I really don't like this guy," Roland interrupted. "Cut 'im loose, Jay. I think it's past time we beat feet."

"I fear not the path to the Great Journey beyond. I embrace it." Though he was bloodied and gravely wounded, the Elite's eyes welled with pride as he spoke.

"'Great Journey,' huh?" Jonah huffed. "What's so great about it?"

The Elite stared directly at Jonah's visor, making eye contact despite the fact he could not see Jonah's face through the reflective surface. "You will never—"

In a blur of motion, Jonah's hand flicked forward, plunging his blade hilt-deep into the side of the Elite's neck.

The creature shuddered and lurched, sick wet gurgles bubbling up from its throat. It lunged for the blade, more reflex than an actual attempt to defend itself. Jonah stood motionless, holding his ground.

Purple-black blood seeped from the wound, dripping from the Elite's split mandibles.

Jonah maintained his stance for a moment—looking down on his latest victim with disgust—then suddenly, violently wrenched his wrist, twisting the blade in place. "It was a rhetorical question, asshole," he said, his voice a mix of disdain and boredom as he slid the blade out of the dying Elite's neck.

In one fluid motion, he removed his M6C from its holster with his left hand, and kicked the alien to the mud- and blood-caked ground with a thud. As the heavy alien body settled, a sudden and silent flash burst from the muzzle of Jonah's pistol as he fired a single round into his fallen enemy's face—the bullet entering through the roof of its still-twitching mouth before exploding out the top of its thick skull, depositing itself, along with a myriad of brain bits and bone fragments, in the soft, soggy turf below.

"Overkill, don't you think?" Roland offered, mockingly.

Jonah leveled his M6C dead center on the dead Elite's chest, firing four more rounds, each whispered *thwip* of gunfire—*thwip, thwip, thwip, thwip*—answered by the kiss of punctured flesh and ventilated lung. "Better safe than sorry," Jonah cracked back as he safetied his weapon and ran his blade along the armor-plating on his thigh, wiping away the residue of a battle well won.

"Yer funny."

"Someone's gotta put a smile on that grumpy face, Rolle, old boy."

Roland checked his sensors and the power charge on his suit's battery. "We got other places ta be and this joint is primed to blow—you ready to roll out?"

"Yeah." Jonah paused as he gave the area one last visual sweep—Covenant carcasses and discarded weapons littered the campsite. "This place is dead anyway—"

As the last syllable escaped Jonah's lips a sudden crackle of energy sparked in the cool night air.

FIVE

SOMETHING NEW

Roland's body quaked—a violent, sudden spasm erupting from his torso and pulsing through his limbs in a series of aftershocks—then he seized as the muscles along his spinal column clinched and froze.

Jonah sprang back, instinctively taking up a defensive stance—pistol instantly off his hip and in firing position, the events before him slowing to a crawl.

For less than a second Roland stood perfectly upright and motionless before his body jerked with another forceful, involuntary start as the dual-pronged tips of a Covenant energy sword pierced his chest, sliding through his body and armor like wet paper. Jonah's eye caught on the flicker of the blade's plasma sizzling red with blood—the weapon's dual blades protruded farther from his partner's chest.

Shaking himself from his daze, Jonah unloaded his Magnum's clip just over Roland's shoulders.

The bullets pinged off something large, but unseen; each round harmlessly deflected into the night. A replacement magazine clicked home in the pistol before the last of the barrage's shells hit the ground.

Roland's muscles relaxed and he let out a gurgled, raspy cough, and a single, whispered word . . . "Clear . . ."

Everything—the blade, Roland, Jonah, the evening breeze—stopped for a handful of seconds—still and eerily serene; the only sound the pop and sizzle of the energy sword as it seared the flesh around and between the wounds.

Then, just as suddenly as it had appeared, the floating sword pushed forward with a quick, deliberate thrust before viciously being ripped up and away, exiting through the Spartan's right shoulder, just below the neck. Upon reaching the apex of its arc, the energy sword shimmered then blinked out. Gone—but not gone.

The force of the swipe nearly cleaved Roland's upper body in two, a thick geyser of blood spraying upward as the mortally wounded soldier slumped to the dirt, lifeless. As Roland fell, the spray of his blood coated a cloaked shape looming directly over his broken body.

Like an apparition, the smattering of crimson life danced in midair. Jonah couldn't make out the exact shape of his enemy, but its weapon of choice suggested it was Sangheili. He brought his pistol to center mass on the red blot and sidestepped toward a downed Unggoy to his left.

The small, dead creature's plasma pistol would come

in handy if Jonah hoped to penetrate the cloaked Elite's shield. Jonah had two additional disruptors, but he would need them at the next target site. Regardless of being a man down—friend or not—there was still a mission to accomplish.

As Jonah retrieved the alien weapon, he was sure his foe would attack.

Instead, the alien held its ground—showing an extraordinarily high level of restraint, even for an Elite. Usually Covenant warriors pressed any advantage—attacking in force until their enemies were overrun and slaughtered, but this one was different. It hadn't taken part in the firefight between the Spartans and the rest of the camp's Covenant contingent. It had stayed back—hidden; waiting.

For what? Sangheili weren't cowards. Unlike the Unggoy and Kig-Yar, whose bravery and ferociousness most often relied squarely on the tide of battle, the Sangheili were uniformly fearless foes. Why would this one in particular wait until its colleagues were beaten before launching its assault?

Jonah wanted answers to these questions—craved the hows and whys—but more than anything he just wanted this creature dead. He wanted to see the life drain from its eyes. Wanted to revel in its death.

He felt rage well up inside—like a weight pressing down against his chest—as he gripped the plasma pistol and began to rise, pointing both of his weapons at the bloodstained blur across the yard.

Motion trackers should've caught him before he got close, Jonah thought, running through the past twenty seconds, grasping for logic in this surprise attack—in his friend's death.

He squeezed the trigger on the plasma pistol, building a charge as he and the alien circled one another. He and Roland liked to goof—liked to have fun—but they were careful. Damn careful. And way too skilled to have their partnership ended in such an ignoble fashion—taken unaware by a lone Elite.

Hazarding a glance at Roland's mangled body, Jonah's mind raced. "Goddamn it," he shouted. "How'd you do it, you sonuvabitch? How'd you get the drop?"

Jonah released the plasma pistol's trigger, sending a large green burst of energy careening toward the ghostly blood smear. The Elite tried to leap out of the way, but the plasma blast tracked its target, catching the alien in its side just below the rib cage. The beast let out an angered cry as its active-camouflage and its shielding sparkled with tiny flecks of electricity and faded, revealing an Elite warrior like none Jonah had ever seen. The Elite seemed like any other in terms of its size and physical makeup, but was made more imposing by the sleek, custom armor that covered its entire body, including a full-faced helmet with a cycloptic visor port wrapping from right to left. There was also an odd shifting in the armor's coloring, as if it were analyzing and adapting to its environment, the base color of the armor adjusting, changing to blend with the background, making it hard to focus on the alien's movements. While not as effective as active-camouflage, this new chameleonlike feature definitely provided a strategic advantage.

Squinting to get a clearer view, Jonah noticed the armor itself was more rounded—more elegant—than the typically segmented Sangheili battlefield attire and was adorned with etched detailing, which was hard to make out in the low light, but seemed to have a purpose similar to war paint—ornate and aggressive. This Elite may not want to be seen, but clearly wanted any who got a good look to understand completely, and without question, that he meant business.

Jonah followed the plasma blast with a barrage of bullets from his pistol, lightly feathering the trigger for maximum rate of fire.

But this Elite was too fast. Jonah hit his mark with a few rounds but the nimble alien easily avoided the rest; an unsettling turn of events for a marksman of Jonah's caliber.

Jonah holstered his pistol and pulled his fully loaded SMG from his back, bringing it to bear on the Elite, cocking the weapon in one fluid twist, but the alien's shields and camo recovered from the plasma hit.

"There's no way," Jonah said, shocked. "Well, Rolle, buddy," Jonah already missed his friend more than he cared to admit, "looks like we got ourselves somethin' new with this one."

Jonah flipped on his suit's VISR enhanced vision. Luminescent tracers marked the edges of buildings, trees, abandoned weapons and corpses, giving a defining edge to everything in Jonah's line of sight.

Wherever the Elite was hiding, VISR would allow Jonah to track him with ease. Problem was, the Elite wasn't hiding . . . and neither were his friends.

Standing where he had faded just seconds ago, the mysterious Elite held his ground, his transparent bodily features indicated by a ring of red as the VISR technology mapped out the creature's silhouette.

Jonah kept his aim on the Elite, but didn't fire.

"Shit," Jonah said aloud to himself, his shoulders slumping a bit.

The Elite laughed, a thick, guttural boom, as the full extent of the danger dawned on Jonah.

Standing to the left and just a few meters behind the Elite were three others sporting the same souped-up armor, as marked by the red VISR-induced glow tracing their outline. To his right, two more Elites stood, almost casually.

These others had been watching the whole damn time. "This wasn't a solitary straggler who'd caught two of ONI's heavy hitters with their guard down," Jonah chided himself.

"This was a goddamn trap."

SIX

FAIR TRADE

Time was running out. Despite the immediate odds, Jonah knew he didn't have much time to make his escape before the base camp was overrun with Covenant regulars, never mind the six hard-asses standing in front of him.

The other squad's gotta be doing better than this, he

hoped, as his mind flashed to the second team of Head-hunters operating on the other side of the valley.

As if reading Jonah's mind, the Sangheili who'd killed Roland spoke. "Your fellow conspirators are dead. Like the one here, slaughtered like pups—helpless and weak."

Jonah was impressed. If the Covenant had such high-level Spec-Ops troops stationed on such a remote moon, then one of two options was true: Either ONI had gotten their intel right and this place was, in fact, a pretty damn big deal to the Covenant, or the Headhunt-ers had been doing their job so well that this whole scenario was one big alien boondoggle devised to draw them out. For a moment, thoughts of Roland's death and six large obstacles standing before him dissipated and Jonah found himself strangely satisfied—if two or more teams of the Covenant's absolute top-of-the-line Elite squads were tied up babysitting a site so far from the frontlines, then they weren't *on* the frontlines, which was a win for the UNSC no matter how you sliced it.

"You idiots set this up," he called to the Elite. "This . . . all of it. You wanted *us* . . . heh. Yer *afraid* of us. I'm flat-tered."

"You are dead," one of the Elite hissed.

"Could be. Don't matter."

"You value your life so little?"

"No. Not really," Jonah explained. "I kinda like be-ing me, actually. But you being here, means yer not somewhere else, get it? All this . . . these resources, all yer skill, wasted on a few 'pathetic' humans makes me feel kinda good—kinda special. And if you think yer taking me out without losing a limb . . . you've lost yer goddamn mind."

"We'll see who's lost their mind, once we have carved your flesh and you've screamed your secrets to the stars," the main Elite replied.

These guys *were* different, and Jonah admired them for it.

Usually Covenant battlefield doctrine was simple and to the point: "Take no prisoners." And while this new brand of Elite seemed to be playing a different game, Jonah was fairly certain that, had they wanted, he would already be dead. After all, they had the numbers and, up until a moment ago, the added advantage of total surprise.

"This ends one of two ways, chief," Jonah said. "I either walk out of here, yer teeth hangin' from a string around my neck, or I die with my fist down someone's throat."

Jonah made a come-hither motion with his SMG, before finishing, "So let's start this party, I'm late for a hot date, and I don't wanna keep yer sister waiting." Jonah was unsure if the familial insult would translate, but by this point he couldn't care less. It was time to dance.

"You can sense your end, human. That is good. If it brings you any peace, the whole of your kind will soon follow suit."

The lead Elite clicked something to his squad in their native language.

Three of the Elites leveled what looked to be modified carbine rifles at Jonah, while two others began moving toward him, igniting their energy swords. As the blades sparked to life Jonah noticed something he'd earlier mistaken as a trick of Roland's blood on the Elite's blade—these energy swords weren't powered by the same blue-white energy source as the Covenant's typical plasma-based cutlery. Instead they were composed of a reddish energy combined with the white flicker of electricity, which caused them to emit a blood-colored glow.

Jonah couldn't guess at the difference between these new swords and the more commonly used blue-variant, but he was sure of one thing: his attackers were full of surprises, and he felt a twinge of fear creep up the back of his neck.

The two sword-wielding Elites moved forward carefully, as if stalking prey.

Jonah laughed. "You know I can see you, right?"

The Elites didn't alter their approach, maintaining their speed and positioning—muscles tensed, ready to strike.

"We are aware of your visual upgrades, human. As stated, we've already been through this with your friends. Lay down your arms and surrender yourself for inquisition."

Jonah shifted his gaze to Roland's body, keeping the Elites squarely in peripheral view. "Twenty credits says yer all dead within . . . let's say . . . the next thirty seconds."

The lead Elite scoffed. "We will end you before you so much as bruise our egos, dog. Now, lay down your weapons—"

"Seriously. I know you might not have any credits handy, but I'm willing to take the Covenant equivalent." Jonah let the offer stand for a brief instant, then dropped his SMG to the turf.

"We got a deal?" The two approaching Elites picked up their pace, as the others steadied their aim.

Jonah relaxed his posture, let his knees flex and his back and shoulders slouch.

The two Elites were almost within reach. Jonah bent into a deep crouch—his muscles contracted, taut—before tumbling back, head over heels, coming up a good ten yards from the nearest Elite. Hunched in a low squat, Jonah held a disruptor in one hand, his charge detonator in the other.

While Roland had been responsible for demolitions on most missions, with Jonah preferring to focus on direct combat, both members of a Headhunter squad were required to carry the proper charges and triggering mechanisms necessary for fieldwork to ensure redundancy should any unforeseen complications arise. And though Jonah would've preferred another way out, he was fully aware that his luck had run dry, and as he and his fellow 'Hunters had been fond of saying since their earliest training days on Onyx: "When in doubt, blow shit up."

Jonah's mind flashed to Roland one more time, and he silently thanked his partner for one last assist— "Clear." Roland's final breath had also been a parting shot at the Covenant bastard who'd run him through.

These special division Spec-Op Elites may have been watching the whole show, but Roland was cloaked when he set his charges, so unless the Sangheili had the equivalent of VISR in those shiny new helmets, they didn't know thing one about the explosives placed on the reactors all around them.

"Clear" meant the primer on the charges had been initiated.

"Clear" meant with a push of a button this entire section of the valley would light up as bright and hot as the surface of a star, nothing but scorched earth and charred bones in its wake.

"Clear," and Jonah had a plan, even if it meant kissing his own ass good-bye.

He raised the disruptor. "Know what this is?"

"Take him!" the lead Elite called.

But Jonah had allowed the two closest Elites to get within arm's length in order to block the line of fire of their three squadmates with ranged weaponry. If they got close enough to cut him he'd still have time to blow the fuse and take them all to hell right along with him.

Jonah activated the disruptor and tossed it in a low arc toward the four farthest Elites while dodging a swipe from one of the energy swords, but he was too slow to avoid the second's grasp.

The Elite yanked him to his feet, ripping his shoulder from its socket. Jonah screamed in pain.

The energy field from the disruptor expanded as it hit the ground at the feet of the farthest group of aliens, shutting down power to their weapons and armor.

The Elite holding Jonah shook him like a rag doll. "You dare defy us, filth? You will suffer for your sins." He raised his sword, using the very edge of the blade to cut a gash across Jonah's faceplate, digging into the flesh beneath. Jonah's left eye sizzled and popped as the blade passed through. For the second time in recent memory, the Spartan screamed, but he still held tightly to the detonator, thumb pressed firmly on the tiny unit's ignition switch.

The second sword-wielding Elite stepped up and grabbed him by the neck.

In Jonah's mind a thousand witty remarks echoed, an infinite chorus of banter to die to, but instead of uttering a word, Jonah simply glanced at the beasts above him, these "elite" commandoes whose body count quite possibly surpassed his own, and thought to himself, *Six of you, one of me. Fair trade*, as he released his thumb from the detonator.

After that everything went white.

THE IMPOSSIBLE LIFE
AND THE
POSSIBLE DEATH OF
PRESTON J. COLE

ERIC NYLUND

PLNB Transmission XX087R-XX
Encryption Code: GAMMA-SHIFT-X-RAY
Public Key: N/A
From: CODENAME SURGEON
To: CODENAME USUAL SUSPECTS
Subject: HISTORICAL/PSYCHOLOGICAL ANALYSIS OF
  COLE, PRESTON J.
Classification: EYES ONLY, CODE-WORD ██████████
  TOP SECRET
Security Override: BLACK LEVEL-IV
Ghost server file-transfer protocol (EXACTION):
  TRUE
AI-touch protocol (VERACITY): FALSE

/file extraction-reconstitution complete/
/start file/

The purpose of this analysis is to find the final resting place of Preston J. Cole (UNSC Service Number: 00814-13094-BQ) for what I surmise to be the answer to *the* political, sociological, and military conundrum the UNSC now faces with the post–Covenant War situation.

Please spare me the plausible denials and "need to knows" about the reason for requesting this analysis.

I know.

Otherwise, you wouldn't have asked me in the first place.

To ascertain if such a final resting place even exists, or if the redoubtable Cole rests at all, is not a straightforward query, and I'm afraid my analysis will be less than straightforward as well.

Even if you pierce the veil of propaganda and discount the vast number of Cole's victories, promotions, and decorations as nothing more than engineered drama to prop up our population's then-sinking morale—Preston Cole *still* has an unparalleled battle record . . . even far and away more impressive than the legendary Spartan-IIs. He was the greatest hero in modern times, a legend before, and in spite of, our meddling.

I shall add commentary for historical context and psychological analysis, but these depend primarily on the available interviews, orders, after-action reports—as well as audio, video, and AI-enhanced holographic bridge and battle logs.

You'll forgive me if I wax long and poetic about Preston Cole. We knew him, we loved him, and finally we hated him for being the less-than-perfect military god that we had come to depend upon.

Cole would not approve of this report—only because he is the subject of the inquiry. He at least would have understood and, also being a cunning bastard of a military strategist, he would do the same in our shoes.

To quote Cole himself: "They told me to fight, and that's what I've done. Let historians sort through the wreckage, bodies, and broken lives to figure out the rest."

Which is precisely what I intend to do.

Codename: SURGEON
0900 hours, December 30, 2552 (Military
  Calendar) \ UNSC *Point of No Return*, Synchronous Lunar Orbit
  (far side)

SECTION ONE: COLE'S EARLY LIFE (2470–2488 CE)

Preston Jeremiah Cole was born to Jennifer Francine Cole and Troy Henry Cole November 3, 2470, in the rural reconstituted township of Mark Twain, Missouri. He was the third child of seven (three sisters and three brothers).

He was described as a precocious child who obeyed his parents, had wild black hair, dark brown eyes, and an unwavering stare that unnerved most teachers and classmates alike.

His father was a dairy farmer with no criminal record, no military background, and followed the Quaker faith with no particular zeal.

His mother was arrested once at the age of twenty-one for protesting taxes (released on one-year parole),

*and both her grandfathers served in the Rain Forest
Wars (one surviving, received the Bronze Star—see attached report on Captain Oliver Franks).*

*Starting in 2310, exploration and colony ships were
built, and the best and brightest people left the safety
of the Earth to make their way to the stars. This was
the "Golden Age" of colonial expansion from Earth.
Within 180 years, the main human colonies had been
established—some becoming huge population and commerce centers such as Reach, while others would remain
tiny manufacturing outposts. This collection of "close"
worlds would later be called the Inner Colonies.*

*The Inner Colonies provided a surplus of raw goods,
materials, and taxes that flooded back to the parent
government on Earth. For most it was a time of plenty,
optimism, and indolence unparalleled since second-
century Rome or the financial bubble at the end of
twentieth-century America.*

*For the Cole family, however, tax records show his
family struggling to make ends meet.*

Preston Cole's Fifth Grade Report Card

Missouri Rain River School District
Wallace Fujikawa Elementary School
Homeroom Teacher: Dr. Lillian Bratton
Preston J. Cole (Student ID #: LB-0034)

Grades:
Physical Education: B-

Pre-Algebra: A
English: B
Art: C
Physical Science: A
Technology II: A

Finchy-Franks Intelligence Quotient: 147

Homeroom Teacher Evaluations:
Sociability: Below Average
Leadership: Average
Classroom Participation: Below Average
Citizenship: Above Average

Homeroom Teacher Notes:
Preston requires guidance to reach his full potential. A boy of high natural intellect, he tends to work too hard even when he plays. He overanalyzes every strategy when he plays baseball, slowing the games to a crawl. If he does not know how to do something, he looks it up, or if possible derives it (in the case of Mr. Martin's pre-algebra class) from first principles. These traits in and of themselves are admirable, but he also needs to cultivate his imagination. In short, Preston never seems to have fun. Everything is a task to be finished. Preston also falls asleep in class on a regular basis; I would suggest that his chores or responsibilities at home be relaxed. He is, after all, only ten years old.

Confidential Note: Wallace Fujikawa Elementary School database / March 12, 2481 (Military Calendar)

The incident in Mr. Martin's pre-algebra class has been settled. A makeup final exam has been given, and Preston was carefully monitored the entire time. He produced *another* perfect test score, proving to William (Mr. Martin) that he did not cheat, although a perfect score (let alone two perfect scores) is a feat that has never been accomplished on the standardized pre-algebra final.

Preston's father continues to defend his son's driven nature and his family's antiquated beliefs, insisting that Preston's education at home has far and away exceeded what is taught at school. He went on to say that his chores were necessary to the family's financial support and absolutely refused any suggestion that they apply for government aid.

Follow-up with a social worker at the Preston household bore no evidence of physical or psychological abuse when they made a visit at the school district's request.

{Excerpt} The Viability of Extended Colonization By Preston J. Cole (age 14)

Freshman English / Miss Alexander
Grade received: B
(Teacher's comments: "Thesis: B / Conclusions: C / Too much speculation and gratuitous use of Yeats quotation")

The metaphor of a biological system, for example a population of wolves or fungus growth in a Petri dish, is tempting to apply to colonial expansion.

There can be three fates for any biological system. It may grow as long as there are sufficient nutrients, a suitable environment, and no over-predation—the system can enter a balanced state of growth and loss—or the system may decline from over-predation, lack of nutrients, environmental disaster, or being poisoned by its own waste products.

Off-world colonies similarly require a stable environment with suitable food and water, and no over-predation. It is considered an open system because there are limitless numbers of habitable planets. (Or at least a very large number within the Milky Way Galaxy. See my Drake calculation assumptions in Appendix B.)

Human colonies, however, differ in one critical aspect: they are, by rule, inhabited by predictably intelligent entities. The values of these entities can diverge from the parent world with each successive generation. That is, while colonies directly seeded from Earth remain very earthlike in social, economic, and political values, they change with successive generations as they adapt to local environmental pressures, and in turn send out new colonies farther in physical distance and values from the original parent.

Such diversification in biological systems is a normal evolutionary process, but it produces offspring that are increasingly alien in nature to the parent.

Such was the case of colonial expansion in early Earth history, most notably in the British colonies in the eighteenth and nineteenth centuries. Those colonies diverged from their parent nations and their resulting different social and economic values culminated in a schism, and in one notable case a war that resulted in a shift in the balance of power, such that one former colony became the dominant military, cultural and industrial complex on Earth for hundreds of years.

How long can Earth and its close colonies extend without producing offspring that differ sufficiently to want to break away from the parent? As William Butler Yeats said: "The center cannot hold."

ANALYSIS

The Cole family farm was an anomaly. Most small Earth farms couldn't compete with colonial agrocorporations that could produce ten times the yield on worlds with constant sunlight and volcanic alluvial soils. The Cole farm, however, still exists (after eight generations) and continues to operate. This family instilled a no-nonsense work ethic and discipline in Preston Cole that made him "anachronistic" in comparison to the population at the time who were enjoying the benefits of the still-expansive colonial era and whose most noteworthy ability was a sense of entitlement.

Perhaps it also gave Preston Cole a clarity which many at the time lacked. Reading his freshman essay, one cannot help but think that this must be a fabrication of ONI Section-II, a remnant fiction from an earlier propaganda campaign. And yet, it has been verified as legitimate. What would Cole have become had his teacher shared even a fraction of his insight and encouraged it? This boy whom the elementary teacher decried as lacking "imagination" was damn near prophetic.

Cole's grades, however, continually slipped in high school—we assume from the boredom of the standardized coursework and the increasing demands of his life on the farm.

No journals have been found from his adolescent years, and it is doubtful that his family situation would encourage such activities, so we're forced to speculate on his aspirations.

Cole was surrounded by a world of excesses and opportunities that were just out of his reach. He was highly intelligent, but had no creative outlet. Given the mass media's predilection for romanticizing off-world adventures at that time, Cole may have seen the colonies and stellar exploration as an irresistible opportunity which he could not pass up.

Given his limited economic means and lack of excellence within the templates and strictures of a standardized educational system, there was only one way for him to seek his fortune off-world.

SECTION TWO: NONCOMMISSIONED YEARS (2488–2489 CE)

The policy at that time was to allow any college graduate or promising student out of high school with superior grades (or the right connections) to enter prestigious military colleges that virtually guaranteed a commission upon graduation.

The requirement of mandatory noncommissioned field experience before application to officer training schools was instituted only later, when it became clear that such officers would be responsible for irreplaceable military assets and personnel—and, in the Covenant War, the lives of millions of civilians on the worlds they protected. Preston Cole was one of the first admirals to implement such a policy, saying, "Those not bloodied in combat have no business leading men and women into battle."

The just-graduated Preston Cole (age eighteen) had neither the grades nor the connections to attend such officer training academies. So he enlisted as a noncommissioned recruit in the Navy. He was ordered to Unified Combined Military Boot Camp (UCMB), and then shipped up-elevator for six additional weeks of vacuum and microgravity training (colloquially known, then, as now, as "barf school"). Upon his graduation as Crewman Recruit Cole he was ordered aboard the CMA Season of Plenty, *assigned to atmospheric reclamation maintenance duty.*

{Excerpt} **Preston J. Cole's Military Service Enlistment Application / September 21, 2488 (Military Calendar)**

WHY DO YOU WANT TO ENLIST? (answer in 100 words or less)

"Humanity's future is among the stars. There is no

single more important thing than to help men and women build new lives on distant worlds. I have no illusion that this is some manifest destiny, but rather, it is the only logical place left for humanity to evolve. I plan to be a part of that, learn as much as possible, and then one day become one of those humans on some distant world, on a little farm of my own under a night sky full of stars that I've never before seen."

Evaluation of Cole, P. J. (UNSC Service Number: 00814-13094-BQ) by Petty Officer Second Class Graves, L. P. (UNSC Service Number: 00773-04652-KK) / UCMB Sierra Largo / November 3, 2488 (Military Calendar)

Completed all requisite physical tests: YES
Displayed any mental aberrations: NO
Combined Arms Skill Test (CAST): 78 (Above
    Average)
Combined Physical Skill Test (CPST): 65 (Average)
Gratney-Walis Hierarchical Aptitude Score:
    (GWAS): 94 (Exceptional)

Remarks: Follows orders without question beyond what is required. Keeps mouth shut. Shows initiative. Hard worker. How often do we see that these days? Move this kid onto NCO track before someone makes him a dammed technical specialist or we lose him to OCS.

*1120 HOURS, SEPTEMBER 22, 2489 (MILITARY CALENDAR) \
COLONIAL MILITARY ADMINISTRATION SEASON OF PLENTY \
SOL SYSTEM LUNA, HIGH ORBIT \ BRIDGE LOG (VIDEO, SPATIAL
ENHANCEMENT=TRUE)*

The tiny bridge of the CMA *Season of Plenty* had view
screens and workstations crammed on every square
centimeter of wall (with auxiliary stations on the ceiling and floor in case the rotating segment failed). The
screens would have provided a simulated panorama of
stars had not they instead been crawling with icons
representing colonists, building supplies, and the raw
materials to jump-start the new city dubbed "Lazy
Acres" on the hellhole of a world called Paradise Falls.

Six ensigns manned their stations, checking and rechecking every gram of mass and fuel, and balancing
the energy flow of the reactors in preparation for launch.
They barely had enough room to turn without bump-
ing into one another—save Ensign Otto Seinmann,
who stood aft of the captain's chair at Lorelei's inter-
face pedestal.

The artificial intelligence hologram stood half a meter
tall. Like all holograms, Lorelei's outer appearance re-
flected a chosen inner personality: a woman wearing a
toga, a sickle in her belt, and a wreath of wheat crowning
her head. She once again shook her head at the young
ensign.

Seinmann crossed his arms over his chest. "We're
not done." He towered over the diminutive hologram,
two meters tall, handsome, and his dark hair short but
stylishly wavy.

"*We* may not be done, Ensign," Lorelei replied, "but *I* am. My apologies; I have a scheduled self-diagnostic to run before the jump."

The hologram vanished.

Seinmann pounded a fist onto the console.

Ensign Alexis Indara tore her gaze from the mass-balance matrix on her screen. "Better ease up, Seinmann. You're going to break it."

Next to her at the fusion monitoring station, Ensign Handford murmured, "Maybe it's Seinmann's breath. These new 'smarter' AIs are supposed to be sensitive to everything."

Lieutenant Commander Nevel stepped onto the bridge. In his mid-thirties he already had that casual air of "don't mess with me" that most officers couldn't achieve until they were at least captains. The ensigns all stood a little straighter but kept on working.

"Navigation reports no input parameters yet," Lieutenant Commander Nevel said. "What's the hold-up, Seinmann?"

Seinmann flushed, not with embarrassment, but with anger. "Sir, Lorelei has shut herself down for routine maintenance—again."

Nevel raised an eyebrow. "Well, we were warned it might take a while for her to come fully online. Reboot the backup intelligence and get those calculations—" Nevel paused, looked Seinmann over, and then told him, "On second thought, this would be a good opportunity to brush up on your Shaw multivariate calculus, Ensign. Do a rough calculation by hand. The captain expects to be under way in ninety minutes."

Seinmann opened his mouth as if to protest—then said nothing, and then finally, "Aye, sir."

Nevel wheeled about and left the bridge.

Ensign Indara whispered, "I think Nevel has an antique slide rule tucked away somewhere if you run out of fingers to count on."

Seinmann growled something unintelligible, grabbed a data pad, and stabbed in calculations.

After a minute of this, he looked among his fellow ensigns (all of whom were busy with their own work) until he spotted a young crewman—or rather the backside of a crewman that protruded from an open access panel to the oxygen recycling intake.

"Cole!" Seinmann barked. "Get over here."

Crewman Apprentice Cole extracted himself from the narrow crawlspace, stood, straightened his gray coveralls, and ran a hand over his shorn hair (which was dotted with drips and spatters of grease).

The fresh-out-of-barf-school crewman looked alert and eager to please. His dark eyes met Seinmann's and didn't waver.

"Yes, sir?"

Seinmann shoved the data pad at Cole. "I need you to run an independent check on these numbers."

Cole's gaze moved to the data pad. He swallowed.

"In case you don't recognize them, they're parameters for a Shaw-Fujikawa manifold collapse."

Cole nodded and took the pad.

"You *do* know what a Shaw-Fujikawa manifold is, don't you, crewman?" There was a dangerous glint in Seinmann's eyes.

Cole didn't look up from the pad, still studying its contents. "Yes . . . sir."

"Good. If you get stuck just look up the formulas on a workstation." With no further explanation, Seinmann picked up his coffee mug and strolled over to Indara.

Cole took the data pad and sat at a nearby station, still not moving his stare from the ensign's equations, but now frowning at them. He tapped in a few parameters, sighed, and erased them.

"You're cruel," Indara whispered to Seinmann.

"And in hot water if the lieutenant commander finds out you're not doing your own work," Handford added.

"Cruel . . . ?" Seinmann mused. "Isn't that what crewmen are for?" He looked over at Cole. "Don't worry about the lieutenant commander. I already have the rough calculation done."

"So why pick on Cole?" Indara asked. "He gets his work done and doesn't bother anyone."

"He bothers *me*," Seinmann said. "Never shows the proper respect. Did you see the way he looked at me? And he's always got his nose in a library access terminal, too, reading ancient history or quantum field theory or stuff he couldn't possibly understand. It's so obviously an act."

"I still think it's unnecessarily cruel," Indara said.

Lieutenant Commander Nevel stepped onto the bridge.

Seinmann instantly pretended to be double-checking the seed stock in Holding Bay 4.

The AI pedestal lit and Lorelei flickered upon its surface, the lines of her face smoothed into the features

of someone just waking up. "Good afternoon, Lieutenant Commander. All primary and secondary neural
links checked. Shaw-Fujikawa parameters calculated
and three-times-three checked. All systems go. *Season
of Plenty* ready for slipstream space transition upon
the captain's orders."

"Very good," Nevel said. He spotted Seinmann and
added, "Oh . . . and link to Ensign Seinmann's data
pad and check his work, please."

Seinmann strode over and whispered to Lorelei, "I
thought you said you had to run a self-diagnostic."

"I did," Lorelei admitted, "but that's not *all* I did.
I'm not an idiot, Ensign."

The AI blinked, and then announced to Nevel in a
loud voice, "His calculations are correct, if crude. The
input parameters would have gotten the *Season of Plenty*
there—albeit 160 million kilometers off course . . . *and*
pathing through a brown dwarf."

The lieutenant commander frowned at Seinmann.
"Ensign, report to the captain that the *Season of Plenty*
is shipshape and awaits his orders."

Seinmann skulked off the bridge, but as he passed
Ensign Indara, she whispered, "What about Cole? He's
still working."

"Let him," Seinmann muttered and left.

A moment later the order came through the bridge
intercom to transition to slipstream.

The bridge officers remained busy for the five hours
until the shift change, and it was only then that Lieutenant Commander Nevel noticed Crewman Apprentice Cole still working at an auxiliary workstation.

"Crewman, what precisely are you doing?"

Cole looked up; his eyes were ringed with fatigue. When he saw Nevel he immediately stood at attention. "Sir, finishing the slipstream space calculations Ensign Seinmann ordered me to double-check."

The lieutenant commander's face contorted with anger, disgust, and finally a hint of amusement. "Very good"—his gaze fell onto the name tag of Cole's jumpsuit—"Crewman Cole. I'll take it from here. Dismissed."

"Yes, sir." Cole gathered his tools and left the bridge.

Nevel chuckled and retrieved Cole's data pad—then halted, gazing intently at its contents.

He moved to Lorelei's station. "Did you help the crewman with this?"

The data pad flickered as Lorelei interfaced. "No." The AI paused for a full half second. "How intriguing. It is indeed a Shaw-Fujikawa manifold calculation, but it uses a method I have never before encountered."

"Is it correct?"

"Yes . . . even good . . . for a crude approximation. But highly impractical. It would take far too long for a human to implement such a method, and I have far superior algorithms at my disposal."

Nevel looked again at Cole's equations. "But let me get this straight—this *crewman* actually came up with a *new* way of calculating input parameters?"

"That is correct."

Lieutenant Commander Nevel traced his fingers over the multidimensional, imaginary-space calculus on the data pad. "Hmm." His face hardened. "Find Ensign Seinmann and have him report to the bridge. I need to remind him of the level of mathematical expertise we expect of our officers on the *Plenty*."

Letter from Crewman Apprentice Preston Cole to his brother, Michael James Cole, October 16, 2489 (Military Calendar)

Mike,

So much is going on, I just have time for a quick note. They keep me twice as busy on the *Season of Plenty* as I was back home—even during calving season, and I'm trying to learn *everything* I can, all at once. This is exactly where I want to be. Where I was meant to be.

And some of the people that we take to the colonies! Most were rich back on Earth. Many have PhDs. But they're risking everything to become blacksmiths and herd sheep and throw themselves out into the great unknown. It's inspiring.

I want to get out there and be a part of this, too. You and Molly should join me one day. Dad would bust an artery if he heard me say that, so don't tell him. Or would he be proud?

The only problem I'm having is with some of the crew—they aren't as easy for me to figure as a math problem. I'm getting along, mostly. I just don't understand some of the junior officers. I'm glad I don't have to. That's one of the advantages of being a crewman apprentice: we just do what we're told.

More soon,

P.J.

{Excerpt} Bi-annual Personnel Review of CMA
Season of Plenty / November 27, 2489 (Military
Calendar)

Junior Officer Summation (continued)
Ensign Handford, W. (UNSC Service Number:
00786-31761-OM)
Average performance
Ensign Indara, A. (UNSC Service Number: 00801-
46332-XT)
Above average performance
Requested management training (Series 7).
Request granted.
- Ensign Seinmann, O. (UNSC Service Number:
00806-95321-PG)
Above average performance
Promotion to Lieutenant Junior Grade
Transferred to the CMA *Laden.*

Additional:
RE: Crewman Apprentice Cole, P. J. (UNSC Service
Number: 00814-13094-BQ)
Shows aptitude for history and mathematics.
Suggested by Lt. Commander Nevel *and* the
ship's AI, Lorelei,
that he would be a superior applicant for the
Academy at Mare Nubium (aka Luna Officer
Candidate School).
One week temporary assignment to Luna,
pending
entrance examination results.

ANALYSIS

It was the end of the Golden Age of human colonization. As of 2494 CE it was still a time of peace and
prosperity, but Earth had begun to overreach its lo-
gistical ability to control her colonies. Several fac-
tors led to the destabilization of the more distant, or
as later called, "Outer" Colonies.

1. There were widely varying standards for recruit-
   ment to the Outer Colonies. "Colonization con-
   tractors" were more interested in staking claims
   to valuable resource rights than providing the
   most-skilled personnel. Some people were ille-
   gally conscripted, and others were law-breakers
   granted pardons if they agreed to go—all of
   which led to these colonists being less than absolutely loyal to Earth.
2. Some colonists struck out on their own, procuring
   by legal or illegal means transport to farther-flung
   worlds, partially or wholly outside Earth's control.
3. Continued taxes, levies, and restricted trade
   practices by the CMA increased friction as the
   Outer Colonies received only a fraction of the
   benefits they were taxed for.

The situation was a problem of physical as well as
psychological dimensions. Mathematically the volume of the sphere increases as its radius cubed, and
so the number of Outer Colonies grew. Given such a
numerical advantage and the fact that they encapsu-

lated the Inner Core worlds, there was the belief that Earth and her close colonies were literally *surrounded* by increasingly hostile forces.

Many now think this was a skewed perception, and that given diplomacy and enough time, Earth and her Inner Colonies could have established more harmonious relationships with her farther-flung cousins. Others point out, however, that had there been no military action, the Outer Colonies might have risen to power and threatened the core worlds at the *worst possible moment* in human history.

All theoretical analysis aside, the United Earth government and her colonies developed new policies and an increased military presence that would provoke further unfortunate responses from the Outer Colonies . . . and lead to an undeclared Civil War.

For that, Earth would need more ships and crews . . . and officers to lead them.

SECTION THREE: LUNA OFFICER CANDIDATE SCHOOL (2489–2493 CE)

Cole's academic record at the Academy at Mare Nubium speaks for itself. He graduated magna cum laude with high degrees of excellence and specialization from the Rutherford Science Magistrate. Apart from minor hazing incidents, and the usual swept-under-the-rug blemishes that are on any cadet's record . . . there is only one incident of particular note.

During Cole's junior year, there was a series of

incidents with Admiral Konrad Volkov's daughter: her
overnight disappearances from family officers' quar-
ters located on base, sightings of the young lady in the
company of a young man, and the biological conse-
quences of these liaisons.

The scandal culminated publicly when six cadets
were brought before a Board of Inquiry.

{Excerpt} Transcription of Cole, P. J. (UNSC Service
Number: 00814-13094-BQ) testimony before Board
of Inquiry, Academy at Mare Nubium JAG Incident
Report (local) 475-A \ June 7, 2492 (Military
Calendar) \ Log (video, spatial, psychological
enhancement=TRUE) FILE *SEALED* (UNSC-JAG
ORD: 8-PD-3861), June 13, 2492 (Military
Calendar)

Seated Board of Inquiry: Colonel Mitchell K. Lima
(UNSC Service Number: 00512-5991-IX), Captain
Maria F. Gilliam, JAG officer in residence (UNSC
Service Number: 00622-7120-RJ), Frank O. Welker
(Civilian Liaison to the Academy at Mare Nubium,
Civilian ID#: 8813-316-0955-G)

[Crewman Apprentice Preston J. Cole is sworn in be-
fore the Board.]
COLONEL LIMA: State your name for the record.
CREWMAN COLE: Cole, Preston J., sir.
CAPTAIN GILLIAM: Tell us, Cadet, where exactly you
were between 1900 and 2300 hours three days ago?

[Cole remains standing at attention and stares up and
to the right. Since Cole is right-handed this
indicates he is accessing the visual memory
portion of his brain (and not lying).]

COLE: I was on watch duty on Shadow Perimeter Three
with Cadets Parkins, Haverton, and Tasov, ma'am.

MR. FRANK O. WELKER: Describe "shadow perimeter
three" for me, Cadet.

COLE: Yes, Mr. Welker. Shadow Perimeter Three is the
colloquial term used for the series of tunnels and
surface tubes that run across the Mare Nubium,
connecting the Academy to the civilian sectors of
Asimov Center. The "shadow" part of the name
comes from the shadows cast from the nearby crater
walls.

WELKER: Why guard that particular section?

[Cole's eyes now lock forward.]

COLE: I was ordered to do so.

GILLIAM: Cadet, speculate as to the reason required for
guarding Perimeter Three.

COLE: Yes, ma'am. There are two reasons. First, we always maintain a guarded perimeter against unauthorized civilian incursions on Academy grounds.
Second, there have been recent reports of unauthorized military personnel and supplies moving into the
civilian territories.

[The five other cadets who await questioning in the
tribunal chamber shift in their seats.]

LIMA: Do you know of any such unauthorized crossing
of our military personnel?

COLE: I have not read of any such occurrences in the incident report, sir.

LIMA: That was not my question.

[Cole pauses, looks straight down.]

COLE: I have never seen any such incidents, sir. If I had I would have attempted to stop them from occurring. If I could not, I would have immediately reported it and been required to make a note of it in the incident log.

[Gilliam leans forward and removes her glasses.]

GILLIAM: You say "never seen," but have you heard rumors or otherwise received any indication of such illegal base crossing on or off your watch?

[Cole swallows, eyes back up, staring past Captain Gilliam.]

COLE: I cannot substantiate any rumors I may or may not have heard, ma'am. I have insufficient evidence to do so.

LIMA: I'm going to remind you once, Cadet, and only once, that obstructing any military investigation is a serious offense that carries a minimum of five years of hard labor.

[Cole gives no response.]

LIMA: I am now ordering you, Cadet, to tell me *everything* you know about any military personnel crossing the perimeter the evening of the twenty-fifth—or any tampering with security devices or recordings of the region during that time—or *any* detail of *anything unusual* that evening.

[Cole inhales deeply, looks directly at Colonel Lima.]

COLE: Sir, no. Nothing . . . unusual.

[Captain Gilliam, Mr. Welker, and Colonel Lima
    confer among themselves.]

[Cole remains standing at attention.]

GILLIAM: If you are trying to protect a fellow cadet
    through some sense of camaraderie or honor—it is
    misplaced. Do not throw away your otherwise ster-
    ling service record to protect someone who, to be
    blunt, does not deserve to be an officer.

[At this time, Admiral Konrad Volkov enters the room
    and sits.]

[Cole faces the tribunal and cannot possibly see the
    admiral, but nonetheless stands straighter and
    begins to sweat.]

COLE: Sir, what kind of officer would I make if I said
    what you wanted me to say just to avoid trouble—
    regardless of whether it is the truth or not? Or if I
    guessed at any wrongdoing to make myself look bet-
    ter? I will not do such a thing.

LIMA: Crewman Cole, you are in contempt of this
    Board of Inquiry. I'll deal with you later.

[(Colonel Lima motions for the court guards. The
    guards move to escort Cole).]

[Cole salutes the presiding officers, turns, makes direct
    eye contact with Admiral Volkov, and is
    marched from the tribunal chamber.]

Certificate of Marriage

The State of Mare Nubium   County of Newton

To any Judge, Justice of the Peace, or Minister:

You are hereby authorized to join:

Preston Jeremiah Cole, age 21, and Inna Volkov, age ███

In the Holy State of Matrimony according to the Constitution of Luna Confederated States and for so doing this shall be your License. And you are hereby required to return this License to me with your Certificate herein of the fact and date of Marriage within thirty days after said Marriage.

Given under my hand and seal this 17 August, 2492.

Quinn Lloyd (Licensing Officer, Newton County), Ordinary.

CERTIFICATE

I Certify that Preston Jeremiah Cole and Inna Volkov were joined in Matrimony by me this Seventeenth day of August, Two Thousand Four Hundred Ninety-Two.

Recorded 21 August, 2492.

In presence of Witnesses:

Michael H. Cole

Admiral Konrad Volkov

Behold by my hand and with my seal, Harold Yates, Ordinary.

Certificate of Live Birth

The State of Mare Nubium Department of Health

Certificate No: 4216

Child's Name: Ivan Troy Cole

Date of Birth: December 12, 2492   Hour of Birth 0445

  Sex: Male

City, Rural Plot, or Station of Birth: Asimov Center

  County of Birth: Newton

Mother's Maiden Name: Volkov

  Mother's DNA Trace: ███████████

Father's Name: Preston Jeremiah Cole

  Father's DNA Trace: SUY-OOU-WYED

Date Filed by Registrar: December 16, 2492

This copy serves as prima facie evidence of the fact of birth in any court proceeding {HRS 550-45(b)}

ANY ALTERATIONS INVALIDATE THIS CERTIFICATE

ANALYSIS

Colonel Lima dropped his charges of contempt and obstructing the tribunal's investigation against Preston Cole two days after the inconclusive hearing.

The record shows Cole married Admiral Volkov's daughter, indicating (at first glance) that he was the cadet who had the illicit liaison.

But why would Admiral Volkov allow such a cadet to marry his daughter instead of having him summarily thrown out an airlock?

DNA analysis of Ivan Volkov (done at the request of the admiralty and codeword classified: NIGHTINGALE) provides incontrovertible evidence that he was *not* Preston Cole's son.

There are three possible explanations for these facts.

1. The admiral knew which cadet was the true father and didn't like what he saw. He found a suitable replacement for his daughter: a cadet who would stand up for his principles even if that meant going to jail.
2. The child's DNA did not match any suspected cadets or other military personnel (civilians transferring to and from Luna were not required to provide DNA samples in their CMA screenings). This would have left the admiral's grandchild still fatherless.
3. Cole was indeed the cadet who had the liaison with the admiral's daughter, but not the father of her child.

Many questions, however, central to understanding Cole remain unanswered. Did Admiral Volkov make him marry his daughter or did Cole—compelled by a sense of chivalry—offer to marry the disgraced young lady and provide a father for her unborn child?

Cole's admirers would say that he stepped up and did the noble thing: a young man with a sense of honor and morality (regardless of any possible indiscretions).

Cole's detractors, though, would claim this incident highlights his strategic and opportunistic nature: a cunning junior officer currying favor with the admiral at his most vulnerable moment, which would result in rapid promotion and assignment to choice (if remote) postings.

Or could it have been a little of both?

Whatever the reasons, Cole remained married to Inna for many years thereafter, fathering two more sons and one daughter (DNA analysis proves these were his), and he remained a loving father to all four children, writing to them often, and providing birthday gifts and support to them for the rest of his life.

After a two-week honeymoon, Cole was reassigned for duties in the Outer Colonies aboard the UNSC destroyer *Las Vegas*.

SECTION FOUR: THE OUTER COLONY INSURGENCY: THE *CALLISTO* INCIDENT (2494 CE)

For decades prior to the end of the Colonial era (c. 2490 CE) Earth-based military forces had focused on colonization logistics, settling minor trade disputes, and perhaps chasing off the odd pirate. UNSC officers had studied how to engage in glorious, large-scale (but as yet hypothetical) battles against enemy states—not how to cope with an emboldened insurgency that could hide in the very populations they were sworn to protect.

One event in particular (among a dozen similar incidents in the Outer Colonies), the Callisto Incident, would shape Preston Cole's early career.

The distant colony Levosia had been suspected of diverting refined selenium and technetium (used in the manufacture of FTL drives), which would yield huge profits on the black market.

Apart from lost taxes, however, Earth realized it could not allow insurgent forces access to FTL engine components. Therefore, Central Command (CENTCOM) ordered the Navy to blockade and search all ships in the system for suspected contraband.

The UNSC corvette Callisto stopped and boarded a trading vessel. The merchant crew was skittish due to rumors of impressments during similar searches in the Outer Colonies (a rumor started, we suspect, by insurgent sympathizers). A weapon was drawn and shots exchanged, resulting in the death of three naval officers and twenty-seven merchant crewmen.

No contraband was discovered.

This sparked outrage throughout the system. Thirty-seven days later, the Callisto ordered a similar merchant vessel to stand to and be searched. The merchant ship allowed the officers to board with all due courtesies. When the officers entered the cargo bay, they found it empty. The bay doors opened and the officers were blasted into space. The merchant crew then swarmed into the unsuspecting Callisto *and murdered the remainder of its crew.*

The Callisto *was taken and its computer system gutted and replaced.*

The insurgency was now armed.

In response, a UNSC battle group of three light destroyers was sent to hunt down the Callisto. *They had weapons that had never been fired in conflict, nor had her crews engaged in any battle.*

Leading the battle group was the UNSC destroyer Las Vegas *under Captain Harold Lewis, with a new assistant navigation officer fresh out of Luna OCS, Second Lieutenant Preston J. Cole.*

0315 HOURS, MARCH 2, 2494 (MILITARY CALENDAR) \ UNSC DESTROYER LAS VEGAS PATROLLING 26 DRACONIS SYSTEM \ BRIDGE LOG OF THE UNSC LAS VEGAS (PRIMARY, VIDEO, SPATIAL ENHANCEMENTS=TRUE)

The bridge of the UNSC *Las Vegas* was a narrow oval of nav, ops, engineering, comm, and weapons stations. Green and blue icons winked on and off, illuminating the faces of the officers, while the shadows around them were full of the red glow of battle station lights.

Captain Lewis sat on the edge of his seat, nervously scraping his thumbnail. The first mate, Commander Rinkishale, stood near, her cap snug on her head, and lines of concern crisscrossing her face.

"Update on target vector," Captain Lewis said.

"Still decelerating, sir," Second Lieutenant Cole answered. His close-cropped hair spiked up with stubborn cowlicks. His gaze was cold iron and only the faintest lines creased the corners of his eyes as he squinted at the screen. Without looking away, he tapped in a double-check calculation of what the nav computer displayed. "Enemy on a direct course *into* the asteroid field."

"We have to engage before they get in," Commander Rinkishale told the captain. "We'll be able to maneuver around a few rocks, but too far into that field . . ."

"And they'll be able to play cat and mouse with us," the captain replied. He tapped in a message on his secure comm to the destroyers in his battle group.

Immediate replies scrolled across his screen.

"The *Jericho* and *Buenos Aires* concur," Captain Lewis said. "So we go hunting. Set course to intercept the *Callisto*," he ordered Lieutenant Cole. "Flank speed."

"Answering 030 by 270, sir," Cole said.

"Reactor answering one hundred percent," Lieutenant Taylor replied.

The *Las Vegas* accelerated and the bridge crew crunched in their padded seats as the *Callisto* grew on the central view screen.

"She's slowing, sir," Cole announced.

"Because they have to navigate through the field," the captain muttered. "What in God's name do they think they're doing?" He turned to the weapons station and Lieutenant Jorgenson. "Range?"

"In twenty seconds, sir," Lieutenant Jorgenson replied. "Firing solutions online for Ares missile system.

The target might bank around that larger asteroid at the edge of the belt, but we have a lock. The missile tracking systems can steer around."

"In twenty, then," Captain Lewis said and started scraping his thumbnail again. "Coordinate firing solutions with the *Jericho* and *Buenos Aires*, and allow computer control to fire at will—silos one through six."

Cole shot a quick glance at Lieutenant Jorgenson, who looked back at him and gave an almost imperceptible shake of her head.

"Arming silos one through six, aye," Jorgenson replied. She opened the button covers and flipped off the safety mechanisms for six of the seven banks of missiles in the *Las Vegas*'s arsenal. She activated the automated control systems. Green acknowledgment lights winked across the board.

"They're a sitting duck," Captain Lewis said with great satisfaction.

Cole stared at the automated control system, the lines about the corners of his eyes deepened, and he frowned.

*EXTERNAL CAMERA 6-K, UNSC DESTROYER JERICHO *
0317.235 HOURS MARCH 2, 2494 (MILITARY CALENDAR)

Eighteen Ares missiles streaked silently through space, leaving feathered plumes of gray smoke behind. For twenty seconds they remained on course tracking the *Callisto*. The enemy vessel moved on a vector directly aligned with an asteroid the size of Manhattan.

The *Callisto* then rolled, her engine cones flaring

white hot, as she executed a slingshot orbit to the far side of the cratered rock.

The missiles split their unified trajectories, each one independently optimizing the best targeting solution, and left eighteen smoky trails that looked like giant fingers reaching out into the dark . . . as if clutching the asteroid.

They never hit.

For the blink of an eye a new sun appeared in the 26 Draconis system.

A wash of white filled the screen . . . which coalesced to a boiling center of ultraviolet.

A nuclear device had been buried in the asteroid, facing outward. It blasted the rock apart, vaporized and shattered iron and ice, and spewed forth a shower of molten metal and plasma—a tide of destruction that rushed into the UNSC battle group.

It hit the *Buenos Aires*, which had been leading the charge. Her antennae and MAC trajectory sensors boiled away . . . as the cloud enveloped her in seething energies . . . from which she did not emerge.

A chuck of spinning rock hit the *Las Vegas*—a glancing blow, but enough to crumple her side and bend the ship's hull twenty degrees—she careened backward, venting atmosphere from a dozen ruptured decks.

A cloud of tiny molten fragments hit the *Jericho*—eventually killing all forward momentum, until she spun slowly backward in space, lights winking on and off.

Camera 6-K spun as well—but in the distance still tracked the prow of the *Callisto*—unscathed as it angled out of the plane of the asteroid field, and turned toward them.

A chunk of iron-silicate rock appeared for a split second in the field of view—moving directly into camera 6-K.

Static.

EXTERNAL CAMERA 6-K FEED TERMINATED

0329 HOURS MARCH 2, 2494 (MILITARY CALENDAR) \ UNSC DESTROYER LAS VEGAS PATROLLING 26 DRACONIS SYSTEM \ BRIDGE LOG (PRIMARY, VIDEO, SPATIAL ENHANCEMENTS=TRUE)

Shards of shatterproof plastic tumbled through the air on the bridge. Captain Lewis, tethered to his chair, hung, arms limp. One emergency light burned and tinged everything bloodred. Commander Rinkishale's body twisted at unnatural angles, floating, and in the strange light looked like an insect trapped in amber during its death throes.

The only stations active were nav, comm, and one winking panel on the otherwise static-filled weapons station.

Second Lieutenant Cole remained at his station, belted in to his seat, his legs wrapped around the pedestal for good measure. His hands flew over the nav controls, checking and rechecking.

"*Buenos Aires* destroyed, sir," Cole reported, his

voice cracking. "I'm reading a debris field along her last reported vector. There's too much radiation . . . but I think the *Jericho* has come about to engage the *Callisto*. Reading multiple missile locks. I'm not sure from whom."

Second Lieutenant Cole waited for his orders.

And he waited.

He then turned and looked . . . and saw his dead captain and commander . . . and the rest of the motionless bridge crew.

He unbuckled himself and moved to each, checking for vitals—finding only Lieutenant Jorgenson still breathing, and quickly tying a tourniquet above her bleeding calf.

He tapped the comm station, cleared his voice, and said, "Any medical personnel, any fire teams on decks four, five, or six—report to the bridge." He looked about once more, taking the carnage in, and then added, "*Any* crewmen who can get up here, do so immediately."

From the flickering weapons station a shrill alarm sounded, confirming missile lock on the *Las Vegas*.

Cole yelled into the comm, "All hands brace for impact! All crew brace—"

The bridge shuddered.

For a split second the air condensed into fog, then explosive decompression blasted out the atmosphere.

BRIDGE LOG OF THE UNSC *LAS VEGAS* (PRIMARY, VIDEO, SPATIAL ENHANCEMENTS= TRUE) / TERMINATED 0332.091

0348 HOURS MARCH 2, 2494 (MILITARY CALENDAR) \ UNSC
DESTROYER LAS VEGAS *PATROLLING 26 DRACONIS SYSTEM *
CAPTAIN'S LOG (AUDIO)

> {TRANSFER CONTROL CODES ENABLED PER MIL JAG
> ORDER TR-19428-P}

Captain Lewis and Commander Rinkishale are dead. The rest of the bridge crew are either incapacitated or dead.

I, Second Lieutenant Cole, Preston J. (UNSC Service Number: 00814-13094-BQ), do hereby assume command of the UNSC destroyer *Las Vegas and responsibility for the actions detailed henceforth*.

Emergency bulkheads are in place on the bridge and the additional breaches on decks one through eight and eleven through fourteen have been contained. Decks sixteen and seventeen remain evacuated and cannot be repaired.

The Shaw-Fujikawa drive is offline. Primary and secondary reactors are offline. There was a major spike in the primary system. Radiation containment protocols are in effect.

We are dead in space.

I have been trained to follow the rules and regulations and enforce our laws.

And even when I broke those rules—it has been to uphold a higher honor.

Now I am faced with a choice: Break those rules, discard honor, or lose. No—this has nothing to do with

winning or losing. I must break the rules and my honor
or die. Or all the crew will die.

With so many lives at stake, I have no choice.

I have ordered our missile silo doors shut.

I have signaled our unconditional surrender to the
insurgent-controlled ship *Callisto* and requested immediate aid for our wounded.

They won't be able to resist the prize of a UNSC
destroyer. They won't fire. They'll answer the distress
signal.

END ENTRY CAPTAIN'S LOG \ UNSC *LAS VEGAS*

EXTERNAL CAMERA A-4, UNSC DESTROYER **LAS VEGAS** \
0406.335 HOURS MARCH 2, 2494 (MILITARY CALENDAR)

Callisto's prow approached the port side of *Las Vegas*
and slowed to a full stop five kilometers away—with
her missile silo doors open.

After three full minutes *Callisto* moved closer and
turned so that the two ships were abeam: Cargo Bay 5
on the port side of the *Las Vegas* aligned with Cargo
Bay 3 on the starboard side of *Callisto*.

Robotic tethers reached from *Callisto*, groping over
the crumpled armor of the *Las Vegas*, until they found
purchase.

The arms pulled the *Las Vegas* within a few meters.
A hard docking collar extended from the *Callisto*—
large enough for three trucks side by side to roll
across—and fitted to the side of the *Las Vegas*.

Orange safety lights strobed along the passage as the seal was established, the interior pressure equalized, and the links locked and checked.

Incoming comm on alpha channel from *Callisto*: Las Vegas, *prepare to be boarded. Offer no resistance and we will evacuate your injured to Lawrence Space Station. Any tricks and we open fire.*

Comm (alpha channel): *This is* Las Vegas. *Understood. None of my crew will fire.*

A moment passed and then more strobe lights flickered along the *Callisto*'s flank, indicating her cargo bay doors opening.

A second shudder traveled the length of the docking passage—from the *Las Vegas* into *Callisto*.

On the port side of *Callisto* explosions blossomed outward from *inside*, obliterating her midsection from decks fourteen to three. Armor plates and bodies tumbled into vacuum . . . along with plumes of gray-green reactor coolant.

Both ships spun out of control.

The docking passage between the destroyers strained and twisted—and the connection snapped.

Atmosphere continued to pump out of *Las Vegas*'s bay, propelling her farther from the now crippled *Callisto*.

The armor on the aft quarter of *Callisto* glowed dull red as her fusion reactor and secondary fission reactor ran rampant and melted.

Thrusters on the *Las Vegas* puffed so she matched the pitch and roll of the enemy vessel . . . but turned so her prow faced the enemy's obliterated midsection.

Missile silo doors on *Las Vegas* opened.

Transmission (alpha channel): *This is* Las Vegas. *You are ordered to immediately seal missile doors and open Security Port 347 and allow our computer to take control of your vessel. Comply—or I will blast your ship in two.*

ANALYSIS

The UNSC was not prepared for brutal ship-to-ship combat in the early years of the insurgency. The light destroyer class, for example, had none of the armament one recognizes as standard today. The titanium-A armor and magnetic accelerator cannons, however, would soon be developed as industrial priorities shifted from building . . . to killing.

More problematic, however, was the application of those new technologies to three-dimensional battles in the vacuum of space.

The use of nuclear weapons in the battle with *Callisto* was not expected. It was believed that fissile detonations in space were nearly useless. Such detonations are extremely low-yield and produced a reduced electromagnetic pulse effect in a vacuum environment (very little bang for the buck, as they say).

But the fact that the insurgency *knew this* and had planted a nuclear device ahead of time in an asteroid that provided the reactive mass to outright destroy one UNSC ship and cripple two more was an astonishingly forward piece of military thinking.

More amazing, however, was Cole's tactical leap of insight. UNSC officers and merchantmen of the era had a near-religious reverence for Common Space Law—most especially pertaining to rendering aid to vessels in distress. The fact that Cole faked a distress signal to lure his opponent closer was both a stroke of genius and a breach of protocol so severe that UNSC CENTCOM dithered over whether to award him the Legion of Honor or have him court-martialed (ultimately, they did neither, to avoid difficult precedent). Cole's moral strategy was drawn from centuries of ambiguity in dealing with the idea of "enemy combatants" and inhabits a gray legal and ethical area, even in retrospect.

Emblematic of Cole's later tactical thinking, we see flexibility with regard to his ship's functional design. He had crewmen remove *Las Vegas*'s last Ares missile from its silo and transport it to Cargo Bay 5—where it could be fired *directly* into the enemy vessel at point-blank range, bypassing her external armor, and destroying her FTL drive and reactor coolant systems.

Cole noted later in his personal log that he would never again be able to send a distress signal in enemy territory. "No one would believe it," he stated. "Surrender, quite literally, is no longer an option for me."

The UNSC, the insurgency—all humanity had been awakened from complacency; we were evolving and learning how to fight again.

Cole was evolving as well, jettisoning antiquated ethical qualms—and learning to do whatever it took to win.

SECTION FIVE: THE OUTER COLONY INSURGENCY: THE *GORGON* V. THE *BELLICOSE* (2495–2504)

Cole was quickly promoted (although not without some protest) to first lieutenant and then commander and given a small corvette to patrol the Outer Colonies. After a dozen successful engagements in five years against insurgent forces and privateer fleets he was promoted to captain and received the honor of commanding the first heavy-destroyer-class vessel armed with a magnetic accelerator cannon (MAC), the UNSC Gorgon.

In Cole's personal logs he attributes his success more to luck than skill in battle, and he wonders if his rapid promotion was warranted. He also notes that insurgent atrocities may have greased the public relations aspect of his promotions.

Cole might have sensed part of the truth. The Navy had latched onto him as a figurehead to quell an unease percolating through the Inner Colonies. Many of the Inner Colonies were beginning to wonder if it was just to hold on so tightly to their Outer Colony cousins.

Earth needed a hero to distract its populace from an inconvenient moral confusion.

Meanwhile, the insurgency had learned how to hide, strategize, and terrorize as well. They had organized (by theft, customization of industrial vehicles, or by wholesale construction of their own ships) a sizable fleet.

Cole's record was not without its blemishes. In particular, the UNSC Bellerophon (a frigate captured by the insurgency and renamed the Bellicose), *engaged Cole thrice: escaping twice, and once, fighting him to a draw.*

Preston Cole's otherwise impressive military record did not come without a high personal cost.

Personal communiqué from Cole, Preston J. (UNSC Service Number: 00814-13094-BQ) to Volkov, Inna (Civilian ID#: 9081-613-7122-P) \ Routing Trace: UNITY 557 \ March 9, 2500 (Military Calendar)

Inna,

Your last letter caught me by surprise.

Is this how you truly feel? After all these years? A divorce?

I know your father would never pressure you into leaving me, so I have to assume this is how you feel, or that there is another person involved . . . or that it is somehow my fault.

Yes. That is it. It *is* my fault.

You never wanted a long-distance military marriage—and neither one of us expected to endure three extensions of my tour of duty. I cannot imagine how you must feel, so far away, with me in danger, not knowing if your husband will ever come back, and always having to wear a brave face for the military social elite that orbit your family.

I wish I could give this up and come home, be a husband for you, and a father for our children who are growing up not even knowing me, apart from the official broadcasts that are sent to Earth.

But the Navy needs me, too. Just by being here, I am

saving lives . . . saving us all by stopping these border conflicts from flaring into full civil war.

Maybe you don't want to understand that, or can't. But I do. I have to stay.

I will always love you. I will always love the kids.

Please reconsider your decision.

I await your final word but I stand by my duty.

Ever yours,
Preston

0700 HOURS JUNE 2, 2501 (MILITARY CALENDAR) \ UNSC DESTROYER GORGON \ THETA URSAE MAJORIS SYSTEM \ BRIDGE LOG (PRIMARY, VIDEO, SPATIAL ENHANCE-MENTS=TRUE)

Captain Cole did not sit in his padded chair on the raised center of the *Gorgon*'s bridge. Instead, he paced, stopped to glance over the shoulders of his officers at their stations, but otherwise kept moving like a shark.

Cole's temples were tinged gray. Where there had once been laugh lines, crisscrosses of concentration now crinkled his eyes. Other than these telltale signs of strain, however, he was the model of calm and thoughtfulness; confidence emanated from him like a magnetic field.

The UNSC *Gorgon* had engaged in two battles in the last seventy-two hours—so when it crossed paths with the insurgent-captured *Bellerophon*, the *Gorgon* had severely depleted munitions and a weary crew.

They battled the *Bellerophon* for the next 34.7 minutes, peppering one another with Archer missiles, and then the *Gorgon* slung around a planetoid to come around at the proper angle for a killing shot.

It was a "kill" shot. There was no other possible outcome.

No ship had yet evaded the new magnetic accelerator cannon, which could accelerate a tungsten-alloy slug to a fraction of the speed of light.

A shudder ran through the *Gorgon* and a flash filled the main view screen, a blurred afterimage of glowing metal that faded into the infrared.

The *Gorgon*'s AI, Watchmaker, flickered upon his pedestal, a wizened old man holding a huge pocket timepiece with a dozen arms and dials.

"Time on target?" Cole demanded.

Watchmaker's eyes riveted upon his clock. "Six seconds to impact."

On the screen the fired MAC slug was visually enhanced so it glowed soft blue—its trajectory a flat line speeding toward the enemy.

"She's coming about—new course 030 by 090," Lieutenant Maliki, at navigation, said. "Her reactors are past the red line."

The *Bellerophon*'s desperate acceleration to avoid destruction was useless, because for all practical purposes, compared to the MAC round, the ship stood still.

"Missile fire detected!" Lieutenant Betters, at weapons, announced.

"Won't do them any good," Maliki murmured. "At this extreme range we can pick off their missiles with the Helix system."

But the Archer missiles fired from the *Bellerophon* prematurely detonated—puffs of fire in the vacuum that made a dotted line in space . . . drawn straight from the *Bellerophon* to the *Gorgon*.

One distant explosion smeared across the black of space, however, and ever-so-slightly nudged the line representing the multiton ballistic projectile.

The blue line then closed on the silhouette of the *Bellerophon* . . . overlapped . . . and continued past the frigate.

"That's not possible!" Lieutenant Betters said, standing.

"It *is* possible," Cole said, "just not very likely."

"Ballistic tracking confirms," Watchmaker said. "We missed."

Lieutenant Maliki turned to face the captain. "They anticipated our firing the MAC, sir? How?"

"A guess," Cole replied staring at the view screen. "An educated guess, though, because we had the right angle on them. Still . . . incredibly lucky." Cole frowned. "And a brilliant defensive use of the last of their missiles."

"Not at all," Watchmaker quipped. "Those detonations were on a vector traced from the *Gorgon* to the *Bellerophon*. A reasonable estimation of the MAC trajectory and a precise gauge of distance." He snapped his watch shut.

"They can explain how they know so much about our MAC after we capture them," Betters remarked.

"And how do you propose we do that?" Cole asked. "Status, Lieutenant Maliki?"

"Archer missiles spent, sir," Maliki replied. "Except

silo eight, per your standing order. No remaining MAC rounds. We have seven Pelicans on standby. The AAA Helix guns are spun up and hot."

Cole stared at the *Bellerophon* as the frigate slowly turned away.

"Incoming message," Watchmaker announced, ". . . from the '*Bellicose*.' Text only."

"To my station, Watchmaker." Cole settled into the captain's chair and turned the view screen so only he could see.

```
Bellicose: I heard you've already used your
    new peashooter twice today. So that was
    your third and last round—unless you're
    going to load up one of your Pelicans in
    that cannon and fire that at me?
```

Cole stabbed his fingers into the keyboard, typing back:

```
Gorgon: You're out of shots, too. Your mis-
    sile silos are empty.
Bellicose: I invite you to take a closer look.
```

Captain Cole considered a moment and then tapped in ambiguously:

```
Gorgon: Not likely.
Bellicose: Well played, Preston. We're a good
    match. If you ever retire from the UNSC, you
    might consider working for the good guys.
```

```
Gorgon: Perhaps you'd like to come over here
  and persuade me?
```

A full fifteen seconds passed without reply, then:

```
Bellicose: Tempting. But another time, I
  think.
Gorgon: I look forward to it.
```

Cole slammed his fist on the arm rest, and yet there was a slight smile on his face.

The *Bellerophon* continued to turn and her engines flared to life as she moved off.

"Sir, we're *letting* them go?" Lieutenant Betters whispered. "That's the third time that ship has escaped."

"Three times," Cole echoed. "Yes. But we'll cross paths with the *Bellerophon*—the *Bellicose*—soon enough. Next time we'll be ready for her."

Personal letter from Captain Preston Cole to his brother, Michael James Cole, September 4, 2501 (Military Calendar)

Michael,

We searched for the *Bellicose* in five systems, laid ambushes, but have yet to find the vessel. In the meantime, there have been more engagements, with two insurgent corvettes, and one merchant privateer that ██████████████████████████████ "significant strategic victories."

Not a word of that to anyone else, or these letters will end up so redacted they'll look like a zebra has thrown up on them. I'm positive ONI is reading this and watching the family . . . and indulging me in this bit of personal communication.

I'm sure the only reason my letters get to you at all is that we're both playing this *their* way.

This undeclared war has worn on me and my crew. Before I let the *Bellicose* become my Moby Dick, I'm putting in to the Lambda Aurigae system on a backwater world called Roost for some long-overdue shore leave.

It's nice, like home . . . if there were red sand beaches in Ohio. It might make a decent base of operations for the *Gorgon* in this sector of the Outer Colonies.

I miss the kids and Inna. Still. Sixteen months since the divorce and I think it's all a nightmare. The hardest thing is not getting any replies from the kids. I've sent letters, but I think Inna burns them all.

Please try to get them a message: Tell them I love them.

—P

{Excerpt} Personal letter from Captain Preston Cole to his brother, Michael James Cole, March 12, 2502 (Military Calendar)

I was talking to Lyra about the *Gorgon*'s fusion reactor. (You remember her? She owns the bar on the beach? Got her PhD in nuclear engineering and moved here to fish and pour drinks? My kind of lady.)

Discussed nothing classified, just the generalities of plasma physics, and she came up with a way to boost our output by at least 5%.

I think we've all underestimated what kind of people come out to the Outer Colonies.

If things ever settle down, you and Molly should see for yourselves. I'm not saying leave the farm—just look.

{Excerpt} Personal letter from Captain Preston Cole to his brother, Michael James Cole, May 28, 2502 (Military Calendar)

That skirmish at Capella was too damned expensive. Thirty-two men and women lost. After so little insurgent activity for so long . . . I thought they'd given up.

I've gotten the okay from CENTCOM on Reach for a month of leave for me and the crew. What could they say? The *Gorgon* is going to be laid up that long in space dock getting patched up.

I'll be on Roost. No pressures. Some fishing. Some time with Lyra.

A little slice of paradise in all this purgatory.

Personal letter from Captain Preston Cole to his brother, Michael James Cole, November 9, 2502 (Military Calendar)

We got married, Michael. Pictures and video attached.

I'm sorry for the surprise. (Or maybe you've known this was coming for a long time, huh?) It was nothing fancy, just a ceremony on the beach performed by the local pastor.

Lyra is happy. She's pregnant, too.

God, I'm happy for the first time since I can remember. I feel like I've finally gotten a real second chance out here.

Even the insurgency seems to have finally calmed down. There've been just a few policing actions near Theta Ursae Majoris. Maybe this thing is finally coming to an end.

Classified communiqué from Admiral Harold Stanforth to Captain Preston Cole \ June 13, 2503 (Military Calendar)

```
United Nations Space Command Transmission
  08871D-00
Encryption Code: Red
Public Key: file / Albatross-Seven-Lucifer-
  Zeno /
From: Admiral Harold Stanforth, Commanding
  Officer, UNSC Leviathan / UNSC Sector
  Three Commander/ (UNSC Service Number:
  00834-19223-HS)
To: Captain Preston Cole, Commanding Offi-
  cer, UNSC Gorgon (UNSC Service Number:
  00814-13094-BQ)
Subject: TROUBLE
Classification: EYES-ONLY (BGA Directive)
```

This is bad, Preston. Sit down if you're standing.

There are new orders coming down from CENT-COM, and you're not going to like them: You're going to Reach.

Let me start with the hardest thing.

The woman you've been having a relationship with for the last seventeen months, one Lyrenne Castilla, is part of the insurgency. Hell, she's not a *part* of it; she's a high-ranking member—we think commanding one of their ships.

ONI has all the details. I've seen their intelligence reports, and I believe those usually-lying-through-their-teeth SOBs. They've been tracking her insurgent alter ego for a long time and just discovered her civilian identity.

It's simple: She's been playing you, Preston.

ONI is going to come after you, too, claiming that she's been pumping you for classified ship patrol routes and technical information.

So here's how it's going to play out:

1. New orders are being transmitted in three hours from Reach CENTCOM.
2. You will be confined to quarters on the *Gorgon* with no access to communications until the Prowler *Edge of Umbra* arrives in system.
3. The *Umbra* will then transport you to Reach where ONI will put you through the debriefing of your life.
4. After that—what happens is anyone's guess. I'll wager ONI can't court-martial unless they can

prove you willingly collaborated, because they built you into a military genius superstar back home. But whatever they're going to do—it ain't going to be pretty.

I'm breaking regs and telling you this because I don't believe for a hot second you would have gotten yourself deliberately involved in this—or that you'd be stupid enough to divulge ship locations or technical secrets to some pretty girl.

You've got three hours. Find Lyrenne before ONI gets her. Bring her in yourself. That'll go a long way toward clearing your name and ending this.

Good luck.
Harold

Personal letter from Captain Preston Cole to his brother, Michael James Cole, July 6, 2503 (Military Calendar)

. . . to follow up on that last quick note, Michael. I need to let you know, in case things end up going badly.

Everything Stanforth said was true.

I got to the bar on Roost and Lyra was gone. Everything she owned in our room had been taken—except one paper she left. It was a printout from a text-only exchange between the *Gorgon* and the captain of the *Bellicose*—something that happened two years ago. Lyra should have never known about it.

One part of that exchange she circled in red: *"We're a good match. If you ever retire from the UNSC, you might consider working for the good guys."*

It was a souvenir. She was the captain of the *Bellicose*, Michael.

All this time. Right under my nose.

Was she using me for information? That doesn't make sense. I never leaked any classified data. And the more I think of it—the insurgent fighting almost died out in the sector since we met.

So is Lyra a spy? Or someone like me? A ship captain who fell in love and wanted more than a life of fighting?

I have to find out, Michael. I have to find her.

—P

{Excerpt} UNSC After-Action Report: Battle Group Tango

AI-enhanced battle summation and casuality reports attached

PRELIMINARY: Battle Group Tango, comprising four heavy UNSC destroyers, engaged one insurgent-controlled frigate in the Theta Ursae Majoris system January 2, 2504 (Military Calendar). Two UNSC destroyers heavily damaged. Insurgent vessel known as the *Bellicose* (aka the UNSC *Bellerophon*) lost control, was caught in the gravitational pull of a gas giant (ref ID: XDU-OI-(1)), and lost with all hands.

ANALYSIS

History looks upon this time as an unfortunate (and perhaps inevitable?) misunderstanding between Earth and her colonies, but those of us fighting for the last decade also realize that it was the most amazing piece of blind fortune the human race has ever stumbled upon. Had we not been armed and learning how to fight in space . . . what would have happened in the years that followed, when we faced an enemy a hundred times worse?

Oblivion, no doubt.

For Preston Cole it was a time when he tempered his brilliance and flexibility into an implacable "do whatever it takes" fighting style, a time of ascendancy when his deeds propelled him (with the help of ONI's glorification campaign) into one of the most beloved public figures of our generation.

On a personal level, however, Cole lost the woman he loved, suffered, found a second chance at love—and lost it all again.

At the debriefing ONI officers read him the After-Action Report concerning the *Bellicose*. I can only believe they thought Cole actually colluded with her and this tactic was designed to break his spirit.

(*Note to self*: find these fool interrogators and transfer them to Kelvin Research Station on Pluto.)

And it did break Cole, but not in the way the debriefing officers expected. For any other man would've given up everything *because* the lady in question was dead. For Cole, however, Lyra's honor had to now be preserved at all costs. Cole remained stoic and silent and utterly stubborn, just as he had when he was a cadet at the Academy at Mare Nubium. Even though he faced a court-martial for treason— even execution—he did the noble thing and kept his mouth shut.

Because of immense pressure from Admiral Stanforth and from Cole's admiring public, he was released (no charges filed), but given strict orders that the entire affair was classified.

So, the greatest hero of the age was sent back to Earth—to sit at a desk.

Cole would have stayed there for the rest of his life if the burgeoning civil war between Earth and her colonies had not been rendered irrelevant by the appearance of the Covenant.

SECTION SIX: THE COVENANT WAR: THE COLE CAMPAIGNS (2525–2532 CE)

Cole was promoted to rear admiral. He agitated for a reassignment that got him back to space (all requests were denied). He proposed new policies to make the UNSC fighting forces more effective against the insurgency (all ignored). After eight months at his desk job, he was quietly offered early retirement with an honorary skip promotion to vice admiral (which he accepted).

In the years that followed, Cole's star dimmed in the public eye, resurfacing for his highly publicized marriages to much younger women (each of which ended in even more spectacularly publicized divorces).

Cole's liver failed from cirrhosis on May 11, 2525, and was subsequently replaced—as were his damaged heart and worn endocrine system—by flash-cloned transplants.

Shortly thereafter the Covenant encountered the human colony world Harvest. Only a handful of farmers managed to escape to warn the authorities. The Colonial Military Administration (CMA) sent a battle group to respond to the alien threat. They survived less than fourteen seconds before two of the three destroyers in the group were obliterated, and the remaining destroyer, the Heracles, *was forced to retreat.*

The Heracles *sensor logs showed an enemy with an overwhelming technological superiority. The CMA was placed under NavCOM for the duration of the conflict and effectively absorbed into the UNSC. Central Command scrambled a fleet of more than forty ships of the line to respond . . . but they needed someone to lead that force.*

Why did they pick Cole?

In hindsight, this was a masterful choice. Preston Cole was a hero and a tactical genius and would be the only person to ever consistently win against Covenant during the long war that followed.

Many claim that without Cole, the Covenant would have carved a path through the Outer Colonies and conquered Earth within three years, and humanity

*would be a memory today. Others say that any person
with the same military assets at their disposal could
have done the job, and perhaps done it better.*

*Cole was one thing our collection of "brilliant" ad-
mirals were not, however—a fallen hero who woman-
ized and drank too much. If CENTCOM's plan to
repel the aliens failed, he would have made an easy
scapegoat.*

*I believe this last point is too convenient an explana-
tion, however.*

*We had to win at Harvest. We were not going to
pick someone solely for the sake of convenient explanations later.*

*No, there was something dark about Cole that ap-
pealed to our leaders. He had a proven stomach for
carnage. Suicidal? Nothing so dramatic—but he did
have a willingness to stare into the face of death, to
sacrifice himself and any number of men and women
and ships—and do so without flinching.*

And that was precisely what we needed.

{Excerpt} Field Report ZZ-DE-009-856-841 Office
of Naval Intelligence
Reporting Agent: Lieutenant Commander Jack
Hopper (UNSC Service Number: 01283-94321-KQ) \
November 2, 2525 (Military Calendar)

As ordered, Lieutenant Demos and I went to offer Vice
Admiral Cole reinstatement to active duty and the job
command of the fleet to retake Harvest.

The admiral's general state when we arrived on his

doorstep was one of indifference. He answered the doorbell in his bathrobe and did not bother to return our salutes. He looked much older than I thought he would. His hair was silver and gray as was his complexion. Gone was the spark in his eyes that I had seen in videos of this legendary man when I was a child. It was as if I'd found the ghost of Admiral Cole, and not the man.

He did, however, read the situation report with interest, not flinching when he got to the part about the *Heracles* and how easily the enemy destroyed her counterparts.

Demos suspects he was drunk—a supposition supported by several empty bottles of Finnish black vodka in his living room.

I believe Cole's mind is as sharp as ever, though. Everywhere on the premises there were stacks of books (real paper books) on military histories and naval battles and the biographies of Xerxes, Grant, and Patton—and theoretical mathematical monographs on slipstream space and other mathematical esoterica that frankly I had a difficult time even understanding the titles of (like *Reunification Matrices of Hilbert Fields Within Spiral Unbounded Singularities*).

After reading the situation report twice, the admiral poured himself a drink, and offered one to Demos and myself. For politeness's sake we took them.

Cole then said, "Three divorces, a cloned liver, two heart attacks—not much left of me, boys . . . Like anyone can help with this slice of Armageddon. But okay. I'm in."

He set aside his drink, untouched, and added, "I think you need me as much as *I* need this." He got up to get dressed.

When he emerged from his bedroom he was in uniform and clean shaven—transformed from the shade of a man we had seen before. He seemed taller somehow, and tougher.

By reflex, I suppose, Demos and I stood at attention and saluted.

Cole took command—issuing orders, asking what capital ships were available, rattling off the specifics of the staff he wanted, AIs that he would need, and then requested *all* the intelligence reports ONI was holding back.

Just like you said he would.

Vice Admiral's Log (written) \ 1215 Hours November 15, 2525 (Military Calendar) \ UNSC cruiser *Everest* in slipstream space en route to REACH

I've digested the data from *Heracles* and the Chi Ceti Incident report.

The enemy has directed plasma weapons and a dissipative energy shield technology, the theoretical underpinnings of which our brightest can only guess at. The MAC rounds fired from destroyers *Arabia* and *Vostok* at Harvest had no effect. They didn't have time to launch nukes ... so their use against these energy shields remains unknown.

My assessment: trouble.

I see the situation as if we are a horde of *Homo ne-*

anderthalensis rushing toward a medieval castle. We will throw our sticks and stones against their unassailable fortifications—and they will rain hot death upon us with crossbow and boiling oil.

Will that analogy hold? Can I find a way to *tunnel* under those walls? Get inside and slaughter the enemy at close quarters?

I have to.

This first encounter with the aliens is a test—for them and us. So far we have failed that test. We have to show them that we cannot be so easily defeated. We have to win no matter the cost.

The super-heavy cruiser they have given me, *Everest*, is a supremely fine ship (although I already see a dozen modifications I wish to make to her). The crew is battle tested and razor sharp.

They believe in me.

God—I can see it in their eyes. They believe that *the* Admiral Cole is leading them into victory.

Maybe . . . but regardless, the truth of the matter is I will also be leading them straight into hell.

0120 HOURS MARCH 1, 2526 (MILITARY CALENDAR) \ UNSC CRUISER EVEREST \ FLAGSHIP BATTLE GROUP X-RAY \ EPSILON INDI SYSTEM BRIDGE LOG (PRIMARY, VIDEO, SPATIAL ENHANCEMENTS=TRUE)

Vice Admiral Cole paced the bridge of the *Everest*, followed by two adjutant commanders. The two dozen bridge stations were manned by officers and their assistants—all to coordinate the activities of the flagship and the thirty-nine other vessels comprising Battle Group X-Ray as they approached Harvest.

The colony world glowed blue and filled the view screens that stretched floor to ceiling in the cavernous command center.

Cole paused before a translucent screen the size of a blackboard, and with deft motions he zoomed back and forth through the spatial planes of this star system.

As the battle group descended below the planetary plane a blip appeared on screen.

"One ship," Cole murmured. He tapped the tactical display and the image enlarged.

The Covenant warship had sweeping organic curves, an odd purple phosphorescence, and was patterned with glowing red ovals and lines—the whole thing looked like a sleeping deep-sea creature of gigantic proportions.

"Two kilometers long, one wide," Cole said. "Energy readings off scale."

"Increase battle group velocity to three quarters full," Cole told one of his adjutant officers.

He pulled the perspective back on the tactical screen so Harvest was the size of a baseball, and then plotted a parabolic course past the enemy to slingshot around the world.

"Navigation inputs completed," Cole told the *Everest*'s AI.

Named Sekmet, the ship's AI's hologram was a lion-headed woman dressed in white Egyptian robes.

"Transmit burn vectors to the fleet," Cole ordered.

"Aye, sir," Sekmet answered, her cat eyes flashing green and gold.

Forty comets flared in the dark as the group accelerated toward the Covenant vessel parked in orbit over Harvest.

"Fire at will," Cole said. There was no emotion in his voice. He stared at the tactical board, watching and waiting.

MAC rounds streaked through space—strikes of molten tungsten alloy impacted the Covenant shields.

The veil of energy shook about the alien vessel and shimmered and resonated . . . but not a gram of metal touched its hull.

Hundreds of Archer missiles fired and filled the vacuum between the opposing forces—blanketing the enemy ship with fire and thunder . . . but not a shred of shrapnel scarred its surface.

Two curved lines on the Covenant flanks wavered and pulled free, oscillating through space.

They enveloped ships on either side of Battle Group X-ray.

Plasma tore through two meters of titanium-A armor like a blowtorch through tissue paper. Explosions boiled through their interiors—blasting out the aft sections, blooming with white-hot secondary fusion detonations as reactors went supercritical . . . leaving smears of fire and burning dust where a moment before there had been two UNSC destroyers.

Officers scrambled to COM stations to relay reports from the fleet.

"Nukes have no effect on the vessel, sir," and one officer shouted.

"*Sacramento* is down, as is *Lance Held High*!"

Vice Admiral Cole remained impassive at his tactical board.

The Covenant ship fired again, plasma lines searing space, boiling titanium and steel, vaporizing the fragile flesh and bone contained within.

"The *Tharsis*, *Austerlitz*, and *Midway* destroyed. My God!!"

Cole squinted at the energy signatures oscillating on the display before him.

"*Campo Grande* is gone! The *Virginia Capes*, too."

"Sound the retreat," one officer screamed.

"Belay that order," Cole barked without looking up.

The fleet arced about the apogee of their parabolic course and engines flared as they came about the dark side of Harvest. The scattered debris of seven destroyers, however, continued on their previous trajectories, sparks and swirls of molten alloy that faded into the night.

Cole jotted down calculations . . . and frowned.

"Damage and casualty report, sir." One of his adjutant officers offered him a data pad.

Cole waved it away.

He leaned closer to his display and drew a curve, numbers scrolling alongside his line as it circled about Harvest—and intercepted the enemy vessel.

Cole nodded and finally glanced up.

His bridge officers looked to him and seemed to absorb some of the vice admiral's implacable self-possession.

"Open alpha FLEETCOM channel," he ordered.

"Open, sir."

"Accept new course inputs," Cole said. "Accelerate to flank speed. Ready another salvo of MAC rounds. Sekmet, we need an Archer missile solution on target 0.1 seconds after those MACs—then a second firing solution for a salvo of nuclear detonations 0.2 seconds after initial impact."

Sekmet blinked. "Understood, Admiral. Threading multiple processing and crosschecking matrices between fleet AIs. Working . . ."

Cole's hands came up in a gesture that seemed part contemplation and part prayer.

"Firing solutions acquired," Sekmet announced.

"Input solutions. Slave master-firing control to *Everest*, and lock," Cole ordered.

"How many of the Archers, sir?" the Chief Weapons officer asked. "How many Shivas?"

Cole glared at the man like he was crazy. "All of them, Lieutenant."

"Aye, sir. Solutions locked and ready to fire on your order."

Cole nodded and laced his hands behind his back. He studied the tactical board as Battle Group X-Ray inched along their new trajectory.

The UNSC ships accelerated about the curve of Harvest, and the sun rose and blazed across the view screens.

The Covenant ship waited for them—plasma lines heating and flaring through space on an intercept course.

"Prepare to launch missiles," Cole ordered. There was steel in his tone. "Release targeting and fire control of the MACs to Sekmet."

He watched as the deadly plasmas sped toward them. "Initiate firing sequence—now!"

Dozens of rumbles shook *Everest*.

"Archer and Shiva missiles away, sir!"

Covenant plasma, so bright it seemed to ignite the black fabric of space, hit the fleet and burned the *Constantinople*, *Troy*, and melted the prow of the *Lowrentz*.

More than a thousand missiles left crisscrossing exhaust trails as they sped toward their target. The larger Shiva missiles fell behind the swarm.

Explosions spread throughout the fleet as new plasma ejected from the Covenant ship—destroying the *Maelstrom*, the *Waterloo*, and the *Excellence*.

"MAC system power at maximum," Sekmet announced. "Automatic firing sequence to commence in three seconds . . . two . . . one."

The remaining ships in Battle Group X-Ray fired their magnetic accelerator cannons—twenty-seven simultaneous lightning strikes that flashed across space and struck the Covenant vessel.

The alien ship blurred behind its shields . . . opaque for a split second.

The Archer warheads hit, splashing fire and fury across the curve of her flank.

And then dozens of new suns ignited—a corona of man-made nuclear violence. It was a cloud of destruction that writhed and contorted and clawed at the enemy ship for a full three seconds as the UNSC group continued at flank speed toward their target.

"Alter course, sir?" a commander asked.

"Remain on target," Cole said.

And in a whisper so low that while it was picked up by the bridge log microphone, no one else could have possibly heard, Cole said: "*Fix bayonets.*"

The fleet hurtled toward the inferno boiling about the alien ship.

The stern of the Covenant ship deformed—blasted outward as the interior shuttered and imploded, and ejected a double cone of blue-white hot plasma.

The bridge crew erupted into wild cheers.

"Course correction," Cole said. "Starboard group about to 060 by 030. Port group to 270 by 270."

"New course transmitted and acknowledged," Sekmet replied.

The fleet split and veered from the spreading fields of churning destruction.

"Bring us about to search for survivors," Cole ordered.

He closed his eyes, took in a deep breath, and then refocused on the tactical board. Cole touched an icon and watched as the names of destroyed vessels—and the thousands of men and women who had served and died under his command—scrolled into view.

Classified communiqué from Vice Admiral Preston Cole to Admiral Harold Stanforth \ May 2531 (Military Calendar)

```
United Nations Space Command Transmission
   102482-02
Encryption Code: Red
```

```
Public Key: file / Vegas-Anaconda-
  Mockingbird-Zero /
From: Vice Admiral Preston Cole, Commanding
  Officer UNSC Everest / (UNSC Service
  Number: 00814-13094-BQ)
To: Admiral Harold Stanforth, USNC Region
  One Commander / REACH CENTCOM (UNSC Ser-
  vice Number: 00834-19223-HS)
Subject: safeguarding navigation data -
  more thoughts
Classification: SECRET (BGX Directive)
```

Harold,

I've gone over this a dozen times: starting with our capture and interrogation of the alien creature my doctors are calling an "Elite" and ending with my tenuous conclusions and recommendations.

It doesn't make sense. My gut tells me the entire war hinges on something that we have overlooked.

First, and foremost, the Elite was xenophobic. The venom with which it spoke of humanity and its one desire—even as it bled out on the table—to find Earth and burn it to hot ashes . . . left zero doubt.

With that in mind, I still believe that safeguarding Earth's position is of vital importance. I plan to immediately implement the directives I drafted and sent to ONI for review, namely:

1. ALL UNSC and civilian ships that come into contact with alien assets must have nav computer

network/AI erased—destroyed, if necessary—to prevent capture of core world locations.

2. ALL human vessels fleeing alien forces must do so on randomly generated vectors away from UNSC core worlds.

3. ONI Section II to begin slipstream space attenuation broadcast of prerecorded human carrier signals from antiquity to prevent triangulation of Earth.

But, like I said, some things about this do not add up.

First, I do not understand why the aliens DON'T know where Earth is. They have technology hundreds of years more advanced than ours. All one has to do to find Earth is stick a radio antenna into space and triangulate on the source. I suspect something is occurring within the Covenant hierarchy that has prevented Earth from being targeted, or perhaps appreciated . . . something our captured alien had no knowledge of.

Second, my recommendation for ONI to obfuscate the radio signature in slipstream space (directive 3) might be our best bet to keep rogue elements within the Covenant military from finding Earth and preemptively attacking. Considering the dangers of any energy manipulation in slipstream space, however, I'm going to need your support with Parangosky to use her assets in what she'll consider an "extreme-risk" operation.

Third, I need solid intelligence on the enemy. Do

they seem to see us as some kind of religious aggressor . . . following some hitherto unknown ritual that accounts for them destroying our Outer Colonies before Earth? Or another possibility—an anthropomorphic gulf—that we have so many inhabited worlds, some more powerful militarily, economically than Earth—what if they're not interested in our *homeworld* strategically—but rather for some other, unknowable reason?

I can fight them, Harold, but only so effectively without knowing *why* they hate us.

I keep thinking of Sun Tzu: "If you know your enemies and know yourself, you will not be imperiled in a hundred battles; if you do not know your enemies but do know yourself, you will win one and lose one; if you do not know your enemies nor yourself, you will be imperiled in every single battle."

I look forward to your thoughts on this, my old friend.

Be well.

Preston

Personal log (audio), Vice Admiral Preston Cole, Commanding Officer UNSC *Everest* \ June 27, 2541 (Military Calendar)

Tonight a bottle of Capellan Vodka and I reviewed some of the old battles.

The Origami Asteroid Field in 2526—My fleet of one hundred seventeen UNSC ships of the line fought twelve Covenant vessels. We won that at the cost of thirty-seven ships.

Xo Boötis in 2528—Seventy ships versus eight Covenant. Another "victory." That time I lost thirty ships.

Groombridge 2530—Seventeen against three. We lost eleven destroyers. Still a win.

Leonis Minoris in 2537—only ten UNSC ships lost, but the Covenant glassed the other two colonies in the system. God—I couldn't save them all; I had to make the choice.

Another twenty-three engagements (or was it twenty-four . . . does Alpha Cephei count?) like those over the past ten years . . . or is it fifteen? So much travel in slipspace. So much subjective time lost to damnable Heisenberg uncertainties and in cryosleep.

It's killing me . . . although I seem to have somehow, technically, lived through it all.

They told me to fight, and that's what I've done. Let historians sort through the wreckage, bodies, and broken lives to figure out the rest.

Yet, how many men and women have I had to watch die? How many would have perished on colony worlds if not for their sacrifice? I look into space and no longer see wonder and stars and the endless possibilities that I did when I was a cadet. I see nothing but a cold death.

I hope CENTCOM can see farther than I do and planned for all contingencies: including *not* winning this war.

If the unthinkable happens—Earth and her colonies reduced to ash as promised by that Covenant Elite—where can humanity escape to? Perhaps there are already plans in motion: a colony vessel en route to some secret distant world where we can start over.

So this sacrifice we endure has purpose.

ANALYSIS

Cole won every major engagement he committed his forces to against the Covenant. On only two occasions did he encounter an enemy fleet he considered too large to take, and then he would return in both cases with reinforcements—most notably at the Battle of Psi Serpentis (more on that fateful encounter in a moment).

The losses of ships and people under Cole's command were staggering. Any normal battle group would have been dismantled and reassigned, and their commander given some rest—but Cole was a victim of his own popularity. CENTCOM could not allow their symbol to fail, so they kept reinforcing Cole with new ships and crews—and kept their fingers crossed that he wouldn't snap from the strain.

Imagine fighting Stalingrad and Cold Harbor and defending the Hot Gates with three hundred Spartans and repelling the Mexican Army at the Alamo—and then having to repeat those lopsided, impossible fights over and over.

Certainly Cole knew this that first time he faced that Covenant super-destroyer at Harvest. His unheard remark on the bridge of *Everest*, "Fix bayonets," is a reference to Colonel Joshua Lawrence Chamberlain's famous charge down Little Round Top at the battle of Gettysburg.

Chamberlain had orders to defend the far left end of the Union line, and had repelled numerous assaults upon his position. When the Fifteenth Alabama regiment charged up the hill toward Chamberlain's exhausted and low-on-ammunition Twentieth Maine regiment, instead of falling back, Chamberlain ordered his men to "fix bayonets" and charge down the hill. That apocryphal moment is considered to have saved the line, the Union army at Gettysburg, and perhaps determined the entire outcome of the first American Civil War.

Likewise, Cole knew he *had to* win no matter the cost in ships or lives or even to his sanity. Because if he failed, the enemy would destroy entire worlds; millions and billions of lives were his sole responsibility.

Mere psychological analysis cannot reveal the nature of what could keep any man going under such never-ending pressure.

Certainly we see in that last personal log that Cole had reached the nadir of his spirits. All he needed was a push to send him to his end, a push which soon arrived—but from something he could never have foreseen.

SECTION SEVEN: THE COVENANT WAR: THE BATTLE OF PSI SERPENTIS (2543 CE)

{Excerpt} UNSC After-Action Report: Battle Group Sierra-3

AI-enhanced battle summation and casualty reports attached.

Battle Group Sierra-3 engages Covenant in 18 Scorpii.

PRELIMINARY: Battle Group Sierra-3, comprising two UNSC destroyers and one cruiser, engaged a Covenant CPV-class heavy destroyer in the 18 Scorpii System, March 6, 2543 (Military Calendar). The UNSC *Seattle* and *Thermopylae* sustained moderate damage, while the *Io* sustained heavy damage. Covenant vessel destroyed.

SUMMARY ADDENDUM: The Convenant ship inflicted heavy damage and Sierra-3 group was unable to peel its shields. *Io*'s FTL drive was inoperative, so I faced a decision to fall back and save two destroyers, or fight and possibly lose all those ships. Reinforcements arrived when unknown friendly ships jumped in-system. Additional firepower penetrated enemy shields.

Lead reinforcement ship's silhouette matched a thirty-year-old UNSC frigate design with major modifications (see technical reports attached). Passive transponder pinged and yielded a ship reg. number, identifying the UNSC *Bellerophon*. Friendlies jumped out-system before comm contact established.

CAPTAIN'S NOTE: I don't believe in ghost ships. But I don't care if it is the *Bellerophon*, or if it was the Flying Dutchman sent by Lucifer himself—they saved our hides. Transmitted thanks to them before they jumped out and wished them well . . . whoever they were, and wherever they were headed.

SECTION PREFATORY REMARKS

I start this section with the Sierra-3 After-Action Report as it was the catalyst for what happened next (or so I believe).

Cole had to have seen the report. He was in charge of military operations in Sector Three, and a man of his exacting detail would not let a report—a report of a UNSC victory no less—pass his desk without a glance.

Cole's analytical mind likely came to two possible explanations for the sighting of the Bellerophon, *aka* Bellicose. *(1) The* Bellerophon *was incorrectly identified. Or (2) the* Bellerophon *escaped or faked falling into the gravity well of a gas giant and its subsequent destruction twenty-nine years prior.*

The captain of the Bellicose, *clever enough to face Cole thrice in battle and live, might have been able to engineer such a deception (although an in-atmosphere FTL jump while accelerating was only a theoretical possibility at that time).*

And given the ONI revelation in 2503 of the public identity of the Bellicose's *insurgent captain, it also makes perfect sense that she would want to drop off their radar in such a permanent and unequivocal fashion.*

But why would Bellicose *rescue Sierra-3? Had the remnants of the Outer Colony insurgency resurfaced to unite with their former enemy to face a greater threat?*

Or was Lyra Castilla's reason personal? Did she reappear to send a message to Cole? Or am I stretching the limits of my analysis with romanticism?

That we will never know.

Cole's personal logs cease after February 2533. His normal pattern of behavior also altered—nothing overtly suspicious, and all within the prerogative of a vice admiral—but as we will soon see, seemingly innocuous actions and orders would culminate in the momentous death of Preston Cole.

Restricted communiqué from Vice Admiral Preston Cole to REACH LOGISTICS \ March 9, 2543 (Military Calendar)

```
United Nations Space Command Transmission
  116749-09
Encryption Code: Red
Public Key: file / Vegas-Anaconda-
  Mockingbird-Zero /
From: Vice Admiral Preston Cole, Commanding
  Officer UNSC Everest / (UNSC Service
  Number: 00814-13094-BQ)
To: Admiral Dale Kilkin, UNSC CENTRAL
  COMMAND, REACH LOGISTICS OFFICE / (UNSC
  Service Number: 007981-63882-GE)
Subject: requisitions, transfers, and favors
Classification: RESTRICTED (BGE Directive)
```

Dale,

Recent prowler reports indicate a Covenant armada massing in Sector Three. I need my ships repaired, refitted, and battle-ready ASAP. Code these orders CRIMSON, and pull in favors people owe me to make it happen. You know what I mean.

1. **Requisition:** 600 tungsten-layered titanium-A armor plates (radiation-absorption rating: 5), replacement and upgrades for degraded armor plates on *Everest*, et al.
2. **Requisition:** Additional "smart" nav AI. Sealed and unbooted. Back-up for *Everest*. Current AI operating at 68% capacity.
3. **Order:** Pull the *Io* out of space dock and tow her to my position. Too far gone to repair, but Captain Wren has an idea to use her as a fire ship.
4. **Requisition:** Ordnance: 105 Shiva nuclear missiles (VE-3 type), 2400 Archer missiles, 45,000 blocks Helix System ammunition (see additional nonordnance supplies in Attachment A).
5. **Requisition:** Detailed stellar survey of Sector Three, subvolume D-6. Emphasis on systems with proto-brown dwarf gas giants.
6. **Transfers:** I can't lead my fleet into battle when half my officers are on the verge of collapse from fatigue. List of crew transfers in Attachment B. List of requested crew replacements in Attachment C.
7. **Favor:** I have a theoretical Shaw-Fujikawa manifold calculation that needs crunching through the ONI AI network on Reach. They're the only ones

in the Outer Colonies with the raw power to get the job done.

8. Wish me luck.

UNSC *Everest*
Preston J. Cole

```
Copy to: Logistics Office, NavCOM, REACH.
Office of Naval Intelligence, SECTION-III,
  REACH
```


0915 APRIL 18, 2543 (MILITARY CALENDAR) \ UNSC CRUISER EVEREST \ *FLAGSHIP BATTLE GROUP INDIA* \ *PSI SERPENTIS SYSTEM* \ THE BATTLE OF PSI SERPENTIS {AI RECREATION BASED ON VIDEO, AUDIO, AND SENSOR LOGS—BLACK BOX RECORDERS—AND EYEWITNESS ACCOUNTS}

When Battle Group India transitioned into normal space in the Psi Serpentis System, it was the largest assembly of UNSC forces ever: thirteen cruisers, twenty-three carriers, seventy-nine destroyers, forty-two frigates, five prowlers—and fifty supply, repair, and rescue vessels (those latter ships remaining in slipstream space for the duration of the engagement).

The wake from the massive transition into normal space sent a ripple outward from the fleet's entry point—a distortion across the electromagnetic spectrum that propagated from their location three million kilometers above the planetary plane of Psi Serpentis.

It made auroras sparkle over the nearest three planets. It caused a visible shift in the smoldering red eye of Viperidae, the gas giant with thirteen times the mass of Jupiter (with gravity nearly enough to crush and fuse the hydrogen churning in its atmosphere).

. . . and the ripple passed through the massing Covenant ships on the far side of the system.

An unmistakable signal to the enemy.

The Covenant ships appeared on radar like a swarm of sharks in the dark—more than a hundred sleek organic silhouettes registered—CPV destroyers, light cruisers, and the hitherto unseen in battle CCS-class battle cruiser.

Their prows collectively turned toward Battle Group India, lateral plasma lines pulsing and illuminating hulls so it looked as if an entire alien fleet emerged from the shadows by sleight of hand.

The UNSC prowler *Wink of an Eye*, having been in-system for seven days waiting for this moment, moved into its proper position and reappeared, only visible because its active camouflage skin could not keep pace with the churning red and orange surface of Viperidae behind it . . . the prowler sent a radar ping to the UNSC forces to verify its position, and then the *Wink* flash transitioned into slipstream space to drop guidance beacons.

Battle Group India one by one moved into slipstream space, the preliminary Shaw-Fujikawa calculations having been done a week previously by Cole himself.

And the entire fleet then reappeared two seconds later, one hundred thousand kilometers on the opposite side of Viperidae—positioned so the gas giant blocked the enemy sight line.

UNSC FTL technology, however, was not perfect—especially over short intersystem hops near gravity wells. A dozen UNSC ships reappeared, scattered from the main group.

The Covenant fleet angled toward the stragglers and accelerated to attack speed.

Cole's fleet split into two wings, both using the gravity of the gas giant to slingshot around either side of the planet—and toward the onrushing enemy armada.

In response, the Covenant fleet also split to track each portion of the UNSC forces on either side of Viperidae.

The starboard wing of the UNSC fleet, however, shifted its orbital burn—arced up and over the gas giant and angled back to meet the rest of the battle group.

Engine cones flaring with the power from overloaded reactors, the human ships reunited and rocketed toward the port-side breach in the Covenant line.

A dozen nuclear-tipped Shiva missiles launched, crossed the space between the two converging forces, and detonated harmlessly before reaching a single enemy vessel.

But as the Covenant loosed their plasma charges, the exploding clouds of superheated gas from nuclear detonations scattered the alien weapons, rendering them ineffective.

Just as the Covenant fleet came into Battle Group India's optimal magnetic accelerator cannon range.

A dozen MAC slugs struck the leading Covenant ships—impacts timed microseconds apart as they hammered down energy shields, punched through hulls, penetrated through and through, and sent thirty-seven of the alien CPV-class destroyers careening through space.

As the two forces closed, however, a cloud of nuclear fire no longer protected the UNSC vessels, and plasma lines lanced through the vacuum, tearing into titanium-A armor and breaching reactors. Archer missiles fired at extreme close range to fill the space with flash and detonations, but this did little to stop the enemy.

Three human destroyers crashed headlong into a Covenant battle cruiser—their hulls splintered and the entire mass engulfed in a blob of plasma.

As the fleets sped past one another, the UNSC ships fired thrusters, spun about one hundred eighty degrees, and launched Archer missiles to provide cover from the Covenant's devastating plasma weaponry.

The Covenant had lost statistically more vessels than was typical in an engagement with the UNSC. Twenty-three alien ships of the line now drifted in space inert or burning from within as their reactors overloaded and vented plasma.

But Battle Group India had lost more than a third of her ships, and nearly every one of those that had survived was now scoured and pitted or had decks breached—

With one noticeable exception: *Everest*, which had led the charge, emerged unscathed.

Meanwhile, the other wing of the Covenant armada that had been outmaneuvered on the first pass came about—spinning in place as the UNSC fleet had done . . . slowing . . . and then pursuing Cole's ships.

Swarms of Archer missiles fired from Battle Group India. Their MAC systems had yet to recycle for another shot. The UNSC ships scattered, moving apart like an opening blossom—

—as the second wave of Covenant vessels opened fire.

The UNSC destroyer *Agincourt* charged headlong into concentrated streams of incoming plasma lines— sacrificing herself to save her sister ships.

And still the alien fleet picked off a dozen more human vessels.

Both sides were now scattered across the system. The first Covenant forces to engage, however, caught up with those now in pursuit. The human ships regrouped and changed course back toward the gas giant, accelerating and keeping just out of effective range of the enemy's plasma.

Cole's fleet might have escaped, and yet the UNSC ships collectively slowed to allow the Covenant fleet to gain a tiny bit—as both groups of ships sped around Viperidae.

The Covenant armada lost sight of their prey due to the curvature of the gas giant.

As they emerged in hot pursuit of Battle Group India they saw brilliant blue flashes of Cherenkov radiation, the result of multiple slipstream transitions into normal space.

A new fleet of human ships appeared, barreling on an interceptor trajectory toward the aliens.

Fifty-five ships—highly modified older UNSC warships, merchant vessels bristling with missile pods, and entirely new designs that neither human nor Covenant had ever seen before—led by *Bellicose* plunged into the center of the Covenant fleet and opened fire.

MAC slugs tore into the enemy vessels as they accelerated toward one another. Plasma lines launched—many deflected by the strong magnetic field of the gas giant in proximity. Ships collided and scraped hulls, and a dozen craft from both sides fell into the boiling clouds of Viperidae's upper atmosphere and perished.

Then the two forces flashed past one another . . . and the Covenant emerged, their forces decimated and wounded . . . less than half the original strength.

The insurgent-led forces had lost one-quarter of their number. They did not turn to fight, however.

They continued on their trajectory out of the Psi Serpentis system where, with dozens of crackling blue flashes, they transitioned back into slipstream space.

Cole's fleet had altered course into a high parabolic orbit, turning toward the enemy, their collective MAC systems shimmering with superconductive sparks of power—aimed directly at what remained of the Covenant fleet.

A mere million kilometers distant, however, space again rippled as new slipspace ruptures appeared . . .

three . . . and a dozen . . . a hundred . . . then a fleet of more than two hundred Covenant ships appeared in normal space accelerating toward Viperidae.

The UNSC ships continued a full ten seconds on their current course, firing neither weapons nor engines.

COM traffic from *Everest* was on a secure and scrambled channel—private, for admirals to captains only—that was then deleted by a viral worm.

The channel closed and the UNSC fleet moved off at flank speed—leaving *Everest* alone to face the enemy.

Everest's engines flared and she slipped deeper toward the gas giant. Her MACs powered down and every external light went off. All her missile silo doors, however, opened.

The mass of the fresh Covenant armada turned to pursue the retreating Battle Group India.

COM CHANNEL (BROADBAND ALPHA-THETA) from UNSC *Everest*: *"Listen to me, Covenant. I am Vice Admiral Preston J. Cole commanding the human flagship,* Everest. *You claim to be the holy and glorious inheritors of the universe? I spit on your so-called holiness. You dare judge us unfit? After I have personally sent more than three hundred of your vainglorious ships to hell? After kicking your collective butts off Harvest—not once—but twice? From where I sit, we are the worthy inheritors. You think otherwise, you can come and try to prove me wrong."*

The Covenant fleet, both damaged vessels and fresh reinforcements, turned to *Everest*. Some ships rushed toward her position, while others skirted around Viperidae—cutting off any possible escape vector.

Everest tightened its orbit and vanished from view as it moved to the far side of the gas giant.

She did not slingshot out as she had done on previous occasions, but rather emerged again on the near side of Viperidae along a trajectory so low, the cruiser could never recover from the inevitable gravity spiral into the gas giant's crushing atmosphere.

The leading Covenant ships fired.

A hundred plasma streams lanced toward their target . . . but spiraled about themselves and dissipated in the extreme magnetosphere of the gas giant.

Laser fire followed from the Covenant ships, peppering *Everest* with a thousand smoldering holes. No atmosphere, though, leaked from the ship, as every outer deck had already been evacuated.

COM CHANNEL (BROADBAND ALPHA-THETA) from UNSC *Everest:* "*Is that the best you can do?*" Cole laughed. "*Watch what one unworthy human can do!*"

Everest launched everything she had.

Archer missiles rocketed out of the gravity well of the planet along with a dozen Shiva nuclear warheads—while another *hundred* Shiva missiles plunged deeper into Viperidae's churning clouds.

The gas giant's hydrogen-helium atmosphere was so dense, so compressed, that if it had a tiny fraction more mass it would have ignited and become the smallest of brown dwarf stars.

The Archer missiles had no effect on the Covenant shields. They did, however, provide a dazzling display of pyrotechnics: flashes of white and blue and red and obscuring clouds of propellant.

The nukes launched out of the gravity well exploded.

The lead Covenant ship was destroyed—an insignificant loss compared to the two hundred remaining Covenant vessels moving closer, now near enough to punch through the magnetosphere and obliterate *Everest*.

But the vast majority of the nuclear ordnance had not been aimed at the Covenant—rather, they fell deeper into the atmosphere of Viperidae.

And detonated.

One hundred dots of light flickered deep within the thick atmosphere, compressing the already superpressurized hydrogen—adding the needed spark of fission that flashed through and around the gas giant's surface, sending helixing tentacles of solar plasma about the planet circumference.

For an instant, Viperidae was a star.

Countless tons of hydrogen blasted off its outer layers and filled space with plasma—washed away everything with a blaze.

The expanding ball of destruction slowed and dissipated.

Until only a cloud of glowing haze remained . . . and in the center, the dark cinder of Viperidae.

Every ship in the Covenant fleet had been destroyed.

As had the UNSC *Everest*, its crew, and Vice Admiral Preston J. Cole.

ANALYSIS

A day of mourning was proclaimed July 28, 2543. Humanity had lost its supreme hero. There would be others elevated to this lofty position (most notably, the Spartan-IIs, who had already gone public in 2547), but for many, Preston Cole was the one man who had stood between life and annihilation at the hands of the Covenant.

It was no coincidence that after a brief pause in alien activity in the Outer Colonies, they renewed their efforts, overwhelmed UNSC defenses, and swarmed through the Inner Colonies. Was that because Cole was gone? Or had his victory spurred the enemy to redouble their efforts?

What occurred at Psi Serpentis, while it was investigated, was not forensically examined in exacting detail at the time. The tactics in the battle were consistent with Cole's previous behaviors: innovations in FTL jump technology, a sophisticated coordination and maneuvering of multiple ships in formation, gravitationally assisted slingshot to excellent effect, and tricking the enemy into exposing vulnerabilities.

As for the real question, what *really* happened to Preston Cole, we must examine the available evidence.

First, the AI recreation of the battle stitched together by ONI Section-III and Section-II was one part scientific analysis and one part propaganda. To be fair, there were many holes in the official record. Speculation and raw glorification of the events were inevitable.

Let us consider some anomalies and curiosities.

A frame-by-frame analysis of the last moments of

Everest captured by external cameras of the withdrawing Battle Group India show the vessel spiraling into the atmosphere of Viperidae just before the detonation of her Archer missiles.

Tactically those missiles served little, if any, purpose. They could not possibly have penetrated the Covenant shields. So why fire them?

Hyperfine enhancements of the video make out the characteristic prow of a UNSC super-heavy cruiser silhouetted against the backdrop of the red atmosphere—but also recorded an aura of bright blue light (which most experts assume is the premature detonation of a cluster of Archer missiles).

But most curiously, there appears for a single frame *another* silhouette behind the *Everest*: that of a UNSC cruiser.

All UNSC ships, surviving and destroyed, were accounted for in the battle, save *Everest* and the towed, never-used "fire ship" Cole had requested, the cruiser *Io*.

Spectroscopic analysis of the radioactive debris field captured in the orbit of Viperidae shows amounts of tungsten-180 consistent with the newly requisitioned and repaired armor of *Everest*—but it failed to yield the ratio of titanium-50 in the mixture that would have been present had *Everest* been vaporized.

No black-box recorder was ever found from *Everest*. While UNSC black-box recorders cannot survive such a nuclear cacophony, standard protocol is for the ship's AI to eject at least one of the redundant five black-box recorders if the ship is in imminent danger of destruction.

Detailed examination of Cole's Shaw-Fujikawa manifold calculation sent to the ONI/Reach super-AI network for number crunching reveals it to be a theoretical in-atmosphere transition from normal to slipstream space while in a severe acceleration gradient—i.e., identical conditions one might encounter in close proximity to a gas giant.

SPECULATION

The Archer missile screen and the anomalous presence of the Io *were smoke screen and decoy. Cole initiated a transition to slipstream space the instant before detonation of the Shiva nuclear ordnance and the triggering of the micronova of Viperidae.*

Everest was not *destroyed.*

Cole faked his death and escaped.

One hole in this theory pertains to the crew of Everest. *Cole's massive personnel transfer prior to the battle might have been intended to fill his ranks with those sympathetic to his motives or, at least, those who had unwavering loyalty to him. But he could never have convinced the entire crew of* Everest *to agree to a wartime desertion. I do not believe Cole could kill his own crew—but perhaps he could keep potential dissenters indefinitely in cryo sleep?*

As to Cole's motivations, that is pure speculation. But the resurfacing of Bellicose and his former lover, Lyra Castilla, point in the right direction—that, and a mental breakdown brought on by years of constant fighting with overwhelming casualties.

Scattered reports and rumors of independent human forces fighting Covenant pop up on the outer edge of what we believe to be nonsanctioned human colonized space . . . reports that track toward the Sagittarius side of the Orion arm in the Milky Way . . . and then these rumors fade to whispers . . . and legend . . . and then die out all together.

SUMMARY CONCLUSIONS

In my best estimation, Cole survived the Battle of Psi Serpentis.

He may be alive and healthy today.

By Earth-normal chronology he would be eighty-two years old, but before the Covenant War he had his liver, heart, and endocrine system replaced with flash-clone parts. Also, so many of his "years" occupied with space travel were filled with periods of cryogenic suspension and minor but additional relativistic effects. Our best guess at Cole's biological age is sixty.

He is likely leading a band of colonists, insurgents, and UNSC defectors to build a new home far outside UNSC-dominated space. He always wanted a farm on some world where he could look up and not recognize the nighttime stars.

I think he did just that.

RECOMMENDATION

While it is remotely possible that my analysis is incorrect (AIs Phoenix and Lackluster have, however, independently corroborated my conclusions within 89.7 percent accuracy), I shall nonetheless give you my informed recommendation on this matter.

For the moment Preston Cole may be living a simple, isolated life—the governor, perhaps, of some unknown provincial farming colony.

But how long will that isolation last, given the highly unstable situation we find ourselves in after the Covenant War? Namely:

a. *The insurgency may rise again (especially dangerous given the UNSC's weakened postwar status); and*

b. *The Covenant (to the best of our limited intelligence of their culture) is in utter chaos now that their religious hierarchy has been removed. What they will do with their independent races, or collectively, is anyone's guess.*

It is inevitable that these coming conflicts will spread to a wider region of the galaxy.

Cole might be found and convinced to fight once more. In addition to possessing great military genius, he would be a natural figurehead for our battered forces to rally behind. Insurgent or Covenant aggressors would think twice before engaging Preston Cole in battle.

But if found, will Cole fight? For us?

There are three possibilities: (1) Cole will see that Earth and all her colonies are in peril and defend them once more. (2) He will fight for humanity . . . but perhaps not on our side. After living for years among former insurgents, he may back those forces should they rise against the UNSC. Or (3) Cole will not fight, having grown too weary to take up arms again, and will flee farther from the conflict.

Neither I nor the AIs can hazard a better than even guess as to the probabilities (plus or minus 4.35 percent, 4.05 percent, and 4.30 percent respectively).

All that can be said with absolute certainty is that Cole will remain a leader—whether leading his people to safety . . . or back into battle once more.

I offer my services, as usual, to pick up Preston Cole's trail, find him, and attempt to convince him to join our cause.

Failing that, if he chooses to side against us . . . well, I leave those unpleasant details to you.

I, for one, have lost my stomach for killing legends.

```
CODENAME: Surgeon
Office of Naval Intelligence (Section-III)
  Operator #: AA2
```

2200 hours, December 31, 2552 (Military
  Calendar) \ UNSC *Point of No Return*,
  Synchronous Lunar Orbit (far side)

/end file/
/scramble-destruction process enable/
Press ENTER to continue.

ACKNOWLEDGMENTS

The amount of work that goes into a project like this defies understanding. The behind-the-scenes of making a multi-author book that ties into the vanguard of modern science fiction could easily make the stuff of bad reality television. Juggling the franchise's wonderfully high story expectations while simultaneously maintaining authors' creative freedoms, all under fun and torturous time constraints, requires heroic actions from many. This book wouldn't have been at all possible without the herculean efforts of Nicolas "Sparth" Bouvier, Alicia Brattin, Gabriel "Robogabo" Garza, Jonathan Goff, Kevin Grace, Alicia Hatch, and Frank O'Connor.

The amazing team at Tor has to be praised as well. Led by Tom Doherty and masterfully marshaled by Eric Raab, the unsung heroes Karl Gold, Justin Golenbock, Jim Kapp, Seth Lerner, Jane Liddle, Whitney Ross, Heather Saunders, and Nathan Weaver and their efforts in the trenches to make it all happen are the stuff of legend. Special thanks to Shelley Chung, Patricia Fernandez, and Christina MacDonald for desperately trying to make every story in here read without a blip.

Additional thanks to 343 Industries, Bungie Studios, Ryan Crosby, Scott Dell'Osso, Nick Dimitrov, David Figatner, Nancy Figatner, Josh Kerwin, Justin Osmer, Pete Parsons, Bonnie Ross-Ziegler, Phil Spencer, and Carla Woo.

ABOUT THE AUTHORS

TOBIAS S. BUCKELL is a Caribbean-born writer who grew up in Grenada as well as the United States and British Virgin Islands. He has written a number of novels, including *Halo: The Cole Protocol*. He currently lives in Ohio with his wife and his two daughters, two dogs, and two cats.

B. K. EVENSON is the author of the *Aliens* tie-in novel *Aliens: No Exit*. He is currently working on a novel based on the video game *Dead Space*. He lives and works in Providence, Rhode Island. Under the name Brian Evenson, he is the author of nine books of fiction. These include *The Open Curtain*, which was a finalist for an Edgar Award and for the International Horror Guild Award, and *Last Days*.

JONATHAN DAVID GOFF is a writer and artist raised on a healthy diet of Saturday morning cartoons and sugary breakfast cereals. After serving in the United States Air Force, Jonathan spent six years developing creative content for action figure, comic book, and entertainment properties at the McFarlane Companies in Tempe, Arizona, before relocating to the Pacific Northwest where he assists Microsoft Game Studios' 343 Industries in all manner of Halo-related goodness. He currently resides in Redmond, Washington, with his lovely and infinitely supportive wife, Maria.

ERIC NYLUND is the *New York Times* bestselling author of *Halo: Ghosts of Onyx* and World Fantasy Award–nominated *Dry Water,* among several other novels, which have sold more than two million copies. His latest novel, *Mortal Coils*, is the start of an epic five-book series.

FRANK O'CONNOR has worked in and around the video game industry for fifteen years, as both journalist-observer and active participant in game development—first at Bungie, the creators of Halo, and then at Microsoft Game Studios' 343 Industries. Frank has been working in and on Halo fiction for the greater part of six years, having developed fiction, stories, and characters for Halo games, comic books, novels, and animation. The thirty-nine-year-old western Washington resident enjoys reading, cycling, and corralling the ever-more-elaborate escape attempts of his baby daughter.

ERIC RAAB was born in the city of Newburgh, New York, which rests majestically on the western bank of the Hudson River. He's currently an editor at Tom Doherty Associates and has been the editor for *Halo:*

Ghosts of Onyx, Halo: Contact Harvest, and *Halo: The Cole Protocol,* among other projects well worth your time and money. His passions include skipping rocks on water and driving nowhere.

ABOUT THE ARTISTS

SPARTH (NICOLAS BOUVIER) has been an active concept designer in the gaming industry since 1996. Born in France, he now lives in Seattle, Washington, working for Microsoft. He has contributed to the development of several released games since 1997, including *Alone in the Dark 4* (2001), *Cold Fear* (2005), *Prince of Persia—Warrior Within* (2004), *Assassin's Creed* (2007), and *Rage*, a project still in development at id Software. Sparth has also utilized his talents to illustrate numerous book covers. His images have been actively chosen by publishers to adorn the book covers of multiple French and English authors. When he is not working, he finds time to relax with his wife, Lorene, and his three children, Arthur, Leopold, and Zelie.

HALO WAYPOINT ART CONTEST WINNERS

JAMES BIBLE's ("Dirt") parents left him at the zoo when he was three years old to be raised by primates. It was there that he honed his illustration skills, sustained by his opposable thumbs while swinging from a tire on a rope. Since his escape, James's artwork has been seen in newspapers, books, game design, the 2002 Winter Olympics, crime scenes for law enforcement, military projects, children's birthday parties, and on the walls of public restrooms.

LEVI HOFFMEIER ("Pariah"), of Gladstone, Missouri, recently received his BFA from the University of Missouri. He is in the process of making the shift (hopefully a speedy one) to the professional art world, setting his sights on the comic book and video game industries. You can check out his work at www.levihoffmeier .com.

ALEXANDER KENT, a.k.a. Grim, ("Stomping on the Heels of a Fuss") is a California-born artist who has been actively drawing for as long as he can remember. His artwork is heavily influenced by his musical tastes, a passion for video games, his heritage, and general nerdery. He currently lives in San Francisco, California, where he can be found at metal shows, art galleries, taquerias, and working on his Web comic: www.6th CircleComic.com.

APRIL MARTIN ("Midnight in The Heart of Midlothian"), of Harker Heights, Texas, is a lifelong gamer with a particular passion for all things Halo. Upon graduating, she would like to work in the game industry as a concept artist. April spends her free time creating freelance concept art and illustrations.

GARRETT POST ("Headhunters"), of Kent, Washington, is known as TDSpiral in the Halo community. He started drawing when he was a wee lad, and decided to approach digital art as a career when he discovered the beautiful concept pieces in *The Art of Halo 3*. Garrett's father was a huge inspiration to him throughout his childhood.

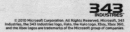

 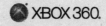